A Quality Street. Christmas

Penny Thorpe lives in Yorkshire where she was the company archivist and historian for her local chocolate factory for more than a decade. She has written four books in the Quality Street series.

PENNY THORPE

A Quality Street Christmas

HarperCollins*Publishers*

HarperCollins*Publishers* Ltd
1 London Bridge Street,
London SE1 9GF

www.harpercollins.co.uk

HarperCollins*Publishers*
Macken House, 39/40 Mayor Street Upper
Dublin 1, D01 C9W8

First published by HarperCollins*Publishers* 2022
This paperback edition published 2023
2

A catalogue record for this book is available from the British Library

ISBN: 978-0-00-853114-0 (PB)

Typeset in Sabon LT Std by Palimpsest Book Production Ltd,
Falkirk, Stirlingshire

Printed and bound in the UK using 100% Renewable
Electricity by CPI Group (UK) Ltd

For Alison Murray, with thanks and love.

Prologue

'Here, Marjorie, look at this! It's come all the way from France, it has.' The lady office clerk held out a letter to her colleague and looked around her to make certain they were neither overlooked nor overheard. The secretarial pool of the Halifax Town Hall did not usually enjoy the luxury of privacy, but it was the dinner hour and, as luck would have it, their office was quiet.

'Yes, it's very pretty handwriting,' Marjorie said down her nose, barely lifting her eyes from her copy of the *Halifax Courier* to glance at the envelope.

'No, no read it.' The lady clerk looked over her shoulder again and then said in a hushed whisper, 'It's unbelievable!'

At this Marjorie's interest was piqued. She turned away from the newspaper and took the letter, an ugly frown of confusion twisting her features. She was impatient for whatever salacious gossip was within to show itself and be quick about it, she didn't want to have to probe too far through a layer of nuance. 'No,' she said, shaking her head and giving up after a few lines, 'you know I don't want to know about any war stuff; I'm not into war stuff.'

'It's not war stuff! Keep reading, Marjorie.'

'I can't make head nor tail of it. Someone's married, or they're not married, and he's never been to England but he wants to find George Hunter.' Marjorie thrust the letter back to her colleague, 'I don't get why he's writing to us.'

'He isn't writing to us.' She held up the envelope so that Marjorie could see who the missive was addressed to. 'He's writing to the Mayor of Halifax because in France that's what they'd do, they'd write to their mayor to ask advice. This is the biggest scandal in Halifax for a decade!'

Marjorie huffed. 'Well then, I'll read all about it in the *Courier* when they print it, but I'm not playing at detective, reading through all that lot,' and she waved her hand in the direction of the letter's two pages of concise information, 'to work out who did what to whom and why.'

'But if you read it now you'll be one of the first people to know. You'll be able to tell everyone that you knew about it before the *Courier* printed it. In fact, it might never get to the *Courier*, they might hush it up. The Mayor's a good friend of George Hunter and don't think he don't know that Hunter's factories employ a good few hundred people in this town – he'll help him hush it up before it goes anywhere.'

'So tell the *Courier*.' Marjorie shrugged. 'It would serve old George Hunter right. Him and his wife think they're so holier than thou with all that philanthropy stuff, and refugee committees, and adopting motherless babies; people ought to know that they're not all they pretend to be. People round here have got a right to know. You go tell the *Courier*. Knock those Hunters down a peg, do the town a favour.'

Marjorie's superior came back from her lunch break with a bright bouquet of Guernsey hothouse flowers to enliven their winter office. 'Anything happen while I was out?' she asked, humming to herself lightly as she trimmed the stems of pink carnations with her box-cutting scissors.

Marjorie and her colleague exchanged a look and slipped the letter underneath the neatly folded copy of the *Courier*. Nothing had happened that they knew of; nothing at all.

Chapter One

Reenie Calder was possibly the most enthusiastic recruit in the history of Mackintosh's toffee factory, and her infectious energy was sometimes a bit much for her friend Mary.

'I ruddy love this job!' Reenie called out from beneath a carton-making machine which had been switched off so that she could get to the motor, her copper hair flopping out of her mobcap as she leant all the way back to get a proper look.

'That's as may be.' Mary waited with her arms crossed against her factory overall and the world. 'But what I want to know is can this machine go any faster without breaking any rules? What's the limiter on the dial for?'

Reenie pulled herself out from beneath the old Rose Foregrove apparatus and tucked her hair back into her cap with both hands. 'Well then, it's a good job I was passing your line, because that machine is in good working order and I don't see why I shouldn't take the limiter off and just whack it up to full—'

Mary stopped her friend short; she was not so easily won over by Reenie's blasé confidence as everyone else. 'If you're telling me that you don't know *why* someone put a speed limit on that machine, then I don't want you messing around with it. I only want speed if it doesn't cause a shutdown.'

'It wouldn't cause a shutdown – you always think the worst. I tell you your trouble, Mary Norcliffe: you're a confirmed pessimist. Don't ask yourself what could go wrong, ask yourself what could go *right*.'

The bustle of the factory production line carried on around them and three girls opened out and assembled card cartons for the next stage of the production line to keep it going while the machine idled. 'Reenie,' Mary said distinctly, 'do not touch that switch.'

'Oh, come on,' Reenie grinned, 'be an optimist!'

Mary took a deep breath, settled her hands on her hips, and bellowed, 'Reenie Calder! I am the overlooker on an emergency production line assembling forty thousand gas masks for a world war which appears to be imminent! I've married a Jewish German whose leave to remain is complicated at best, and I've inherited two stepchildren who barely speak my language and who I might have to smuggle out to America in my luggage if there's an invasion – which it seems highly probable there will be! How the ruddy hell do you expect me to be an optimist?'

The bustle around them faltered. Factory production lines are noisy places, and even if an overlooker can make themselves heard over the din they have to work hard to make the girls pay attention. Not so on this occasion. The gas mask production line was a hand-making assembly line, and with their only machine switched off for inspection an eerie quiet could fall over the hall if the girls stopped talking and slowed their work. The girls stopped. Over a hundred pairs of eyes were turned on Mary, the work before them only continuing in a cautious slow motion because Mary had dared to mention the topic they all avoided on this line: what if these masks they made, what if these air raid drills they were made to do . . . what if they were needed? A chill fell over the brightly lit factory floor which was ordinarily such a lively place and Reenie felt it. This wasn't good for any of them and she decided to raise her voice a fraction when she replied.

'Look at it another way,' she said as she led Mary in the direction of the cloakroom door, 'we've got so many gas masks now that it probably wouldn't be worth Hitler's time to drop gas on us so he might not bother. Or, if he does bother, we'll have done so many drills that we'll have our masks on before you can say *We Are The Ovaltineys*, and the gas won't do us any harm at all. He'll have wasted all his time and money on some gas which doesn't touch us, and he'll have less time and money to spend on guns and boats.' She steered Mary down the production hall, past another overlooker who was chivvying her girls on to get their speed up again. Reenie pushed open the heavy sprung doors which led to the empty cloakroom.

'I'm not saying it won't be tough, but I think we're tougher. Just look at all we've done here since we started out? The place burns down and we have scratch production lines back up and running again in a couple of days; there's a royal visit and the royal gift goes missing and you conjure up a new one overnight; there's an outbreak of scarlet fever and Diana has us all tested and quarantined before you can sneeze and the whole outbreak is quashed before it can reach Wakefield. We've got a good track record in our gang and whenever there's trouble we always fight our way out. Just look at your wedding – that was no mean feat in the circumstances.'

'But war is a very different prospect. If there's an invasion—'

'Then it would have to cross the sea. We're an island, remember, we've got that in our favour, the sea would slow them down. And so would your sister if she started flirting.'

'It's not a joke, Reenie, it's serious. Look at what's happened everywhere else, look at Spain, and Czechoslovakia, and Austria—'

'Look at Mack's. Look at all those girls who work fast as lightning when the whistle blows, organise themselves without any fuss, know by instinct what the girl next to them is going to do and sort themselves out accordingly, and then – when the whistle blows for the end of shift – they know how to let their hair down and have fun and make friends, and keep friends, and take care of those friends. If there's got to be a war – and I've got no control over it either way – I reckon we're in the best shape we've ever been to face it.

'I'm so worried, Reenie.'

'You're *always* worried; I'd be worried if you stopped worrying.'

Mary crossed her arms tighter. 'What are we gonna' do?'

'Well, we're gonna' cross each bridge as we come to it, and not before. Our next job is making sure the girls look smart for the *Halifax Courier*. They're sending a reporter first thing in the morning to see the gas mask line and write about what a great effort we're going to for war preparedness.'

'Since when? Who said the *Courier* could come here? Have we not got enough on our plates?'

'Since just now. It's why I came to see you; I've got to tell all the overlookers. It'll be reet; the line's ticking on well and you've got a good bunch of girls on assembly. I reckon you can be reet proud.'

'I don't want to be proud, I want to be left alone to get on with running my line in peace.' Mary slumped down on one of the cloakroom benches and automatically set to cleaning her glasses with angry vigour.

Reenie knew that there was very little point in trying to chivvy Mary along, but she did it anyway. 'Just think where we are compared to two years ago; we've got Diana practically running the Women's Employment Department, so we know we can always go to her for help if we're in trouble; you don't have to worry about your sister or Albert's kids anymore because the kids are at your new house and your sister's minding them, so that kills two birds with one stone; and then if there's any problems on the production line you know you can always rely on me to come and fix them for you because my department has gone to pot and I'm doing more or less what I like.'

'The idea of you doing "more or less what you like" doesn't reassure me.'

'Well, it should, because I've got such big plans for this place. If we go to war I'm gonna' bring in all the mothballed machines from store and then convert them to do all sorts of jobs we're doing by hand now. We won't know ourselves! It'll free up more girls to do more important jobs and Hitler won't stand a chance against the girls of Toffee Town – we'll be a force to be reckoned with!'

'Somehow I don't think Adolf Hitler is going to give up his plans of world domination because Irene Calder has made a toffee twist-wrapping machine seal up boxes instead.'

'Oh ye of little faith! If we bring in a machine to speed up gas mask assembly we might have an extra 10,000 masks a week, and that's an extra 520,000 masks in a year, and before long everyone's got a gas mask and there's no sense launching an attack with gas. It's like that poem where they lost the war for the want of a nail; if we're all trying to just make a tiny improvement somewhere—'

A siren howled a painful alert and Mary gripped the frames of her glasses in panic. 'They didn't say they were doing a test today.'

'They're not announcing drills anymore, they're a surprise.' Reenie said it lightly and didn't suggest that it could be a real gas attack. It could very well be a real gas attack. 'Where's your mask?'

'Under my chair on the production line.'

Reenie pulled her own mask out of the cardboard carton which hung at her side on a knitted string strap. 'Come on then, let's get it sharpish.' Reenie was confident this was just a drill to test their readiness; they'd sit in the factory shelter for a bit feeling bored and then they'd all emerge again into the dim light of a November Wednesday and everything would be just fine. Mary was trembling as she pushed through the other girls to retrieve her mask, and Reenie felt more convinced than ever of the importance of her own mission: bring back more of their mothballed machines and increase gas mask production. The year was 1938 and just over a month ago their Prime Minister had promised 'peace for our time' but Reenie didn't know a soul who believed him. Reenie's task was simple: she had to do what she did best, and make absolutely certain she didn't get sacked before she could do it. The problem was that she was Reenie Calder . . . and trouble always found her.

Chapter Two

'Factory life will be just what you need to take you out of yourself, you just wait and see.' Ada's father couldn't see the look of disappointment on his daughter's face as he said it because he was crouching at the fireplace in the parlour, sweeping out the ash and preparing to build it up again for the evening. He had changed out of the suit he habitually wore to his place of work and was dressed in flannels and a pink floral woman's apron to keep off the coal dust and soot. 'They've got everything there at Mack's; they've got youth clubs and hobby clubs, they go on outings – it's not like factory work was when your grandma was your age. She used to work twelve hours a day for six days a week and if she lost a finger in the loom they'd dock her pay! You'll have factory dances on Saturdays, music in the workrooms, and a slap-up dinner every day in the canteen. You'll be really looked after. Your cousin's done well there and he said he'd look out for you.'

Ada moped quietly behind her father. She wished she had the courage to ask not to be sent to a noisy toffee factory, but Ada Helliwell was constitutionally incapable of saying no to anyone. Besides, what sort of person would turn down a job at Mack's? Positions at Mackintosh's toffee factory were like gold dust. It showed just how much her father and her cousin Harry cared about her that they had gone to the immense lengths it must have taken to secure not only a job for a new starter, but a nineteen-year-old new starter with no experience.

'I thought about getting you a job in the filing room at my place, but it would be ever so quiet.' Mr Helliwell heaved himself up with a bucket of pale cinders to carry out to the yard, unaware that he had mentioned the dream which was closest to Ada's heart: a nice quiet job with no music or rowdy factory girls.

Mr Helliwell disappeared into the darkness of the yard behind their narrow galley kitchen and returned with the now-empty cinder bucket. Ada hesitated for a moment in the doorway, her mouth open and her breath held. 'What is it Ada? Come on, spit it out, girl.'

Could she say it? Could she ask for him to undo all the trouble he'd been to, waste whatever favours cousin Harry had called in, show an ingratitude that no one but her would understand? Could she ask him to give this chance to a girl who would appreciate it – any girl on Warley Street would think they'd won the pools if they got an offer letter from Mackintosh's – and get her that job in the file room?

'I'm getting cold out here.' Mr Helliwell rattled the ash pail.

'Sorry, Dad.' And she moved out of the doorway to let him pass, along with the moment.

'You'll be with your friend Caroline too, she's leaving that wet fish shop at last. You'll start on the same day.' Ada's father was busy washing the ash off his hands at the kitchen tap, but he must have sensed his daughter's reluctance because he tried to encourage Ada to look forward to her new adventure. 'Your friend Caroline's got the right idea. Get stuck in there at Mack's, have some fun, meet some nice lads, live while you're young. You don't know how lucky you are; there are girls who'd do bloody murder to get a job at Mack's and to have a father who'd give 'em a latch key and tell 'em to seize the day. Get yourself out there, go to the dances, walk out with some lads!'

Ada followed her father into the parlour where he quickly set to, vigorously twisting sheets of old news-paper to pile up in the grate before he rapidly piled on the kindling and the coal. She supposed she ought to think herself lucky that he didn't make her do it, but her dad was so obsessed with absolute economy in heating that he'd never have let any of the kids mess about with such a precious commodity as coal. They had heating with radiators in his office and Ada was willing to bet that he kept the temperature turned right down low and told all the bookkeepers to wear an extra jumper: that would be typical of her dad. Ada wouldn't have minded wearing her coat indoors if it meant she had a chance at working in an accounting firm instead of Mack's. Ada thought about bringing her late mother into the discussion, but her father got there first.

'Your mother would say exactly the same if she were here – God rest her soul – she'd tell you that you'll be married before you know it. You might as well make as much money as you can for your bottom drawer.'

'I'm only twenty, Dad, I might not be married for *years*.'

'You'll not be waiting years. You've got a pretty little face when you make a bit of effort with your hair, and if you're not too fussy you'll be snapped up by a nice lad in no time. You just want someone with a steady living who's kind to his mother, and you'll be settled down to make a home in no time, mark my words.'

Ada resented the implication that she was neglectful of her hair. She kept it clean and tidy; what more did people want? Her friend Caroline sometimes curled it for her with tongs if they went out to subscription dances together, but Ada couldn't be expected to do that for herself, and certainly not *every day*. Ada's hair was mousy, fine, and utterly flat. Life was all right for people like Caroline who had clouds of hair like spun gold that just billowed round their faces with barely a moment's effort, but Ada didn't have that luxury.

There was no time for further discussion because the house was suddenly rowdy with the noise of boys. Ada's elder brothers were home from their football practice, and they'd brought with them her two younger brothers who they always took to watch from the sidelines. The house would be a chaos of competing voices for the rest of the evening and well into the night when it would become a chaos of competing snores. There was no hope of her being heard now and she'd only be seen if someone was teasing her for something.

Ada took up her usual place on the faded rag rug in front of the fire which was just beginning to warm the room as bronze flames licked the coals. She had an old favourite from the library: *Regency Buck*, a romance and a mystery all in one, with Beau Brummell for added colour. The librarian – knowing how much his readers liked the illustrations on the jackets – had covered this one in a gummed cellophane and Ada could just discern, through the yellowed cover and the grime of other borrowers' hands, a gentleman in a top hat and tailcoat, striped silk socks and a cravat so ostentatious that it foamed forth from his collar like a waterfall. Behind him were the domes of an exotic-looking palace that was a world away from soot-black Halifax. In Georgette Heyer's books she found a warm comfort; a feeling that the stories themselves were a kind of home, the characters a kind of family, and that she could slip into the books like a steaming bath, and believe she was among

17

her people; well-mannered, softly spoken people who wouldn't dream of putting their muddy football boots on the dinner table, or talk over the ends of her sentences. Ada had never explained to her father the reason she so desperately wanted to work in a solicitor's office and not a factory, because she thought he wouldn't understand. In a busy, noisy factory she would – at best – be as roundly ignored as she was in her busy, noisy family; at worst she'd be teased and picked on. In a little office somewhere there was a chance that she would be noticed, perhaps make friends with a nice middle-aged manageress who had always wanted a daughter of her own and who would ask what she was reading, or give her dress advice, or teach her how to talk nicely, and introduce Ada to her polite, well-educated nephew. Perhaps in an office she would be the heroine of her own story for a change, and find a world just a little bit like a Heyer novel.

A smart rap at the back door made Ada look up from her book and her dream.

'It's for you, Ada!' her father called out from the parlour where he was boiling the kettle ready to serve bread and Bovril to his brood. 'Caroline's come to see you!'

Ada's heart gave a jolt as she saw her best friend was waving her curling tongs and grinning enthusiastically. Tomorrow was their first day at Mack's, and if that wasn't worrying enough, she was expected to have her hair done in honour of the occasion. A bulging cloth bag under Caroline's arm told Ada that she was going to be forced to try on a selection of her friend's dresses and shoes to see which mode of factory chic suited her best. This was so much worse than even the subscription dances Caroline dragged her to.

The solace of an evening immersed in the world of *Regency Buck* had been snatched away from her. More than ever, Ada missed her mother.

Chapter Three

Diana tried to hold a picture in her mind of how the old production line had looked before they'd hurriedly changed it over. Row upon row of stainless steel tables with two-inch lips to catch the molten toffee before it could flow like volcanic lava onto the asbestos floor; hundreds of girls happily gossiping as they worked. She tried to capture the aroma in her memory of rich, hot butter and burnt sugar which had long since melted away. She tried to hold on to the memory of laughter, singing, and the clatter of the porters' trolleys as they wheeled away the finished sweets ready to be wrapped. Above all, she tried not to look at what they were making now, and not to think about what it meant. Everything had changed.

'I've visited the factory before,' the journalist said, 'but I don't think I've ever been in this production hall. It's quite a lot bigger than—'

'It's the biggest hall we have. Across all our factories both in England and abroad. We've been given a large order to fulfil, and we've created the necessary space to fulfil it.' Diana was careful about what she said to the journalist; her instructions were to show him how quickly and efficiently the factory production line had been changed over, and to show him lots of smiling girls happily pitching together to get the job done. The former was easy, but the latter was damn near impossible. All of them – even hard-as-nails Diana herself – were soldiering on in a sort of horrified daze.

The journalist – Mr Chester 'Sleepless' Parvin – a tall stringy fellow with a pencil-line moustache and an honest look to him, was taking rapid notes in shorthand. 'How large is the order the government have placed with Mackintosh's?'

'We're making forty thousand of them.' She did not say the words; she would *not* say the words.

Chester Parvin nodded grimly and noted the number down. 'How will Mackintosh's keep up toffee production with their biggest toffee line shut down and turned over to special government projects?'

That question Diana could answer easily. As assistant to the Head of Women's Employment she had taken a role in organising it herself. 'Our German factory in Dusseldorf is ramping up production to make up the shortfall. They will be shipping us container loads of wrapped toffees daily, and a temporary staff of married women have been retained to repack them into Quality

Street cartons. Our customers won't notice any difference in the sweets they enjoy.'

'How long will it be before people start to see shortages of your sweets in the shops?'

'We don't anticipate any shortages for our customers.' Diana smiled confidently, but her smile didn't reach her eyes.

'But if you're reliant on European transport routes for your continued trade—'

A large bogie carrying pallets loaded with finished boxes clattered past Diana and the journalist, separating them for a moment. Diana stepped backward and steadied herself on the end of one of the trestle tables where the girls worked on the assembly line. She had tried not to look at what they were making, she had tried so hard. But there on the table was all her worst fears come to life in vivid scarlet casing. A horrible, alien face; a gas mask in the garish shape of a grinning Mickey Mouse. As far as the eye could see, on table after table, girls she had chosen for their dexterity were assembling gas masks to be worn by tiny children. Masks with blind, glassy eyes and hideous, dangling snouts. They made her heart race every time she remembered that one of them was destined for her secret daughter.

'Is there any difficulty about obtaining shipments from Germany?' Sleepless flicked through his notes looking for the other question he'd meant to ask.

'Not a bit of it. We're not at war with Germany as far as I'm aware. If war is declared that might make a difference, but until then we continue as normal.' Diana played it straight. She made a point these days of not asking people which camp they were in or if they thought the threat was real or just scaremongering. She was disheartened daily by the seemingly intelligent, well-read people who were determined to believe that Adolf Hitler was a peaceable man, and that they were all making a fuss about nothing, and that because they were British they would be the exception, would be safe and considered his friends. So many people didn't want to think about preparing for war, and so many more took active steps to stand in the way of reasonable preparations. This was the time when the people of the town needed to come together and use their immense pool of talents and resources to ready themselves to hunker down. But no, the community could not be persuaded to see a common enemy, a common goal. Despite appearances on this production line, time was being wasted.

Sleepless and Diana looked back up over the endless rows of gas mask assembly. War had yet to be declared, but for the Quality Street girls it had already begun. Hundreds of women had been taken off the toffee packing lines at Mackintosh's to assemble 40,000 gas masks in readiness for the deadly attacks the government warned were imminent. Air Raid Precautions – which were now a legal requirement – were swallowing up great swathes of the town, and great swathes of the people; volunteers were donning new uniforms and changing the face of Halifax. The public parks had been dug over to provide enormous air raid shelters; gas decontamination tanks had been installed in the swimming baths; underground first aid stations had been built below the main shopping streets; and Stoney Royd cemetery had been turned into one of the biggest anti-gas training centres in the country. They lived with the certainty of an uncertain war, but they were all expected to put a bright face on it, like the face of Mickey Mouse which grinned out horribly from every child's gas mask. It was November 1938, and in Halifax war had begun.

'These girls over here look as if they're working faster than the machines.' Sleepless nodded to a trestle table where gas masks were piling up, ready to be put into card cartons which were assembled by a Baker Perkins machine. 'Makes a nice change to see the machines struggling to keep up with the workers and not the other way around.'

Diana wasn't as pleasantly surprised as the journalist and called to the girl from Time and Motion who had accompanied them on the tour: 'Reenie, can this machine go any faster without blowing a gasket?'

Reenie Calder, who had nearly turned blue from biting her tongue for so long, was glad of a chance to speak up and offer to be useful. 'That's got a limiter on it to stop the girls turning the speed up, but I can take that off and crank it up easily. It's electric powered, not drive band, it's as simple as . . .' Reenie crouched below the machine, removed the cover on the dial which controlled the speed of the machine, and turned it up to its maximum level. The machine growled as it caught up sheets of flattened card cartons, flipped them open, and folded them together at a phenomenal rate.

The journalist was evidently impressed and made rapid pencil notes in his book. Reenie smiled at Diana, her delight at helping her colleagues beaming from her honest face. The smile was short-lived, however, as the motor on the Baker Perkins machine began to overheat and smoke mingled with the familiar smell of burning tar began to billow from the machine.

Dolly Dunkley had a little pocket of power in the Mackintosh's factory, and she exploited it for everything it was worth. Sometimes she used her power to gain something she wanted, like a nicer desk, or a more comfortable office chair, but other times she used her power just to show others that she had it, could wield it, and wasn't afraid to make her colleagues lives more unpleasant if she could. The trouble with Dolly was that she had very little notion what her motives were because she was too stupid to give them any thought and pursue a goal. Dolly was simply motivated by the enjoyment she felt at being top dog, and the kick she got out of making trouble.

It was not surprising, then, that she should use her new-found autonomy in the Mackintosh's workplace to take up indoor smoking. Dolly did not like the taste or smell of tobacco, and she felt no enjoyment in the physical action of drawing smoke into her lungs – if anything, it made her a little nauseous – but she loved the looks people gave her when they came to her office to ask a question, and she blew smoke in their faces instead of giving an answer. Dolly was only twenty-two, but thanks to her thickly, ill-applied make-up she looked a good deal older. The frequent puckering of her lips around the filter of a Craven "A" caused creases round her mouth into which her lipstick melted, mingling with her face powder and giving her the appearance of either premature wrinkles, or someone who had kissed a starfish. It was a shame, Dolly thought, that so few colleagues had the opportunity to see her in person and admire her magnificent dress sense; working away in an office gave her so few opportunities for flaunting her wardrobe of carefully chosen clothes. That morning, for instance, she was wearing a wonderful new frock made from a custard-yellow satin with a high, frilled collar, under a puce-pink cardigan. She looked like a burst boil, and she didn't know how lucky she was to be tucked away from ridicule.

Dolly's office was really an antechamber, a desk in a waiting room outside the office of Cynthia Starbeck. She occupied a windowless place between two doorways, a gatekeeper between the good people of the factory, and the malevolence of her manager. The two of them did not enjoy the art deco splendour of the main manager's office block and had to make do with the utilitarian virtues of the Time and Motion Department corridor instead. Bare floorboards, greying with age, green doors and frames revealing layers of paint in red lead beneath, and white walls which Dolly was determined to yellow with nicotine.

'Is she in?' Diana Moore marched through, barely pausing to wait for Dolly's answer before rapping smartly on Starbeck's door. 'Wait here,' she said to Reenie who had followed a pace behind.

Reenie waited, eyeing Dolly with the hesitancy of someone who wants to think the best of everyone, and wants to be everyone's friend, but who had too much experience of working with Dolly to be caught out. They knew each other of old. Reenie strained to hear the conversation on the other side of the door, but it was indecipherable.

There was a silence as Dolly smirked at Reenie because she could see the other girl was evidently in some trouble, and she'd have been delighted if she could have found a way to make it worse. Reenie tried to think of something to say which could pass the time without becoming contentious but it was Dolly who broke the silence in the end. 'I bet you don't know what this flag is.' She pointed to her desk where an ugly vase held a clutch of small flags in place of an arrangement of flowers. Nestling between the Union flag and the St George's Cross was an unusual standard which Reenie admitted she didn't recognise.

Dolly's over-made-up face took on a self-satisfied sneer which threatened to crack the crust of whiteish powder and paste she habitually wore. 'It's the Burma flag. My fiancé is out there with Burmah Oil. He sent it to me. What's your fiancé doing these days?'

Reenie said nothing. Dolly had always had a nasty streak, but Reenie had always been Dolly's superior, and therefore impervious to her malevolent activities to a certain degree. What worried her now was that if she was being demoted she could end up under Dolly's thumb, and that would be unbearable. Diana had said that she would be demoted if she wasn't sacked and a part of her hoped she was sacked.

A door slammed. Diana had re-emerged. 'Reenie, follow me. Dolly, send Reenie's pay chit on to Engineering and Fitting – she's moving departments.'

Dolly smirked at Reenie as she left with Diana. A smirk which said she would bin the chit if she found it among the mess of her filing, and Reenie could whistle for her pay until her new office wrote her a new one.

Dolly Dunkley enjoyed her new position of power – small though it might have been. She could order the best stationery from the factory store cupboard; she could order the Estates Department to bring her an office chair with wheels on; she could blow cigarette smoke in her colleagues' faces just to see them wince. Truly, this was the elevated world she had always known she deserved to inhabit.

The only problem was that something was missing; there was a hole in Dolly's emotionally stunted heart, and she could feel it more and more with each passing day. Unbeknownst to Dolly it was the sort of hole which other people filled with the love of their family, or acts of compassion for the needy, or even hard work towards a noble cause. Dolly, on the other hand, was going to fill hers with flags.

She'd recently attended a lecture at a meeting of the British Union of Fascists (now insisting they merely be referred to as the British Union because the f-word was getting a bit of bad press) where a man, who claimed to have simple answers to complex problems, advocated the putting out of more flags. Specifically he believed in the efficacy of waving the BUF's own flag and also the banner which he incorrectly identified as the Union Jack, apparently not knowing that this was its moniker at sea only. For every occasion he prescribed flags. Difficult neighbours? Fly flags. Uncle dead? Wrap the coffin in a flag. Lost dog? Lure it back with half a dozen really good flags. There wasn't a situation which couldn't be improved, or a problem which couldn't be solved, by the simple introduction of more flags. When the lecturer heard about Halifax's recent epidemic of scarlet fever he dismissed it as a trifle – it could all have been solved with the judicious application of *more* flags.

Dolly had caught on to his way of thinking immediately and enjoyed not only the displaying of the St George Cross, but also the act of policing other people's flag-waving. She was keeping a list of people who hadn't put up flags, and they came in for heavy criticism. Dolly enjoyed the smug feeling she got whenever she saw a Union flag flying in a part of the factory where it hadn't been seen before she complained about its absence. Unfortunately, Dolly did not know which way up the Union flag was meant to be flown, nor that flying it upside-down was an old maritime signal for a vessel in distress. Hence the whole of Halifax could see that the workers in the Mackintosh's factory were flying a cry for help from their windows. To whom they were appealing, goodness only knew, but perhaps they were appealing to God to deliver them from Dolly 'Flagging' Dunkley.

Dolly's problem – though she didn't know it – was not that she had an insufficiency of flags, but that she had an insufficiency of friends. Dolly had worked at Mackintosh's for over a year and she had been given ample opportunity to win people over, but she would insist on spreading hatred instead. She hadn't made a single friend in all that time, but her luck was about to change. She was about to make a friend for a lifetime.

Chapter Four

'I don't have time for this.' The slim young man in blue overalls was just in the act of taking a stubby pencil from behind his ear to amend a shift rota when Diana marched into the engineering break room with Reenie Calder in tow.

'You'll have to make time.' Diana was not in the habit of being shooed away easily and she pressed on with the purpose of her errand. 'This is the extra pair of hands I promised you. She was on the production line before the fire in '36, then she went to Norwich to help set up a Quality Street line in '37, and now she's done eighteen months in Time and Motion with Mrs Starbeck. She knows her way round, but she's just burned out another motor so don't leave her unattended with 'owt expensive.'

Reenie resented the suggestion that she needed baby-sitting, but she was so miserable at being demoted that she couldn't bring herself to object. She'd always liked and respected the engineering maintenance crew, but being sent to work with them was a heavy blow to her plans. Surely Diana couldn't mean to demote her for long? Reenie's talents lay in planning the layout and execution of entire factory production lines and she'd proved those talents again and again despite her youth. The factory had benefited from her ideas on many an occasion and surely they had to expect that, every so often, there would be an accident? It wasn't arrogance on Reenie's part which caused her to make these mistakes, it was just a well-meaning enthusiasm. She was, after all, just eighteen and couldn't be expected to know everything yet.

Reenie looked around at her new place of work while Diana Moore negotiated with the supervisor in strained whispers. Reenie knew she was lucky not to have been sacked, and the fact that Diana Moore – assistant to the Head of Women's Employment – was a friend of sorts was possibly all that had saved her this time. All the other managers who had championed her over the years had left the factory and Reenie felt very much alone when Diana left with a final disappointed frown at Reenie.

The new workroom was shabby to say the least, smaller than her mother's farmhouse kitchen by a good measure, and dingy through lack of natural light, a single narrow window having been painted over across the lower panes. Reenie wondered if the rest of the crew ever thought to lobby for better accommodation. She supposed they didn't spend much time there, the work of the maintenance crew being mostly spread over the various factory machines in situ, and those which had to be taken off the line for big repair jobs went down to the repair workshop beside the stable yard. Reenie expected her new job would be to report to the break room each morning, check her list of duties on one of the many crumpled rota pinned to the walls, and then go off on her own with a box of tools and a can of oil. Reenie was very much mistaken.

'All right, if you're all they're giving me I suppose I'll have to make do.' Harry Swallow rubbed his face as though to wake himself up, and Reenie wondered if she should tell him that he had smeared a line of black engine grease down his left cheek. She decided not to. She knew that lots of the sillier girls on the production line had a pash on him, and – believing he played up to it in his own grumpy sort of way – she thought it would serve him right to be taken down a peg in their estimation. Who was he to belittle her and suggest she was anything short of an excellent asset to his crew of engineers? *All* they were giving him? She would show him! But she wouldn't, because Harry Swallow was about to lay out her terms of employment in his department.

'I don't want you going off and doing any experiments or fancy footwork with the production line. I'm seriously short-staffed and I need everyone to just do the work that's on their list, and nothing else, do you understand me?'

Reenie nodded, conscious of the looks of open hostility she was receiving from the two old men who were packing up their lunch tins and getting ready to go back on shift. Back when she had first started at Mack's Reenie had found it hard to work with girls who didn't know her, and didn't always trust her to have their best interests at heart, but this was something else altogether. Working with older men who appeared to dislike her from the outset would take a kind of courage she wasn't sure she had.

Arthur Pardew, the most ancient of the maintenance men threw down his lunch tin in frustration. 'You tell them we need five more men and they send us one lass who's burnt every machine she's ever touched?'

'I'll work hard.' Reenie was keen to try to win the respect, if not the liking of her new crew, her good nature winning out over her bad mood she tried to promise them that she would be a greater catch than they thought she was. 'I'm not afraid to get my hands dirty, and I'll do twice as much work as you expect me to. I'll surprise you with some of the things I can improve—'

'Oh no you bloody won't!' Harry Swallow pulled his cap down over his brow and tucked his chestnut hair back under the band. 'You'll do no more, nor less than I tell you. No surprises, no extra jobs you think might help, no improving things, and no little projects of your own that I don't know about. I think it's best you stick with me for the first couple o' weeks until I know you'll not play silly buggers.' Reenie worried at this; was she really going to be demoted for so long? Surely it couldn't be permanent, could it? This had all happened so fast. Perhaps Diana was just trying to shock her into being more careful. 'Now, pick out one of them boiler suits you think'll fit you and come along with me; we've got four drive bands to change before the next whistle.'

Reenie looked to where her new supervisor had pointed. A locker of sorts held a dozen blue boiler suits in a variety of lengths, all hanging from metal hangers stamped with the Mackintosh's logo. The suits were made for men and not women's figures and Reenie realised she was going to have to pluck up the courage to ask to take some of them home to alter on her mother's sewing machine if they expected this to be her daily uniform. Was she really going to have to get used to this? She wondered if the engineers were making her first day in their crew as deliberately awkward as possible. 'Where's the nearest place for me to change?' she asked with so much apology in her voice that it cracked a little.

'Gordon Bennett!' Harry Swallow evidently hadn't been expected to be held up while he waited for his newest recruit to go and find the nearest ladies lavatories. 'Can't you just put it on over your clothes? We don't have time for you to dress up and make yourself look nice.'

Tears stung Reenie's eyes. It was such a silly and inconsequential thing, but she was realising fully now the consequences of her demotion. She supposed that this was the team who had been given the job of repairing not only the last machine she'd burnt out the motor on, but every machine she'd ever broken through her enthusiasm to try better ways of doing things. This team knew precisely what her abilities were because they had been clearing up after her for the last two years each time she'd got things wrong, and when she thought about it like that she wondered if some of their hostility wasn't justified.

Reenie hung her head and muttered quietly, 'I can't. It would roll my skirt up.'

Harry Swallow sighed with the exasperation one might show a child. 'I can't hear you, what are you saying?'

Reenie raised her voice, straightened up, and tried to sound as neutrally professional as she could. 'I said that I'm not able to put this on over my clothes. I'm wearing a skirt and it will roll up under the boiler suit because the boiler suit has trouser legs. I have to go and change my clothes.'

Reenie was surprised to see Harry Swallow blush and his hostility and that of his two colleagues was replaced by a very human embarrassment. They might all be in a very bad mood, but they were not monsters. Harry cleared his throat and said, 'All right, we'll go out to the hall and let you change in here.' He walked over to the grimy window and pulled down the blind and then ushered his crew out of the door. 'You come and call us in when you've changed into your boiler suit and you're ready to come out. I'll stand guard and make sure no one disturbs you.' He closed the door behind him leaving Reenie almost in the dark. For the first time since she had walked through the door of Mackintosh's two years earlier, she desperately wanted to walk back out again.

Chapter Five

There were plenty of fresh faces at the factory that morning, but Ada didn't see any she recognised. The enormous iron gates which proclaimed the name of *Mackintosh's* were parted at a quarter to eight o'clock and Caroline squeezed Ada's hand and squealed at the thrill of it all. Caroline clutched her letter of employment so tightly that Ada thought it might dissolve; but no, of course it wouldn't, Caroline would never suffer from clamminess. She stood out as a perfectly polished pearl among the crowd of clog-shod workers, and she would probably look just as freshly pressed when the whistle sounded for the end of their shift at half past four. Caroline always shone, and Ada was always invisible in her shadow.

'Please let us be in wrapping,' Caroline prayed aloud in a whisper, 'please let us be in wrapping, please let us be in wrapping.'

Ada didn't care where they were so long as she didn't have to get dressed up like this every morning. After much deliberation Caroline had settled on a cream and rose print cotton dress for her friend, which was hard-wearing, but not dowdy. Ada – for the love she bore her best friend – had agreed to submit to a full head of curls which she had known full-well would drop out before Caroline left, and certainly wouldn't hang on until morning, even if she slept face down on her pillow. It had all eaten into Ada's reading time and she wasn't sure that it had been worth it for a job she didn't want anyway.

'Do you think we should push our way through to get closer to the front of the crowd?' Caroline asked, but had clearly already made her decision as she forced her way through the press of other workers, towing Ada behind her.

'I don't think we should try to do anything that might get us a reputation—'

But it was too late, Caroline was already calling across the throng of people to the gatekeeper in his cabin and waving her employment note: 'Can you let us through, please? We're just *so desperate* to get put in sweet-wrapping.' Caroline's wide, open smile and sparkling blue eyes made it so easy for her to cause the sea of people to part, and the gatekeeper wink as he pointed her in the right direction. Ada was used to all of it. Caroline Caffrey would have no trouble fitting in at Mack's. She had always been supremely confident, and her winning smile somehow let her get away with absolute murder. Caroline was ready to take the factory by storm and Ada knew that her friend would want to be the new 'It' girl at Mack's, just as she'd tried to be at their school, and she'd be doing her best to create a sensation. Caroline wasn't interested in the technicalities of factory work, the art of sweet-making, or the grander scheme of things in the world of business and industry – all she cared about was the factory dances, the factory outings, and the factory boys. Mackintosh's was the perfect place for Caroline, and much though Ada would be sorry to be separated from her best friend, she still didn't think life as a factory girl was for her.

'Come along, Shrinking Violet,' Caroline giggled as she almost ran across the stone flags of the vast, busy courtyard which lay beyond the gates and the crowd of arriving workers, 'this is our big chance!'

Ahead of them loomed the many storeys of the Albion Mills building and the modern office block, and judging by the queue of young people clutching letters the modern building was where they needed to be. These were the keenest of the keen, boys and girls who'd sought advice from relatives and neighbours about which gate to come in through on their first day, which shortcut to take, which door to wait at to make certain they were top of the queue to be placed in the favoured departments and didn't end up mucking out the factory stables or mopping floors somewhere. These were Caroline's people and the excitement on their faces was infectious.

Reluctant though she was to join that particular work-force, Ada couldn't help but catch a little of the eager anticipation in the air, and feel a thrill at entering into this world of grown-up and serious endeavour. She wondered if the first day of work in the factory always felt this momentous; as though they were all embarking on a great adventure together, full of endless possibilities and heavy with significance. Although Ada planned to go on to another workplace eventually, she supposed this was her first day in a real job and she should try to enjoy it a bit while she was there. She felt gratitude to Harry, her cousin in the Engineering Maintenance Department, who had cared enough about her to get her the job, and to get her friend a job at the same time so that she wouldn't be alone. The late October sun shone butterscotch-bright in a cloudless sky over the factory courtyard, and it seemed like an omen of promise, washing over the enormous sign on the factory roof which read, 'Mackintosh's'.

A lump rose in Ada's throat and she felt more than a little pride that such an important company should have started in her home town, and that she could tell her grandchildren she'd worked for them once, if only briefly. Perhaps this was how young lads felt when the recruiting officer stirred them up with a passion to fight for King and Country; all she'd done was walk up to the gates of the factory with Caroline and the place was already starting to go to her head. But then life with Caroline was like that; Caroline was a gossip, a flirt, an outrageous dancer, and an absolute scream. Everything seemed so much more exciting with her friend. *Perhaps*, thought Ada, *working at Mack's might not be so bad with Caroline to look out for me*. But then Caroline did one of those things which always made Ada want to curl up and hide under a rock:

'Does anyone here know what I've got to do to get a job in sweet-wrapping for me and my friend?' Caroline called out enthusiastically to the young people who queued outside the offices. Her voice echoed out across the courtyard and faces appeared at the windows of the office block two storeys up, to which Caroline's voice had clearly carried.

Ada wished she had the confidence of her friend, but she also wished her friend had less confidence. Ada sometimes wanted to be a little bit more noticeable, but not like this; this was excruciatingly embarrassing and a well-bred Heyer heroine would never have behaved like this. Just when Ada thought she wanted to stay by Caroline's side a while longer, Caroline reminded her why they really couldn't work together. This was Caroline's sort of place, but not Ada's.

Chapter Six

When Diana Moore – as a loudmouthed sixteen-year-old – had first walked through Mackintosh's gates over a decade earlier she had not thought she'd grow up to be the sort of young woman who took notes in meetings. But here she was in the Mackintosh's boardroom. listening to important men and women discuss how many tens of thousands of pounds they would spend in 1939, and how much money their toffee factory could make them.

It was one of those days when the view from the window showed autumn colour, but the air had winter's bite. The boardroom – all wood-panelled walls, lined with oil paintings of the Mackintosh family and carpeted in the richest red wool – was stuffy and the air felt dry. The art deco office building at the heart of the vast toffee factory complex was always rather too warm for

Diana's liking. She had grown up in, if not the worst of the town's slums, then at least somewhere life was still hard. Heat had been a luxury she had learned to use sparingly. She had learned to use most things sparingly, even speech. Her wits, though, were another matter. Her wits had kept her among the fastest wrapping girls in the factory for years; her wits had helped her conceal a pregnancy when she was twenty, helped her conceal that child's identity in one way or another and had got her the job of assistant to the head of Women's Employment. Her wits had given her a life she could never have dreamed of, and now she knew that she was going to need them more than ever, because she planned to steal back her child from the kind people who had adopted her, and she was going to run away. It hadn't been an easy decision, but circumstances had conspired against her. All sorts of things had happened to shake her belief in the life she had been living, and the latest among them was a letter from her stepbrother, which had cut through her like a knife.

'Mrs Wilkes,' the wizened old director of finance asked from behind a stack of inky ledgers, 'how much are these gas mask girls costing us? And I don't want you fobbing me off with their hourly rate, I want to know how much they're costing us in real terms. How much money are we losing on the toffee lines by substituting them with slower workers while they assemble these blasted masks, and how much extra are we having to spend on recruiting and training their understudies?'

Diana stole a discreet glance at her manager. She knew Mrs Wilkes well enough by now not to expect her to rise to the bait. She'd give as good as she got, but wouldn't give any ground. Diana would be sorry to leave her when the time came, but that was the least of her worries.

'Is there something you would rather have my girls do than make provision for the safety of the nation?' And now Mrs Wilkes spoke with an almost apologetic tone, 'I would remind you that these gas masks are being assembled at the request of His Majesty's Government. It is the Ministry for the Co-ordination of Defence which has sent us this work, not the Mackintosh's Women's Employment Department.'

The finance director began turning rapidly through his ledgers to a relevant page of figures, 'Yes, but you don't have to put our best people on it! Speed costs money and, in my opinion, it is a senseless waste to use our fastest girls to make gas masks for a war which will never happen, hamstringing the Quality Street production line in the process. The Quality Street toffee selection is now so popular that demand outstrips supply; our best workers should be on Quality Street.'

Sir Harold, owner and chairman of Mackintosh's, cleared his throat loudly and raised an owlish eyebrow at his animated director. 'Our best workers belong where I say they do, and I'd rather be safe than sorry.'

Diana discreetly lifted an elegant hand. 'Would you like me to minute that, Sir Harold?' Diana knew that her manager would want the pronouncement in writing so that she could use it as ammunition later if necessary.

'If you wouldn't mind. Thank you, Miss Moore.'

The meeting rumbled on and Diana noticed that the finance director was unnecessarily combative on several points as he bristled from not getting his own way. He reminded her of her stepbrother in that respect; yet another one of those people who couldn't believe that a thing was true if it was also something they disliked the idea of. Tommo hadn't said anything to her in his letter about the war preparations, but knowing him as she did Diana suspected he'd be in the same camp as the finance director; the brigade who insisted that the government were just scaremongering.

Diana hadn't seen her stepbrother for two years, and she was partly responsible for his absence. Tommo had been caught fencing a variety of stolen goods on the same night that he and his friend crashed a stolen car, and Diana – after years of tolerating Tommo's criminal activities for the sake of somewhere to live – informed on him to the police. Diana had visited Tommo in Wakefield Prison to tell him that she had been forced by circumstances beyond her control to put her daughter up for adoption and Tommo had been livid, had sworn to find little Gracie and to take her back as soon as he was released. It was typical of Tommo that he should show little care for his niece when she was in his house, but become powerfully possessive when she was taken away.

'Should we be recruiting more young women than we ordinarily might?' Sir Harold's mind was clearly still on the matter of war preparations. 'Last time we lost a good deal of the younger men right at the start because so many wanted to volunteer for the fighting, and then we lost them in waves after that. If we're to assume that the same will happen this time, ought we to mitigate the potential loss of men by hiring more women? Perhaps even training our existing women for men's jobs, like running the boiler house or some such thing.'

The conversation rumbled on around Diana and she scratched out minutes now and then. The directors argued firstly about whether or not there would be a war, and secondly whether it would be anything like the last one, and thirdly whether they should try to hedge their bets.

Diana couldn't believe that important, well-educated men and women could be so blind. Of course the war was coming, of course it would be worse, and of course they needed to act. Diana had seen things they hadn't. In order to stay close to her secret daughter, Diana had volunteered to help Gracie's adoptive mother – a local philanthropist – to organise a fund to help refugees of the Spanish Civil War come to England. Diana had met these refugees as they arrived, shocked and frightened, in Halifax, and she had heard in detail about the way the Fascists were behaving all over Europe. Diana was convinced that there would be war, that there would be gas attacks – and then the united fascist alliance would invade England. Diana wouldn't allow her daughter to stay here and risk that. She'd rather sell herself to a New York sweatshop to keep her daughter safe than bide her time in Halifax like a sitting duck. In her desperation she had turned to one of Tommo's old associates to get her tickets on a boat to America under false names, with false papers too. Now she wondered how long it would be before her stepbrother found that out.

The letter from Tommo had only made her see that she needed to accelerate her plans. It had been sent from a halfway hostel in Wakefield. It said that he had come to Halifax on the bus looking for her, but when he went to their old house she wasn't there.

No bloody warning that my house was full of bloody Irish. Not a word to me that you'd moved. How do you think that made me feel? I'm your own brother, almost the only family you've got, and you don't tell me you've cleared out. Well, don't think you can hide away because I'll be back for good once I've got this parole woman off my back and it'll go better for you if you don't make me look for you. I want to know where to find you, and where to find Gracie.

The letter had been sent to her care of the Mackintosh's factory post room, and it was only a matter of time before another found its way to her new home. She couldn't hide in her boarding house forever.

Chapter Seven

The kitchen of the Calder family farmhouse was filled with the tang of cider vinegar and contentedly bickering children. Reenie, Kathleen, and John had spent their Sunday afternoon wrapped in winter coats – for the first time that autumn – picking plump wild plums from the hedgerow in the lane beyond Ruffian the horse's paddock. It was a Calder family tradition all through the autumn for the children to go out foraging after a leisurely Sunday lunch, and then they would argue around the fire while their mother simmered up their bounty into fragrant jams, fruit wines, and ketchups which she bottled for the coming year. The argument this time was rather more grown-up than in previous years; Reenie, just eighteen, John fifteen, and Kathleen, who insisted she 'would be fourteen next birthday', were discussing the difficulty of going out to work.

'I'll have you know I'm very useful to them.' Kathleen was pulling off her old grey mittens and jamming them into her coat pockets so that she'd know where they were next time she needed them.

John scoffed, 'As what, tea lady?'

'What's wrong with being a tea lady? They need tea ladies. I didn't join because I expected to be given a bayonet and lookout post on Beacon Hill.'

'The Air Raid Precautions unit wouldn't be the ones to man lookout posts.' John seemed to know an awful lot for a boy who claimed to take no interest in the government-led preparations for war. 'That would be the army. If you wanted to be left to freeze your ears off at a lookout post you'd need to join up as a cadet, and they wouldn't have you because you're too young.' He didn't add, *I know because I've checked.*

'Well, it's a good job I don't want to sit on a hill with a bayonet waiting for Germans,' Kathleen said, as she draped her coat over a wooden crate full of jars of pickled cauliflower, the coat hooks being all of three yards too far away. 'I want to be a tea lady and give out biscuits to all the nice folks who are doing their training in the parish hall to be ARP Wardens and the like.'

'Oh, *now* it makes sense!' Reenie's nose glowed red with the change from the cold of the lane to the warmth of the kitchen. 'You're sitting in on all the training! You joined the ARP, you probably said you knew you were a bit on the young side, but you could just do something a bit helpful and make an urn of tea, and *that* got your foot in the door and now you're sitting in on all of the training pretending that you're just making sure the tea urn doesn't hiss, but really making sure you're ready to step in at the opportune moment like an understudy who's learnt all the lines. That's it, isn't it? You're trying to make yourself the youngest-ever ARP Warden by stealth.'

Kathleen pursed her lips. 'I am *not* trying to be an ARP Warden. I don't want to be a warden.'

Kathleen's father chuckled with pride and slapped his hand down on the sack of sugar which had been temporarily propped between his kitchen chair and the table. 'You're just like Reenie, you are. You're a right pair. Don't think you can pull the wool over our eyes, we know you. Out with it, tell us what you're planning.'

Privately Kathleen objected to being compared to her sister. They were nothing alike as far as she was concerned. Reenie was big-hearted enough to volunteer to help without really thinking about what the consequences might be; Reenie was always trying to 'make things better'. Reenie might have a short-term plan, but never a long-term strategy. Kathleen, on the other hand, was all long-term strategy. She didn't go volunteering for things and hoping for the best; Kathleen engineered the outcome.

She adopted a casual tone now. 'I'm expecting they'll want more messengers than they've got. I've sat through all the training on being an ARP Messenger and, should the need arise, I could let them have some of my time.'

Mr Calder hooted with laughter, Reenie sighed as though she'd suspected as much, and John rolled his eyes.

'I don't know why you think it's so funny. I'm being very public-spirited. Reenie ought to be joining – she's old enough *and* they'd want her mechanical experience in the gas decontamination centre up at Stoney Royd.'

'I wouldn't have the time, I've got enough on my plate at Mack's and I expect I'll be a reserved occupation anyway.'

'You must have more free time now you're not going to the cinema half the week with your Peter,' Kathleen said unthinkingly.

'Kathleen!' Mrs Calder, who had been enjoying having the children together, even if they were bickering, took exception to this unintended little barb. Reenie's broken engagement was not to be discussed so lightly in her kitchen.

John hastily changed the subject in an uncharacteristic act of sensitive diplomacy. 'Have you got any more of them war magazines in the loft, Dad?' He gestured behind him with his thumb at a tatty, yellowing pile of publications from the Great War with stirring titles like *The Boy's Own Paper* and *British Lads*.

'What do you want with all that old stuff, John. I thought you liked reading the Funny Pages you got from the lads up at Stebbins' farm.' Mrs Calder had noticed her son's changing reading habits and worried. She always worried.

John shrugged convincingly. 'I've read all they've got.'

Kathleen caught his eye and an unspoken communication passed between them, unseen by the rest of the family. She clearly didn't believe her brother, but she wasn't saying anything. 'Can I get the loan of Ruffian and the wagon next Wednesday night, Dad?'

The abrupt change of conversation took the company by surprise and made Mrs Calder – who was pressing plump indigo fruits through a metal sieve – suspicious. 'Since when do you borrow the horse and cart?'

Kathleen sat up a little straighter and tried to sound mature beyond her years. 'There's a first time for everything. Besides, it's in a good cause. The ARP Wardens have got another couple o' thousand gas masks coming from Mack's and they need them taking round the parish halls where they're doing the fittings for the public. I said I could do a bit o' delivering.'

Reenie's ears pricked up at the reference to her own employer. 'Why can't they get a motor van, or a man with a barrow? Why are they calling on the services of a fourteen-year-old girl from a neighbouring farm? Why don't they ask Dad to do it if they're so desperate?'

'Well, it's a difficult time.' Kathleen deftly skirted over the matter of her age, knowing that she was legally old enough to drive a horse and farm equipment if she had her parents' consent. 'Everyone needs wagons. There's all the preparation for food shortages, there's people moving out to the country, there's—'

'Yes,' Reenie pulled her up short, 'but the work you're talking about is an essential war preparedness activity. They get priority. They can get a motor van, and if they can't find one to hire they can just requisition one.'

Kathleen was only too aware of this and had an answer ready. 'You'd have thought so, wouldn't you? But they've tried requisitioning one and there's nothin' doin'; the motor wagons they're trying to requisition have already been requisitioned by other people doing other things for war preparedness. So here we are and it's a good job I'm so public-spirited or those gas masks would have to sit in your factory taking up space, wouldn't they?'

'Public-spirited my eye. You just want to get inside my factory to remind Diana that you want a job next year and ask if you can come to the factory dance.'

Kathleen reclined in the old oak dining chair she'd pulled up to the fire, confident that she'd won this argument. 'Might not have to wait that long if there's war before Christmas. They'll close the school and I'll be free to work.'

'There won't be a war!' Mrs Calder didn't object to all the war-preparedness committees – she said the people who turned up to them were wasting no one's time but their own – but she objected to this pessimistic talk in her home. She said, with desperate tears welling in her eyes, 'The Prime Minister has secured Peace for Our Time and everything will simmer down now. It's been a difficult few years, but now we can all just go back to normal.'

Behind her back it was the turn of Mr Calder and his son to exchange a look of unspoken communication. The kitchen they sat in was crowded with the provisions Mrs Calder had stockpiled 'just in case I can't get to the shops in the snow'; years and years' worth of extra preserves she'd made from the berries she'd insisted the children go out to forage – long after the normal season was over – because 'it's been a good year for fruit, we shouldn't leave anything on the trees'; and in the dresser drawer, wrapped in a tea towel, was the service revolver her father had brought back from the front which she'd suddenly felt the need to have professionally cleaned 'because it's not nice to have dirty things knocking about the house.' They were all of them preparing for war, but for some it was easier to admit to than for others.

Reenie sighed. She had been holding something back and this seemed like the moment to share it. 'I've been demoted at work.'

Reenie's parents looked shocked and her mother asked, 'What on earth have you done this time?'

'Burnt out another machine.'

'Oh, Reenie.' Mrs Calder said. And for a fleeting moment their fears of war were forgotten.

Chapter Eight

'The trick is to rub cornflour into the roots of your hair. If you don't want your hair to fall flat like a matron's bonnet you need to rub the cornflour in *before* you use the tongs.' Caroline Caffrey was holding court in the girls' changing rooms after her third shift at Mack's. She sat with her legs crossed on a bench below a coat hook and a crowd of other teenaged girls huddled round her to hear everything she had to say. It had taken so little time for her to capture the hearts of the other girls, and to become the centre of attention and the authority on all matters. Caroline had moved swiftly from talk about the timing of the next factory dance, to thoughts on dress, advice on complexion, and now a seminar on hair styling.

A girl of about fifteen piped up from the end of the coat rack: 'What about setting lotion? Do you use Amami, or Wave Set?'

'Yes,' chimed in another equally eager voice, 'do you just dip the comb in the bottle, or do you have a special method?'

Caroline smiled confidingly; this was the secret of her success. People confided in her because she invited them to by appearing to share her own secrets. She made people feel they wouldn't be ridiculed; quite the reverse, she made them feel that trusting her with their confidences would win them Caroline's approval and love. People wanted to make Caroline beam her warm and loving smile at them, and so they shared their plans and their fears and their woes and their shame at their shortcomings, and she chatted with such intimacy that she made everyone feel specially chosen for her attention. She treated every stranger like an old friend and it was intoxicating.

But it was also rather hard on her original old friends, the ones who had thought they might be entitled to a little more care and attention than the people she'd met only moments before.

'If I were you,' Caroline said, leaning forward just a little to press the arm of a younger girl in sisterly reassurance, 'I'd use the tiniest drop of glycerine. I think it will be just the thing, and,' she looked over her shoulder as though to make certain no one was listening, though who she was looking out for goodness only knew because the entire shift of minnows was crowded round to hang on her every word, 'I've never told anyone this, but I promise you I had exactly the same trouble and I read in a magazine that glycerine worked miracles and it honestly did.'

After Caroline had cemented her intimacy with the room of thirty-odd girls by sharing a few of her greatest secrets (a small but unsightly rash under her left elbow of which she was ashamed; her fear of dying in a motor accident; and her burning passion for the Maori scrum half in Halifax Town rugby league team), she was ready to find out the information she really wanted from the factory girls, which was: who were the most eligible boys at the dances, and who was her competition. She said, with a bluntness which would have been met with cold reserve had anyone else asked it, 'So, who's got a pash on who?'

The girls blushed, giggled, whispered to each other, pointed away from themselves, gave each other playful digs in the ribs, and generally warmed to the subject with an appropriate degree of coquettish reticence. A few of the more confident souls talked in general terms about lads who were well-liked, and Ada slipped away from the group without anyone noticing, to go and stand by the window and take a last look at the factory court-yard glowing golden in the dying evening light.

It had been another horrible day for Ada. She and Caroline had secured the coveted places in sweet-wrapping (as Ada had never doubted they would) and while Caroline squealed with laughter every time something went wrong, clearly having the time of her life, Ada was desperate for it all to stop. The noise was so intense that it had a claustrophobic quality and Ada felt that somehow her peripheral vision was narrowed by the din. She had kept up a reasonable pace, but had cringed a little every time anyone moved close to her, as though she thought the people walking across the factory floor were staggering about on deck aboard a ship and might lose their footing and crash into her at any moment. The noise and movement of her fellow workers was disorientating to the point of nausea and Ada didn't know how she would manage a fourth day of it.

Ada really had been determined to try to make an effort once she'd met her new colleagues and realised how nice they all were, and she hoped they hadn't noticed her distress on the production line because she had tried so very hard to bottle it up, but it was all just so rough and rowdy. Caroline was good at throwing herself into conversation with people she hadn't been introduced to – it seemed like the factory way – whereas Ada shrank from the informal atmosphere of shared confidences and shouting over the top of each other.

Ada gazed out at the Halifax skyline, every brick of it black with coal soot, the crowded jungle of factory chimneys standing out against the orange sky. Ada longed to get away, longed for the reassuring social rules of her Regency romances, and a civilised ball in the Assembly Rooms at York, where the soot didn't cover every surface and the windows shone. Instead she was faced with the prospect of factory dances which sounded to her like mayhem.

'I cannot *wait* for the next factory dance,' Caroline said, breathless with carefully dramatised excitement. 'After the year we've all had, I think we just need to throw ourselves into everything. I've been learning the jitterbug; have you learned the jitterbug yet? Is anyone doing the jitterbug at the factory dances? I would just *scream* if I got to be the first to do the jitterbug!'

Ada also thought she might scream.

She was desperate to talk about how frightened and overwhelmed she felt by all the noise and bustle in the factory, and how invisible she felt among the mass of workers. She wanted to tell Caroline about how unhappy she was at home and how she missed her mother. Ada wanted to tell someone, *anyone* that she felt as though she didn't exist because people talked *at* her but never *with* her. Ada wanted to feel like someone had heard her and seen her, but on *her* terms and not by making herself as rowdy as her brothers or the girls in the factory. Ada wanted to say so many things, but it was as if she was invisible.

Ada noticed something crooked about the window frame. The small square panes of glass were secured in the windows not by wooden dowelling, but by rusted cast iron. The iron was flaking off in great russet brown curling scales, and Ada thought it would only be a matter of time before someone caught themselves on it and got a nasty cut. She saw something she might do to help; if she hooked a loop of wool from her mitten around one of the protruding flakes she could yank it out of the frame and prevent a nasty accident later. She braced herself against the frame, got a good grip, and then pulled hard.

It all went wrong. The whole rusty iron section came away and the pane of glass slipped.

'Ow!' Ada jumped back as the pane of glass cracked in two and tumbled first through her hands, and then onto the floor where it bounced and shattered almost simultaneously. A cut, no longer than a match, was already beginning to bloom red on her arm.

The other girls looked up, suddenly anxious at the sight of blood and broken glass. Caroline was pushing the girls aside to tend to her friend. 'Ada! What happened? Did someone throw a stone through that window? Quick, someone fetch the first aid kit! And someone call the factory watchman, or the managers! Quick!' Caroline enjoyed taking charge and bossing everyone about, and the other girls scurried about fetching clean handker-chiefs, iodine, and being generally attentive to the girl who, for that moment, they all wanted to care for.

Ada stood stock-still and gazed at the cut in disbelief. It was magic. She wasn't invisible anymore. She felt oddly calm in the noisy chaos which ensued, even felt charitably toward the girl who attempted to take some of the attention away from her by pretending to faint at the sight of Ada's blood. Ada felt elated, focused and real again – and all it had taken was a little cut.

Chapter Nine

'Can I have a go on the Ewbank?' Bess asked enthusiastically, not waiting for her sister's answer before she began thrusting the mechanical carpet sweeper across the hall floor with gusto. To Bess there was evidently still a novelty in seeing the domestic appliances her elder sister had acquired through marriage. Mary's husband was not a wealthy man, but his salary was enough to secure them the lease of a modern family home so far above the squalor which Mary and Bess had grown up in that it seemed like a fairy palace. Long gone was the darkness of their one-up-one-down, back-to-back terrace slum with no sanitation, and no heating but the stove in the parlour. Now Mary had not only running water, but *hot* running water with a fixed bath to put it in. The front door didn't open straight into the sitting room, but into a neat little hallway with a carpeted staircase (supported by brass stair rods which gleamed from Mary's regular and possibly over-enthusiastic applications of Brasso). A three-bedroom semi-detached house with a small square of garden, electric lighting, and a telephone might not have been everyone's idea of paradise, but to Mary it was a better life than she could ever have hoped for or imagined.

'Albert's bought a little one for Greta, too. Look at this.' Mary wouldn't ordinarily have shared any of the details of her domestic arrangements without significant reluctance, but her sister was always the exception. She reached into the cupboard under the stairs and pulled out a miniature version of the 'Parlour Queen' – Ewbank's most expensive model – and ran it over a crumb of dried mud near the doormat to show that it was a working toy. 'We're trying to help her feel at home here, but she's not settling.' And, with uncertainty in her voice, she went on, 'I don't think she likes me.'

Bess stopped messing about with the Ewbank and looked quizzically at her sister. 'Why wouldn't she like you? You're her new mother.' It seemed so simple to simple Bess. An automatic affection, like the automatic lighting.

This, Mary thought, was the problem. She was barely old enough to be Greta's mother, let alone little Max's. They were wonderful children, and she loved them, but the whirlwind romance with their father had been topsy-turvy, and the wedding had been hastened to help the Baums escape Germany at speed. She'd married Albert before she'd even met his children, and the children had found themselves in a new country, in a new house, making new friends and starting new lessons all at the same time as gaining a new mother.

Mary had been forced to give up the job she loved at the toffee factory where they'd met – Mackintosh's didn't allow married female workers – and make do with a temporary position on the gas mask assembly line for as long as that lasted.

Mary walked ahead of Bess into the sitting room. 'Greta, Bess is here to mind you while I go out to work my shift. Do you want to greet her?'

The little girl looked up from her toys reluctantly. She had constructed a house for her Minnie Mouse puppet using a variety of household objects, including an emptied magazine stand, a sewing basket, and a book of Co-op divvy stamps. '*Ich bleibe hier,*' she muttered, and scowled at her new stepmother.

'What does that mean?' Bess asked in a whisper to her sister.

'I don't know, but she's not best pleased.'

'I'm not surprised.' Bess had a lot of sympathy for the little girl who had arrived with so little of the local language. 'Her clothes are all too small for a start, so she must be ever so uncomfortable.'

'I know, and I tried to tell her, but she only wants to wear clothes that make her look like Minnie Mouse. I bought her some new things, but she turned up her nose at all of them and we can't afford to go off buying endless new clothes. They arrived with hardly anything and then they grew out of it all in five minutes flat.' Mary sighed. She didn't understand the little girl's fixation with the American mouse. Greta had insisted on wearing her black hair in two tight little buns on the top of her head to make her look as if she had Minnie Mouse ears. She had a polka-dot skirt with a torn fastening which she had worn almost to rags, and a pair of white gloves which had turned grey. Mary knew she would have to tackle the wardrobe matter eventually, but she was half afraid of little Greta.

'Can I look in the kitchen?' Bess swished her skirt as she bobbed from side to side in excitement at one of her favourite novelties.

'It's no different since the last time you saw it, and I need to get the tram in five minutes.'

'Oh, but can you just turn the hob on for me, just quickly. Just until it goes orange. I want to see it go orange.'

Mary sighed and led the way through to the kitchen. If she was honest with herself, she too loved to see the black coil of the electric cooker hob turning orange as it heated up. She had worried about it a lot at first because it didn't feel as safe as the coal stove she'd always known, but the confectioner's kitchen at the toffee factory had one too and she'd had to grow used to it when she worked there. The electric cooker was just one of a host of modern conveniences Albert had lavished on her when they'd moved into their new home.

Albert said that he didn't want Mary to be burdened with domestic chores just because she had married him. He was of a mind that domestic work was too hard on women, and the idea that she would have to get down on her hands and knees every Monday to black the range had horrified him so he'd immediately signed up to buy an electric cooker on instalments. An electric iron had been discussed, but Albert had instead insisted that the launderette call to collect their laundry and bring it all back, washed and pressed, to give her one less thing to do. The butcher and grocer were to deliver their orders so that Mary wouldn't have to traipse back and forth to the shops each day, and Albert was a marvellous cook; he was, after all, the head confectioner at the largest toffee factory in Halifax.

Mary switched on the electric light in the empty kitchen and noticed Bess's growing anticipation at the thought of seeing her favourite magic trick. She was glad that she could do this one tiny thing for Bess. Mary had felt guilty every day since their mother had died and half a year later the burden hadn't lessened. Bess had never been able to look after herself, but rather than invite her into her new home, Mary had allowed their friend Diana to persuade her to leave Bess in a boarding house with a colleague who needed a companion. Mrs Starbeck had been unwell and Bess was to stay with her to help her until she completely recovered, but Bess herself needed minding and steering away from trouble. It was an imperfect arrangement, but so far it seemed to be working.

Bess began to giggle as the coil on the hob glowed. She reached out to touch it and Mary quickly batted her hand away. 'Don't do that! You'll burn yourself. Even Greta knows not to do that and she's five.' Mary turned off the cooker, ushered Bess out of the kitchen, and went to fetch her coat from the hall. 'Max should be home from school at half past three, and Albert will be back at five. There's bread in the crock if you're hungry, and milk in the larder for you both.'

'I know, don't worry, I'm quite at home. Can I give Greta a biscuit with her milk?'

'Yes, why not? She could do with cheering up. And don't be afraid to turn the fire on in the sitting room if you get cold.' It felt nice being able to say that. Mary was living the most comfortable life she had ever known, but it wasn't all roses. Sometimes in those long hours when she was left alone in the new house she would find herself crying for no reason. After all those years of hardship she had finally arrived at safety, but it wasn't the safety she'd imagined she would reach. Her mother was dead, her sister was a companion in a boarding house, and all Europe was on the brink of war.

Mary valued her work at the factory more than she could ever have imagined she would. She clung to it to keep her ties with her old life. It felt monstrously unfair that married women weren't allowed to stay on as permanent workers at Mack's – or at any other work-place for that matter. Casual and seasonal jobs for married women were in high demand, and Mary hadn't secured hers without difficulty, but she'd got it, and that was the main thing. She had forged an identity through her work and her expert skill, and although she wasn't allowed to keep her old job in the Confectioner's Kitchen with her husband, she could at least supervise a shift to help war preparations, and see her old friends in passing. She could feel like the old Mary, the Mary who was a person beyond the domesticity, and that meant everything. But she knew that it was only temporary and that any day now they'd finish assembling their order and she'd have to let go of the life she loved at Mack's.

Chapter Ten

Reenie Calder had arrived early to the factory dance, not because she planned to attend – her broken engagement was too recent for her to think about being seen dancing with other young men – but because she knew that one of her favourite people would be making an appearance and she had looked forward to seeing him.

Major Fergusson, resplendent in a fine black silk evening suit with a precisely straightened bow tie, was a sight for sore eyes. Absent from the factory corridors for too long he had chosen this occasion to return and, as usual, he brought smiles to people's faces simply by being there. His silver moustache curled up like a grin from the Cheshire Cat, and a number of new girls commented that he seemed very dapper for an old gentleman.

Reenie had known in advance that when he arrived he would be in a wheeled chair, but she had not quite prepared herself for the sadness she would feel at seeing her old friend and mentor so very much reduced in size. Major Fergusson had at long last been discharged from the cottage hospital, but his catastrophic illness had been too serious for him ever to return to full health. He put a brave face on the evening, but Reenie realised with a pang of disappointment that he wouldn't be coming back to work at the factory.

'Reenie, you're still in your overalls!' the Major exclaimed with a knowing chuckle. 'You've left it very late if you are intending to gallop home on your horse and transform into Cinderella.'

Reenie blushed a little with embarrassment as she crouched low beside the Major's chair, hoping that she would not be noticed by the other young people who were arriving early to the ribbon-strewn hall in excited dribs and drabs. 'I'm not stopping for the dance, Major. I just wanted to see you.'

All of a sudden Reenie was lost for what to say next. She wanted to tell the Major some happy news, or make some enthusiastic comment about the paper flowers which decorated the hall, but she found that all she could think about was how sad she was feeling, and how much she didn't want to bring her sadness to the Major. 'I knew I had to say hello before the band started up because I'll never hear you once they get going.' Reenie rolled her eyes wryly in the direction of the band leader who was unpacking his music and straightening his bow tie. He had a look of Duke Ellington about him, which Reenie was almost certain he cultivated.

'I think it's a miracle they can play loud enough to be heard over the dancers!' Major Fergusson chuckled again, but this time the chuckle turned into a cough which appeared to be painful.

Reenie rested her hand on his back, instinctively wanting to help him somehow, but not wanting to hurt him either. 'Can I get you a glass of water, Major? Or lemonade, they have lemonade.' She looked around her for something she could fetch or do to help her friend but knew there was really nothing she could do.

The Major took in a deep breath through his nose, closed his eyes, and appeared to be mastering the coughing fit by a supreme act of will. Beneath her hand Reenie felt him shake a little, and then he was still. 'You're very kind, Reenie, but I shall be quite all right.' The Major smiled reassuringly and Reenie was glad to see that the smile reached his eyes, even though the twinkle was gone. 'The world seems rather a fearful place at the moment, but it makes me glad to know that there are still good-hearted people like you in it.'

All of a sudden Reenie felt herself overwhelmed by a wave of guilt. She experienced that so often these days. She felt that she had broken off her engagement to Peter out of selfishness because she hadn't wanted to give up her factory life just yet to be a young bride and she had told herself that she was staying to do important work to help her country, but now that she had been demoted she found it harder to justify her choice. Reenie blamed herself for burning the machine motor and getting herself demoted, and she felt that all the things which she had built up into the purpose of her life were gone, and it was all her own doing. She was having to start all over again, but at the worst possible time because the factory and the country needed everyone to give their best, and here she was, trying to find her feet again.

'Oh Major, I've made such a mess of everything,' she said quietly, shaking her head. 'I've been demoted and I don't know how to work my way back to where I was.'

'Who says you've made a mess of everything, my dear? Surely you wouldn't still be here if that were true. I hear that the maintenance engineers are pleased to have a capable extra worker. What do you think to their department? Have you started trying to improve it yet?'

'No, Major. No schemes this time,' Reenie said sadly. 'I've just got to do as I'm told and keep my head down.'

'What? No process improvements or reorganisation of the coat hooks? That's not the Reenie Calder I know. Perhaps that's why things seem so blue – you don't have anything to aim for. A good hobby project to get your teeth into would do you the world of good. You leave it to me and I'll have a talk with your manager, and—'

'Oh, no! Please no!' Reenie didn't want to seem ungrateful, but now that she'd been demoted so far she was terrified of being let go altogether; it was therefore imperative that she do as she was told and be clearly seen to do as she was told. 'My new supervisor is quite strict and I don't want him to think I've been complaining.'

'Harry Swallow? Quite strict? Are you sure we're talking about the same young man?'

'I think he thinks I'm trouble.'

'Perhaps you caught him on a bad day – we all have them. I know he has a lot on his mind at the moment as so many lines are being converted so quickly to other uses. Give him another chance, Reenie. I think you two will get along quite well together.' The Major shifted himself painfully in his chair, and then changed the subject to other painful things. 'I had a letter from Peter this morning. He seems to be doing very well.'

Reenie was surprised at how pleased she was to hear this. It was bittersweet for her. She had been engaged to be married to Peter until Easter and had resisted setting a date for their wedding, then hastened it, then called it off. She felt so much regret for her own part in their parting, but after worrying about how much she had hurt her former fiancé she truly hoped that Peter was starting to build a new life for himself in Norwich. 'Is he?' she asked earnestly, her throat constricting.

'He's got his place at Sandhurst to train to be an officer and his engineering experience is opening a lot of doors for him. He sounded very happy.' The Major looked past Reenie and towards the door. 'Ah, I think I see your new manager. I'm going to summon him over and see if we can't thaw out that frosty reception you've been given.'

Reenie didn't have time to object. Harry Swallow had arrived in his Sunday best for the factory dance with a couple of other young bachelors from engineering. His warm brown hair was slicked back so neatly and cut at the nape of his neck with such precision that he looked as if he'd stepped out of the pages of *Picturegoer* magazine, not just scrubbed up after a long week in a factory.

Harry greeted the Major warmly, and grinned when he saw Reenie still in her overalls. 'You make me feel overdressed, lass. Am I not paying you enough to get yourself some glad rags?'

Reenie flushed crimson with embarrassment, her pretty copper waves clashing with her glowing cheeks. 'I'm not stopping for the dance. I just wanted to see the Major.'

'Give over, I'm only messing wi' you. At least we know you're not vain.' He tried to give her a conciliatory smile, but Reenie felt too flustered to answer. She hadn't got off to a good start with Harry and somehow she couldn't get herself back on the right foot even when he seemed willing to.

Reenie made her excuses to the Major and tried to slink discreetly out of the hall before the band could start up. The floor around the entrance was crowded now and she tried to push her way around the lemonade table to get to the door but a last glance back over her shoulder to make certain that Harry wasn't watching her was her undoing; she bumped into the corner of the lemonade table and sent a jug of sugary liquid sloshing onto the skirt of a nervous-looking young woman.

'Oh no, I'm so sorry!' Reenie leapt forward and tried to rescue the girl's skirt with a handkerchief. 'I was looking behind me and I—'

'It's all right.' The lemonade victim tried to wriggle away from Reenie's enthusiastic attempts to make amends. 'It's an old dress.'

Reenie did think it looked old, but her natural instinct to encourage everyone made her say, 'That's as may be, but it's ever so nice and I wouldn't want to spoil it for you. You've gone to all this trouble to come here for a dance.'

The young woman shrank back a little further. 'I wasn't dancing.'

'Well, you should, it's one of the perks of the job. Make the most of it.' Reenie said, trying to encourage the girl, but as she herself was still in overalls she realised she wasn't the best advertisement. 'Don't mind me. I'd be dancing if I didn't have work to do. I'm Reenie Calder, I work in Time and M—' Reenie stopped and corrected herself. 'I'm one of the Maintenance Engineers. Are you new?'

The girl nodded, her big eyes wide with apprehension. 'I'm Ada Helliwell. And I don't think I'm in the right place.'

'Don't you worry,' Reenie reassured the mousy-haired girl, 'everyone finds their place at Mack's; it'll be reet.

You come and see me if you feel lost or out of your depth and I'll remember to look out for you.'

But Reenie would soon find that the girl, like trouble, would find her.

Chapter Eleven

The jitterbug was, as Ada had feared, a favourite dance among the young people at Mack's factory, and when the Friday and Saturday night dances were in full swing the young workers linked arms to perform it in a long line just like the American dancers in the legendary Cotton Club in New York. Albion Mills main production hall had been transformed from its mid-week work as a gas mask assembly line into a dancehall of modern splendour. Decorative garlands of pastel-coloured paper flowers had been suspended from the ceiling and a vivid violet banner on the far wall declared that this was The Quality Street Dance. A low stage had been fashioned beneath the banner and a big band of stylish-looking musicians in white dinner jackets were going red in the face energetically blowing into saxophones and trumpets.

Halifax might have been a long way from New York City, but thanks to the magic of cinema it didn't always feel that way. *Jitterbug Party* – the latest Cab Calloway hit – was being played seemingly on a continuous loop at the Cosy Corner Picture Palace on the Queen's Road, and Ada thought she might be the only young person left in Halifax who didn't know every line of the last big hit: *Minnie the Moocher*. Girls and boys mimicked the dance routine they'd seen Betty Boop stumble through on the big screen, while mouthing the song to one another theatrically, their eyes wrinkling with laughter. From where Ada was standing beside the lemonade table she could see Caroline singing to a lad from the factory boiler house. The songs were all such nonsense; Ada knew everyone else liked them but her orderly soul rebelled against singing gibberish and wiggling about in a disorderly manner. Ada was prepared to attend as chaperone to Caroline, but she was deuced if she was going to take to the dance floor for anything so uncouth.

Caroline broke away from her partner after a particularly energetic swing dance to check on her friend. 'Have you finished that yet?' Caroline pointed to the half-full glass of lemonade which had become warm in Ada's hands through long nursing. 'I've got heaps of lads who would dance with you if I said they could dance with me after. You don't need to be a wallflower all the night.'

'I don't want to dance with anyone,' Ada retreated further into the wall, 'I'm quite content to rest here while you dance.'

Caroline harrumphed. It was obvious that she felt her unoccupied friend was a millstone around her own neck and she couldn't possibly enjoy the dance while the other remained a spectator. 'Oh, come on, Ada, you'll love it once you give it a try. I know you'll have fun, I promise you will. This would be just your sort of thing if you'd let yourself go, I promise it would.'

Ada wrinkled her nose, looked over her shoulder as though she were about to impart some shameful secret to her friend, then whispered in Caroline's ear, 'I've got lemonade on my dress.'

'You've what?' Caroline shouted over the din of the dancehall.

Ada pursed her lips and blushed before mouthing again, 'Lemonade on my dress!'

With an embarrassing lack of discretion Caroline leant back to take a good and obvious look at the patch on Ada's emerald green skirt which ran under her arm, down her side, over her hip, and down to the hem. 'Oh, don't mind that, you can't see it in the dark. Dance with one of these lads for me so's I can dance and not worry about you. He says he'll give me a kiss if we can sneak off down to the bike sheds for a bit. Go and dab it with some paper from the ladies loo and then come back and dance with one of these lads.'

Ada reluctantly went off to join the queue for the ladies lavatories in the corridor beyond the dancehall. The electric lights were bright here, and although the sound of the band reached her, it had a mercifully muffled quality. She could hear the excited, gossipy conversations of the women who queued ahead of her, discussing their dance partners and their hopes of walking out with them in the park on Sunday at the old monkey parade. They talked of what they wanted for Christmas, and it seemed everyone wanted a new dress to wear to the dances come the spring. Would there still be dances in the spring? Or would it be war instead. The conversation took a turn to gas masks.

There was one bright glow of happiness shining through the dark mood in Halifax, and it was the factory dances. Halifax was a factory town, and the managers were no fools: they knew that if the workers were unhappy, their production numbers would suffer, and that in the trying days of 1938 everyone needed something to look forward to. Friday and Saturday night dances had been started all over the town in factory dining halls but the Saturday night dance in the Mackintosh's dining hall was the biggest of them all and the Quality Street girls spent their weekdays eagerly discussing it. The dances served another purpose; the anxious young men who expected to be sent off to fight were hurriedly collecting sweethearts, anticipating that this might be their only chance.

Ada wondered what her mother, who had valued peace and quiet as a nourishing balm, would think of all this. If Mrs Helliwell were still alive, Ada would have spent this evening sitting quietly by her side, perhaps working away on the embroidered tablecloth she'd started last spring, or perhaps reading to her mother about the quadrilles and courtly dances of a ball in Jane Austen's England; a dance where the noise didn't feel like as though it was beating inside your chest, and the people didn't seem like they were closing in on you in the low, low light.

Ada's mother had been bedridden for five years when she died. It was a stroke which had incapacitated her, and then another had finally taken her. They ran in the family on her mother's side and Mrs Helliwell had always been careful to avoid any agitation. That first stroke had coincided with Ada's final school board examinations, and as soon as she finished them she took up her place as her mother's nurse, and remained by her side until the summer just gone when, out of a clear blue sky, her mother had slipped away. Ada wished *she* could slip away now, but Caroline had found her a dance partner and she couldn't disappoint her friend.

Chapter Twelve

It was public knowledge that Diana had a stepbrother who had been sent to prison a few years earlier for theft, among other things, and that Diana had given evidence against him at his trial. He was a nasty piece of work and she never spoke of him. Diana was a private person who rarely talked about herself, but there was more to it than that; her stepbrother represented an old life that it was too painful to remember.

Ten years earlier, when Diana's father was still alive, she herself had lived for trouble. She'd stirred up the girls on the factory floor, and stirred up the boys in every pub in town. She'd been impossible to tame, and she'd liked it that way. Her stepbrother Tommo and his best friend Stuart had been part of her usual set, but it was a friendship built on shared pastimes in low places, and not any respect or liking on Diana's part. Diana had let Stuart show her a good time now and then, but it was no great love affair. The great love of Diana's life was her daughter, Gracie.

Born just as her life seemed to be falling apart, Gracie had changed her. Diana had weathered the battering storm of grief which raged inside her when her father died, she'd swallowed her pride and her frustration at moving into a crumbling, dirty terraced house with her stepmother and stepbrother, and had used their help to raise the secret daughter that neither she, nor Stuart, had ever wanted. They all agreed to pretend that Gracie was a younger sister to Diana and Tommo, and Gracie believed that too. Diana had made the arrangement work for six years; her stepmother had cared for Gracie while Diana worked, but they all knew that it was Tommo's money – money from fenced goods he stored in the house and heaven knew what else – which kept a roof over their heads. Stuart drifted by with Tommo now and then, but Diana had kept him at arm's length; disappointed with her former self for ever stooping so low.

This precarious life gave Diana the only thing she had ever wanted: a way to keep her child close, even if she had to pretend she wasn't her mother. It was Tommo who brought it all tumbling down. He and Stuart had been driving a stolen car around town when it skidded on black ice and crashed into the side of the Mackintosh's factory. Stuart had been killed instantly, but Tommo had survived to limp home and lead the police to his large stash of stolen goods. Diana had lost the only family she had, and her only means of keeping her daughter. Her daughter had lost the only mother she'd ever known.

Tommo Cartwright had now served almost two years at His Majesty's pleasure in Wakefield Prison and he was looking forward to his first Christmas on the outside. Ordinarily she wouldn't care a fig that Tommo might be planning to come in search of her – Diana had stood up to him plenty of times and she'd have no qualms about going for the police and letting the chips fall where they may – but the last time Tommo and Diana had spoken it had been about Gracie and Tommo had made a very specific threat. His most recent letter had done the same.

Gracie was nearly eight and she looked more like Diana every day. Of course Diana had always claimed that they were half-sisters, but Tommo knew the truth. When he and his mother had been sent to prison Diana had been left with no one to help care for the child while she was at work, and barely enough money to support herself, let alone rent a place which would accommodate both of them. Gracie was a delicate child; a bad bout of whooping cough had damaged her lungs, and the black mould in the crumbling slum dwelling had only made it worse. Gracie needed clean air, good food, expensive medicine, and regular checks from the doctor. Diana could only dream of providing these things on her own. She had been caught in an impossible situation; if she admitted to being Gracie's mother and tried to find them a boarding house together Diana would lose her job on grounds of immoral conduct and they would be destitute. Even if, by some miracle, she had kept her job she'd never have made enough money to support herself and her daughter. Instead, Diana had made the stoic decision to allow her daughter to be adopted by a family who believed she was Gracie's elder sister and encouraged her to visit. Diana continued to work hard so that she could earn enough to rent a shabby room in a respectable boarding house and visited Gracie at the Hunters' house whenever she could. Diana had even gone so far as to volunteer to help Mrs Hunter with secretarial and administrative work for her various charities in an attempt to give an excuse to be near Gracie more often.

All had gone well until Easter, when, in an uncharacteristically emotional outburst brought on by worry for her child during a scarlet fever epidemic, Diana had blurted out the truth to Mr Hunter. As the cherry blossom fell in the garden of the Hunter house, so had Diana's disguise, and she knew that nothing could be the same again. The months which had followed had been profoundly uncomfortable in the Hunter house. Mr Hunter had greeted Diana with reserve whenever she had visited, and she felt that she was being always watched.

Diana had been helping Mrs Hunter to arrange transport and accommodation for Spanish refugees coming to West Yorkshire, and she had a sense that once that work was complete Mr Hunter would reveal to his wife the secret her volunteer secretary had been keeping, and there would be no more opportunities to see Gracie.

'I'll not be more than an hour with her,' Diana told the nanny as she collected Gracie from the Hunters' porticoed mansion. 'The fitting is quick enough, it's the queues which take time.'

'You tell me!' Nanny Watson agreed as she pulled a woollen hat down over Gracie's golden head. Nanny Watson had originally been charged with the errand of taking all the Hunter children to be fitted for their gas masks, but Gracie had wailed in fear and fought everyone off so fiercely when she'd seen her own Mickey Mouse mask that they'd had to take her home without one. An appeal to Gracie's sister to attempt the errand again had seemed the only way. 'I think perhaps she was tired from the queuing last time. I'm sure she'll be all right with you. Better to send her with her sister.'

Diana nodded in agreement. The opportunity had come at just the right time. Of course she wanted to be the one to take her daughter for her gas mask fitting, but she also wanted to put in place one more element of her plan. 'Oh, I almost forgot,' Diana mentioned as casually as she mentioned everything, 'I've booked an appointment at the photographer's on the main street to have my portrait taken. Can you tell me if my parting is straight? I got caught in a gust of wind on my way here, and I don't want to turn up looking like the Bride of Frankenstein.'

Nanny Watson was happy to oblige and confirmed that Diana's perfect, glossy hair was as enviable as ever.

Her striking good looks were memorable, and that was something Diana had decided to play on. Diana wanted Nanny Watson to remember the detail about the portrait photographer in case Gracie should mention it later. Diana planned to explain it away as a surprise Christmas present for Mr and Mrs Hunter to complete their collection of family portraits on the hall stairs, but of course that was only an excuse. Diana knew that she would need a photograph of Gracie to affix to the various papers she would have to produce when they left the country, and this was only the first part of her plan.

Diana and Gracie made their way towards the tram stop hand in hand. 'Are we going to have lunch together?' Gracie asked with enthusiasm while she tried to keep up with Diana and keep her gas mask carton from slipping off her shoulder on its makeshift strap.

'Yes, we'll have lunch after we've finished our errands.' Diana cast another look over her shoulder as they drew closer to the tram stop. 'Where would you like to go? You always like those cucumber sandwiches at Coney's, don't you?'

'Can we have French food?'

'If you like. I don't know where we'd find any, though. What sort of things do you think French people eat?'

'I don't know, but we might be going to Canada where people speak French and we'll need to be used to the food.' Gracie said it so matter-of-factly that the words dealt an even greater blow to Diana. Just as she had been planning to snatch her daughter away, her daughter announced that someone else was planning to do the very same thing.

'Canada's a long way away, what would you be going there for?' But Diana thought she already knew.

'Mummy says that she's seen all the awful things anyone can ever see with her refugees from Spain and she's not going to keep us children here like sitting ducks practising air gas drills when her cousins in Canada would take at least two of us.' Gracie's mimicry of her adoptive parent was so perfect, and so clearly unconscious that it left Diana in no doubt that what she said was true.

Diana tried to keep her tone light for the sake of her daughter. 'And do you think you'd like to go to live in Canada, Gracie? It's a long way away.'

'I would if all the French food is sweets. I don't like the squeaky leeks cook makes us eat; they taste horrible and they get in my teeth. I want to live somewhere where they don't have any leeks and you can have pudding instead.'

'I don't know a lot about Canada, but I don't think they'll give you more pudding.' Diana swallowed hard and prepared to say the thing which would hurt her most, but which she knew would be best for Gracie. 'You would be much safer in Canada if a war came, and it would be very kind of the Hunters if they decided to send you.'

'Well, I might not go. Their cousins are quite old and they can't take us all, so they have to choose which of us to send.'

This sounded to Diana as though plans were already well advanced, but it was the first she was hearing about it. 'Do you know if they've already booked passage on a boat? I should think they need to do lots of planning for a big trip.'

'I don't know. They probably have. Aunty Celia has come round lots to help Daddy with writing letters because his French is just *not up to all this*.' The little girl mimicked her adoptive father, but without understanding the meaning of his words. 'And now Daddy's gone to France and he says he never would have—'

'He's gone to France?' Diana blurted out, cutting her daughter short and looking back at the house, the menace of which was somehow suspended in the air around her.

'Yes, he had to go because you can't do everything by letter. He has to *know* things for himself.'

'What things does he have to know for himself?'

Gracie shrugged. 'I don't know. Daddy things.' And the tram rattled into view.

Chapter Thirteen

'I was worried we'd lose you altogether when you got married.' Reenie passed her friend a bag of broken shards of mint cracknel across the clubhouse they had formed in Ruffian's designated stable at the factory. He snorted when he saw that he was not being offered misshapen confectionery.

Mary – who had been pacing up and down with her hands shoved deep into her overall pockets – took the sweets and slumped down onto the opposite hay bale. 'Well, at least they haven't sacked you altogether, that's the main thing. If you keep your nose clean and do as you're told you might get your old job back one day. You're in a better position than me – I have to be grateful for a bit o' temporary work now that I'm a married woman.' Mary looked different and the same. The same old look of hard determination in the face of adversity; the same black hair pulled back tight for practicality's sake; the same livid red birthmark on her cheek like the flash of a comet, or the flash of anger she might loose if anyone threatened her family. She was the same old Mary, but she had a little more confidence in herself now; she was better fed and had a healthy glow, and there was more of that dry sense of humour beginning to emerge. 'I don't know what they think'll happen if they let the married women work the regular shift – perhaps they're worried we'll corrupt the minds of the unmarried girls by telling them all the scandalous details of how to read an electric meter and calculate how much you've spent for the week.'

Reenie grinned. 'Are you going to tell me the scandalous details?'

Mary scowled. 'Are you sure you want to hear them? They're not what you think they're going to be when you're all doe-eyed and innocent and you don't know what married life is really like.'

Reenie put down her lardy cake, sat forward on the bale of straw which served as a bench and said, 'Tell me everything!'

Mary took in a deep breath, huffed, and said, 'Well, the first thing you don't expect is that the electricity board sometimes installs the meter in a box on the floor of your larder, so you have to move all of your tins out the way to—'

Reenie threw her dinner bag at Mary's head.

'Well, you said you wanted to know the details.' A slight smirk creased Mary's lips; she wasn't so het up that she couldn't make a joke.

'You know what I meant, you chump.'

Mary made a show of ladylike delicacy. 'I know that you're far too well-mannered to ask me anything uncouth.' She sounded in good humour, but her foot tapped out a restless beat. For all Mary's newfound blessings – a caring husband, a family, a home – there was an undercurrent of anxiety. Mary could not be still anymore, and Reenie had never seen her like this. If she wasn't pacing up and down she was twitching her foot, or tapping her fingers. Below the surface at all times there was a tightly wound cord of fear.

A rowdy clatter in the stable yard beyond made Mary jump half out of her skin and Reenie went to the door to see what the racket was. She ducked back in and resumed her seat. 'Just a wagon. They're moving a load of concrete buttresses. I think they're putting in more air raid shelters because the first lot aren't big enough.'

Mary nodded solemnly. 'You'd made me forget for a minute that we were on the brink of invasion.'

'You don't think they'll invade England, do you? Surely if there's war we'll be all right here.' Reenie herself didn't know how much of her own opinions were wishful thinking. Perhaps if Mary – ever the pessimist – had a notion there'd be an invasion then the reality would lie somewhere less extreme.

'Well, the merry dictators of Europe are busy invading

everywhere else, so why wouldn't we be on the list? Albert's doing his best to get us permits to emigrate to America, but he's had no luck yet.'

Reenie felt a stab of anguish at this news. She didn't want to see her friend go so far away, but she also didn't want her to stay when Europe felt like such a dangerous place for her and her new family.

The inevitability of war had crept up on the good people of Halifax. Some people had been muttering about it ever since '33 when Hitler had reached the top spot in the German parliament and pulled Germany out of the League of Nations; others saw the writing on the wall in '35 when Germany reintroduced conscription and announced a massive rearmament programme. 'Why,' some suspicious souls asked, 'would he want more soldiers and more weapons if not to wage war against someone?'

In '36 those soldiers and weapons pitched up in the Rhineland – throwing the Treaty of Versailles out of the window – but the British and French didn't act to prevent it, as they had agreed to do in that hard won treaty, and Hitler announced to the world that, 'Neither threats nor warnings will prevent me from going my way.'

Even then there were people who still didn't think there'd be a war; there didn't need to be a war, they said.

In '38 Hitler invaded Austria on the eve of their refer-endum, just in case the Austrians voted for an outcome he didn't like, but still there were plenty of people in

Britain who shrugged and said, 'But they're all German speakers, aren't they? Why shouldn't the Austrians let themselves be ruled by Germany?'

Then Hitler's ranting about Czechoslovakia reached a fever pitch in the autumn of 1938 as he wailed over the rights of 'ethnic Germans' living on the country's fringe; the Sudetenland. These 'ethnic' Germans – white Europeans with no discernibly different characteristics to their neighbours beyond their spoken language – were apparently desperate to be brought under German rule, and on the 1 October 1938 they got their wish; if it really was their wish. News of violence and persecution against Jewish people, among many others, followed wherever Hitler's regime went, but the position of the British government was to make excuses for the Nazis wherever possible. The Prime Minister – Neville Chamberlain – made a pact with Hitler: the Nazis could keep Austria and Sudetenland, but they had to leave it at that. No more invading other countries, or the British would have to consider it an act of war.

Hitler invaded the rest of Czechoslovakia and the British still did not act. The Czechs had feared that this would happen, and so, on the eve of the invasion of their own country, they sent all their military aircraft to England to prevent them falling into enemy hands. They hoped the British would use them to fight the Nazis one day.

'There's always a chance there still might not be a war,' Reenie said with a note of speculative hope.

'Someone might stop Hitler. His people might kick him out of power and get someone else to be Chancellor. Or he might just simmer down when he runs out of steam.'

Mary was quick to respond. 'But then there's all the other dictators who will just carry on where he left off, there's Mussolini, and Franco, and the Romanian fella. They're like the heads of Hydra.'

'How do you know about the heads of Hydra?'

'You're not the only one with a library card, Reenie Calder. My point is that this train isn't stopping, it's built up too much steam now. We have to get the kids out of England, and I honestly don't know how we can do it. We still haven't been able to get Albert's sister out of Germany.'

'Can I help? I got you that marriage licence, maybe I can get you into America.'

'Only the Americans can get us to America. They don't want Jews, and that's that.'

There was a long silence and the injustice of the situation tightened Reenie's throat. What right did any country have to refuse entry to someone fleeing for their life? It wasn't as if Mary wanted to go to America, she'd said often enough that she didn't think she'd like the food. 'Well, at least you're eating well,' Reenie said, trying to look on the bright side as usual.

Mary wriggled her shoulders defensively. 'Who says I'm eating well?'

'Your overalls. I can hear the seams groaning.'

'You cheeky madam!'

'Well, I think it's a good thing.'

'That I've run to fat?'

'Not fat,' Reenie sounded like she was working hard to find the correct turn of phrase, 'just healthy looking.'

Mary was unimpressed. 'I hope you weren't planning to ask me to help you get your old job back because I doubt I'll have time now that I'm going to be busy taking out my overalls.'

'Oh, give over, I didn't mean anything by it. Besides, I've already got a plan for how I'll get me job back. I don't need anyone's help.'

'Reenie, please don't try anything. The world isn't ready for another of your plans.'

'It's nothing to worry about, it's very simple. I'm just going to find out as much as I can about my new supervisor and work out what would impress him, then impress him so's he recommends to Diana that I be given my old job back.'

Mary, still smarting from the suggestion that she was looking plump, said, 'Why don't you tell him how his overalls fit; see where that gets you?'

'Well, I'm sorry I ever mentioned it now.'

'Who is he, your supervisor?'

'Harry Swallow in Engineering Maintenance.'

Mary raised an eyebrow. 'His overalls do fit very well.'

'Mary Baum, you're a married woman!'

'I've still got eyes,' she said, through a mouthful of sugary peppermint. 'He's got dancer's hips.'

'Not you as well! I don't know what all the lasses see in him.'

'Our Bess threw herself at him. He took her dancing once, but she said he walked her home at a reasonable time and didn't try anything.'

'I bet she was disappointed!' But Reenie felt a little bit glad. She didn't think she liked her new supervisor, and she didn't like the thought of her friend having been too closely mixed up with him.

'Seriously, though,' Mary said, 'watch yourself with that one. He's got a reputation.'

'Reputation for what?'

'For never dancing with the same girl twice.'

'Well, I'm not dancing even if he's asking, so there's nowt to worry about there. Besides, it was Diana who put me in his section. If she thought he was trouble she wouldn't have moved me.'

'*Diana* moved you? As in our Diana? Diana Moore?'

Reenie nodded and fished about in the paper bag for another piece of mint cracknel. 'She walked me round to his department herself.'

Mary stopped fidgeting and frowned. 'Well, there's got to be more to that move than meets the eye.' She took a piece of cracknel from her friend, 'There's something afoot here. There's something afoot and I'll be blowed if I can work out what it is.'

Chapter Fourteen

The Engineering Maintenance Department was shrouded in a fog of pipe smoke as the older men circled a Rose Foregrove fondant depositor machine trying to decide what to do with it next. 'I don't think it can be salvaged,' Arthur Pardew said, between puffs on his clay pipe. 'It's jiggered, if you ask me.'

Reenie hovered in the background, desperately waiting to be asked for her thoughts so that she could explain precisely how she would repair and then redeploy this troublesome old machine. However, Reenie had learnt the hard way that in this department she needed to wait to speak when she was invited to, and it left her with an almost permanent feeling of indigestion.

'Reenie,' Harry Swallow called from the doorway of the workshop, 'come here a minute.'

The sunlight in the courtyard beyond cast Harry in silhouette and Reenie wished that Mary hadn't put that thought in her head about Harry fitting his overalls well. And there was that inevitable thought, the one she always returned to: that he was very different to Peter. Where Peter had been a hearty advertisement for the bone and muscle-building properties of Norfolk milk, Harry was lean and moved with a cat-like grace. There had been an open honesty to Peter's face which had made Reenie trust him from the moment she met him, but Harry was a beast of a different stripe. She knew that he'd worked at Mack's for about ten years (assuming he'd joined at fourteen as most lads did) and he'd risen to a position of responsibility, so he must be trustworthy in the professional sense, but was there another sense? She often heard girls talking about him in the cloakrooms. Did he toy with their affections, or did he step out with a different girl every night of the week precisely so that he could not be said to toy with them? He had a face she couldn't read; dark eyes which might be impatient, or might be irritated, or might even be cruel. Harry made Reenie feel an anxiety, a nervous flutter in the stomach, and a tightness in her throat which she tried to explain away to herself as the fear that he might stand between her and her old job. Well, Reenie would show him and everyone at Mack's just what she was capable of, and she'd be out of his department and back into Time and Motion in no time at all.

Harry beckoned Reenie out into the factory yard with the merest tilt of his head. 'I want you to do a job for me,' he said quietly as he led her away from the others.

'Before I do it, can I just say that I think that fondant machine would be perfect for a line my friend works on down at—'

'Leave the machine, I don't want you getting distracted by fancy projects.'

'But I want to really impress you with what I can do so that you'll recommend me to go back to my old job when I've shown that I'm up to it.'

'I'm not impressed by anything except hard work, so just stick to the jobs you're given.'

'But surely you'd be impressed if I could fix a machine that no one else could get running?'

'Today I'll be impressed if you find out where Ada Helliwell is working and see if you can help her settle in. She's new.'

Reenie felt her heart race and a cold chill run up the back of her neck. She recognised the name, and if this was someone she was intended to impress she had already gone very far wrong; if Reenie was not very much mistaken this was the young woman on whose dress she had spilt almost an entire jug of lemonade at the last factory dance, and then abandoned without really putting it right. 'Settle in here with us? Is she another pair of hands from Diana?' It would be just Reenie's luck if she ended up working with her day in day out, but she tried to look on the bright side, 'It'll be nice to have someone else to—'

Harry glanced over Reenie's shoulder at the men in the workshop who were well occupied with their work. 'No, she isn't working here. This is a personal favour to me. Find her, and make her feel welcome.'

Reenie wasn't sure what to say and so she asked again to be certain, 'Ada Helliwell?'

'Yes, can you do that? I've heard you've got friends everywhere so can you introduce her to some? Help her find her feet?'

Reenie tried not to show reluctance, but this was an awkward request. She feared this might be one of her manager's conquests, a dancing partner he'd stepped out with once and now didn't want to see again.

'She's my cousin,' Harry explained, to Reenie's relief. 'Her dad says she doesn't like it here much. She's had a difficult few years and it might take her a bit longer to make friends. She'd been nursing her mother since she left school, and then her mother died this summer. She's twenty, but she doesn't seem it – she's not worldly-wise, you understand? I'd take it as a personal favour if you'd take her under your wing. She doesn't like the noise of the production line by all accounts, but I doubt there's much we can do about that.'

Reenie was delighted at the suggestion that there was someone, somewhere, who she was legitimately allowed to help, and launched immediately into her plans. 'Oh, no, I'm sure there's lots we can do; we can try her with some earplugs first, and then if that doesn't work I could make her a booth or some such thing to go around her workstation which would muffle the sound of the rest of the line.'

'No building things,' Harry sighed, 'just take her to the canteen at dinnertime and let her sit with you. She doesn't need owt fancy, she just needs friends her own age to talk to and confide in. Make her feel at home. She's got her friend Caroline, but Caroline's a bit of a social butterfly and she forgets about Ada when it suits her. Settle her in with a couple of friends, that's all I want you to do.'

'Diana, you have to help me!' Reenie burst into her friend's office and immediately plonked herself down in the chair opposite her desk. 'I've got a chance to impress my new supervisor, but he doesn't know that I've actually already ruined my chances by spilling lemonade on his cousin, but if I find his cousin quickly I might be able to put it right before he finds out that I started off wrong, so I need you to look in an employment file and find Ada Helliwell so I can make a start.'

Diana stamped a memorandum with the date and sighed. 'And there was I thinking I'd put you in a department where you'd have no scope for hare-brained schemes, or experiments, or grand plans. Just a nice, safe, steady job where you could use your skills and stay out of trouble.'

'But it's not a hare-brained scheme, this is something

my supervisor asked me to do and it's a chance to impress him by doing it well.'

'Impress Harry Swallow?' Diana put down her date stamp and frowned. 'Harry Swallow isn't the type to be impressed. I put you in his department for the very specific reason that he doesn't care about anything except getting a day's work done, then clocking out and going to a dance.'

'No, really, truly! He asked me to help his cousin make some friends because she's new and doesn't know anyone and isn't settling in. He said he wants me to take her to the canteen at dinner, and I thought I could take her to the stable to meet Ruffian.'

Diana looked as though she were mulling something over and finally conceded, 'I suppose that sounds innocent enough. Just don't do anything elaborate; you get yourself into trouble when you're elaborate.' She paused and turned to a pile of papers on her desk which she looked through as she talked. 'Try to remember that I might not always be here to get you out of trouble if you get into it, and keeping your head down in Engineering Maintenance is a steady job.' Before Reenie could ask why she might be talking about not always working in a department where she could get Reenie out of trouble, Diana said, 'Here she is, Ada Helliwell, staff number 7429. She cut her hand and got sent home, and she's on post room duties until it's healed. Go and find her in the post room, but don't bother Postmaster Pinkstone – you know what he's like.'

Reenie, filled with enthusiasm for her new project – which was already taking on elaborate proportions in her mind – thanked Diana gushingly and went in search of the girl who needed a friend.

Chapter Fifteen

'Ada,' Caroline said with a directness which suggested that she was about to reveal something, 'I have the perfect young man for you to go to the factory dance with. You are going to adore him! He loves to read, just like you – *such* a bookworm, he just loves books; he's tall – don't they seem more handsome when they're tall? I think they do! He's Roman Catholic – just like your poor mother; wouldn't she have loved you to walk out with a Catholic? And he's ever so good looking, like Basil Rathbone – you love black hair, don't you? And he earns pots of money at Crossley's Carpets choosing the silk and fine wool for their best rugs. Doesn't he sound just right for you? You love him already, don't you?' This last sentence was blurted out with a force that suggested it was more of an order than a question. Caroline, pausing only to eat a mouthful of crimped cod while it was still hot, did not look as though she expected any answer but gratitude.

Ada did not feel inclined to discuss the matter in the middle of the Mackintosh's staff dining hall at the height of the lunchtime rush. She had only just settled down with her own plate of dinner (a plate which she was not pleased to see was getting lighter as Caroline reached over with her fork to steal both helpings of tartar sauce and wilted spinach) and didn't like to have such matters discussed where other people might hear them. Even if Ada had liked the sound of this young man (and she was reserving judgement), she was a private person who would not want her possible romantic forays known publicly.

Ada didn't say anything about the food either. She didn't like Caroline taking her dinner when she herself was hungry after a hard morning shift, but she also didn't want to be seen to be mean. It was a monstrous imposition of Caroline's and she ought to have had better manners. Ada opened her mouth to change the subject, but before she could finish her first syllable, Caroline had launched into further eulogy of young Sidney Otter, the lad she had in mind for Ada.

'I've been friends with him for *ages*, and he's honestly such a good friend, he's become like a brother to me and I would just love it if you two got married and had babies and—' Caroline scooped another forkful of spinach onto her plate before blurting out excitedly, 'Wouldn't it be wonderful if we could become mothers at the same time and do everything together? I would *adore* it!'

Ada was suspicious of Caroline's motives, but she tried to persuade herself that she was merely confused. Why had she never heard about this Sidney Otter before now if he and Caroline had been such firm friends for so long? Caroline and Ada saw each other almost every day and had done for years. Granted they didn't spend every waking hour together, and there were plenty of evenings when Caroline had gone off to the cinema with another friend because Ada had needed to stay at home to nurse her mother. It seemed odd, though, that this was the first she was hearing about the firm friend with good prospects.

'How long have you known him?' Ada asked, trying to sound casual even though her old-fashioned manner of speech made everything she said sound like a line from a legally binding contract. 'Can you truly vouch for his bona fides?'

'Oh, completely!' Caroline covered Ada's hand with her own on the table between them, and leant in with an air of sharing a confidence. 'He's a proper gentlemen, like the kind you're always talking about, the ones from your books. We've really only become close friends since that little holiday my parents took me on to Bridlington – you remember when I went to Bridlington? Well, he's the son of my father's friend, so we've known him simply ages.'

There was something not quite right about all this, but Ada couldn't put her finger on it. On the one hand it seemed so unlikely that Caroline, who talked constantly about herself, and who would often recount the same news to Ada eight times for want of something new to say, would fail to mention such a close friend; but then again, the thought that there was a gentleman with whom Ada might discuss books, and perhaps walk out, was something Ada so wanted to believe in. 'He might not want to go to the factory dance,' Ada did not say 'with me', although that was her principal fear. 'Crossley's have their own dance.'

'Of *course* he'll want to come to the Mack's dance! He was actually already going to come to this one with me,' Caroline's eyes flicked furtively away and then back at Ada, 'He'd asked me if I knew any nice girls and I promised to introduce him to one at the dance.' Caroline's voice went up an octave at the end in that telltale squeak which Ada knew of old. It usually meant Caroline was concealing something. Ada tried to tell herself that it didn't necessarily mean she was concealing something bad, it might be a nice surprise or something good which Caroline hoped would come off, but which wasn't certain yet. Ada knew she had a tendency towards pessimism and must try to assume the best from Caroline who was, after all, her oldest friend. If she couldn't trust Caroline to have her best interests at heart, who could she?

'So can I tell Sidney that you'll go to the next dance with him?' Caroline was evidently doing her best to help her friend settle in. She'd even bought them a bag of Toffee Pennies to share after they finished their main.

'Couldn't I meet him somewhere first? Somewhere quiet, like?' Ada took the sparkling toffee her friend proffered, but she didn't unwrap it. She still hadn't finished what was left of her dinner after her friend had heaved into it, but she didn't like to say so in case she hurt Caroline's feelings.

'Oh, come on, Ada, what's there to be shy about? I'll arrange to introduce you somewhere in a café first to prove he doesn't bite if you really insist. He's really ever so nice and I promise you'll like him. *Do* say you'll go with him. I'll be there with my young man, and—'

'*Your* young man?' This was news to Ada, and made sense of why her friend was so keen to partner her off. Caroline didn't want Ada playing gooseberry if she had a promising prospect herself. Ada was about to ask who this young man was when an interruption occurred.

'Are you Ada Helliwell?' a red-haired girl in blue engineers overalls looked relieved to have found her, and stretched out her hand. 'I've been looking for you everywhere. Your cousin Harry sent me.'

'Is he all right?' Ada rose to follow the interloper, throwing a look of concern and apology in the direction of her friend Caroline, but saw that she was already deep in conversation with a passing stranger.

'He's fine, but he wanted me to come and find you. I'm Reenie, by the way; I'm going to give you the time of your life.'

Chapter Sixteen

A silence stretched out ahead of Reenie, and so did the corridor to the confectioner's kitchen. She had tried chatting away to Ada in what she thought of to herself as a warm, encouraging, and friendly way, but the more she talked, the more Ada seemed to retreat. Eventually Reenie realised with reluctance that Ada looked less like she was going to bolt if they walked along without saying anything. No wonder this girl hadn't made friends yet.

Reenie felt peculiarly sorry for Ada because the lass was obviously lost in life, and Reenie knew that she was resisting the pull of the one place where she could find herself: Mackintosh's toffee factory. Reenie had felt lost during her last years of school and had wanted to be useful somewhere. The factory had given her that chance and it had been a dream come true. She'd found a purpose in life.

There was something so wonderfully consoling and energising about having an honest-to-goodness purpose; and not in a small sense, but in a way which helped her family, and her community, and now even her country if they'd let her. It was this last point which most strongly motivated Reenie at the moment: she wanted to help Ada find her place so that her cousin Harry would be grateful to Reenie and would send her back to her old job as a reward, where she could improve the gas mask assembly line and help to equip her country for whatever the future held.

'You'll love the Confectioner's Kitchens,' Reenie said as she led Ada through twisting factory corridors. 'They're ever so quiet – your cousin told me that you don't like noise – and hardly anyone's seen inside them because you have to have a job there to go in.'

'Am I getting a new job in the kitchens?'

'No, we're just visiting. I've got a friend there, actually it's the head confectioner, Mr Baum. I was at his wedding while Easter.'

'Why do we need to visit the kitchens?'

'We don't *need* to, I just thought it would be a nice treat for you, you know. Help you feel more excited about working for Mack's. If you've not managed to fit in maybe it's because you don't realise all the good things what happen at Mack's. Today they're making samples of a new sweet for Christmas and they've been getting folks to taste it and fill out a questionnaire saying what they thought of it. It's walnut marzipan covered in plain chocolate. It's right nice. You can try it and fill in the questionnaire.' This last offer was intended to create anticipation, but Reenie could see that she'd only succeeded in making the girl puzzled. Was it the idea of a marzipan made with walnut which made her screw up her eyebrows, or the prospect of being asked to fill in a questionnaire? Reenie was saved the trying prospect of dragging the conversation out because they had both arrived at the door of the confectioner's kitchen, and found an unusual visitor waiting for them.

'Is that a bee or a wasp?' Ada asked, looking at a rather fat specimen skimming its way back and forth across the windowpane opposite them.

'I don't know.' It was Reenie's turn to screw up her eyebrows. 'It's bit late in the year for either. I wonder how it got in.' Reenie knocked on the door of the kitchen and, finding no one at home, gave the door a shove. 'Just make sure that you shut the door quick behind you Ada, so we don't let the—' But it was too late. Ada had a dawdling, apologetic way of entering a room and it left the bee – and Reenie could see now that it was a bee – ample opportunity to fly into the sugary paradise of the kitchen. Which surface would it alight its unsanitary paws on first? Perhaps the marble-topped chocolate tempering tables; perhaps the copper dragée pan; perhaps the uncovered trays of five hundred walnut marzipan samples which had been left to set in the empty room while their maker went to eat his dinner.

'Don't worry!' Reenie said, possibly more to herself as Ada didn't seem at all concerned that they had let a bee get into the confectioner's kitchen. 'We can let it out of the window if we just . . .' Reenie waved her arms around above her head to encourage the bee to fly in the direction she wanted it to go, but it circled a little higher. She picked up a wooden spatula from one of the countertops and lunged upwards a few times, edging nearer to Ada who stood still waiting awkwardly, apparently ignoring the bee, because when Reenie lunged for the final time Ada did not anticipate her move, did not dodge out of the way, and chaos ensued.

Reenie, realising too late that Ada was not stepping aside, tried to stop her forward motion in the last second, but only succeeded in stumbling forward and then toppling sideways with Ada into the free-standing coat-stand by the door, which in turn toppled onto a nearby bench, sweeping an assortment of utensils onto the floor with a clatter. Reenie pulled herself up and then Ada with effusive apologies.

'Don't pick those up just yet. Just stay over there out of the way while I see to the bee first.'

'Wouldn't it be easier to get rid of the bee if there weren't things on the floor?'

'It might, but it might land on something while we're cleaning up. It's imperative that we shoo it out of the window before it can contaminate a surface. It's the first rule of food factories.' Reenie darted forward, keeping her eye fixed on the bee, and opened the window ready to shoo it out and let in a gust of wind which blew a neat stack of handwritten notes off the table beside the window. Reenie would think about that later; for the moment she was going to get rid of the bee.

The bee circled still higher, and from behind her Reenie could hear another sound, the sound of the door opening.

'There's another one out here,' Ada said, letting in a second bee.

Reenie tried not to show her disappointment and focused on the task now ahead of them, 'All right. Well, keep that door closed for now and pick up that there book. You use that to bat your bee towards me, and I'll try to coax them both in the same direction.' It wouldn't be easy, but Reenie was confident that if they kept trying for long enough they would eventually clear the air. Suddenly Reenie saw an opportunity to catch the two bees together and she shouted, 'Get it! There! Whack it! Just there!' She lunged again and slipped on one of the sheets of notepaper which had fluttered to the ground earlier and landed on a sack of sugar which burst an inch-long split in its seam and began to leak with something like a sigh. Reenie slapped her hand over the split and attempted to bung the hole with the handle of her spatula, which slowed the flow of sugar for long enough to let her get up.

This was not going according to plan. Reenie had intended to show Ada something which would be a treat for her, but would also be a talking point to help her establish some friendships if she struck up conversation with anyone around the factory. Above all, this was intended to impress Ada so that she would tell Harry that she was impressed, so that Harry would acknowledge that Reenie's talents lay in another department and he would return her to it. So far Reenie had not put her best foot forward, but where there was life, there was hope, and Reenie knew that if she could just think of a clever way to drive the bees out of the window she would still have achieved her aim. A sharp gust of wind blew in from the open window and knocked over a glass jar filled with sticky, crimson jam. Ada looked as though she felt a little sorry for Reenie.

'I've got it!' Reenie dashed over to the door. 'You were right to open the door in the first place. If we just hold the door open while the window is fastened open it should create a through draught with the open door downstairs and that will suck the bees towards the window, might even suck them right out of the window!' Reenie took up position beside the door, took a firm grasp of the handle to prevent the door slamming shut with the draught, and carefully turned the handle. 'Ready? Watch this.'

Reenie opened the door and felt the tug of the draught which would otherwise have slammed it shut. The bees bobbed along the ceiling.

'I don't think it's working,' Ada said.

'We just need to give it a bit o' time. It's basic science, really. You read a lot about science when you work in engineering. If we hang on they'll be drawn towards that open window in no time.'

The pair waited, and Reenie found her arm beginning to ache as she held the door fast to prevent it slamming. The bees took an interest in the light fitting, then the electrical flex, then each other. 'Any minute now . . .' Reenie said, detecting again that look of pity and patience in Ada's expression. Still the bees did not move toward the window.

'What was that?' Ada asked, alarmed.

'What was what? Did you think they were moving?'

'No, I heard a bang far off, like a bomb exploding.'

Reenie frowned, and then realised that the door was slack again – the through draught had slammed shut the front door of the factory downstairs and Ada, acutely sensitive to noise in a way which would embarrass a bat, had heard it. The bees took the opportunity to circle back towards the door and hum back out to the corridor from whence they came to pursue their inexplicably unseasonal existence in peace. Reenie shut the door.

'Should we start tidying up now?'

Reenie demurred. 'I think actually we might need to hide.'

'From the bees?'

'No, from the confectioner, Mr Baum. I've just seen him at the other end of the corridor. I think we're for it.'

Chapter Seventeen

It was Wednesday morning, and the Baum household were entering into tense negotiations in three languages over the return of little Greta's most beloved toy and their strongest bargaining tool: her Minnie Mouse puppet.

'We do not have toys at the breakfast table,' Albert Baum told his daughter firmly, but not unkindly. 'You may play in the afternoon, but first you must eat up your eggs and complete your English lesson with Mother.' Albert pointed to the eggs and the buttery toast soldiers which would likely go cold before his daughter relented. 'Be a good girl, Greta.'

'*Ich bin nicht Greta! Ich bin Mina Maus!*' Greta folded her arms tightly and pulled her chin inside the collar of her frock.

Max rolled his eyes at his younger sister and, for Mary's benefit, explained, 'Again she tells us that she is

Minnie Mouse, not Greta.' Maximillian might only have been seven, but he was determined to carry himself with the bearing of a university professor. He leant over to mutter something discreetly in his father's ear, but his father reached for his coffee cup and said, 'English only, please, Maximillian.'

Mary thought she detected the other language that Max sometimes tried to speak with his father when he didn't want to be understood by either his sister or his new stepmother. She felt inexplicably shamed by this, and left the little dining corner of their drawing room for the sanctuary of her kitchen. The serving-hatch doors were closed and so Mary's new husband couldn't see her wiping hot tears from her flushed cheeks. She looked around at the gleamingly clean workspace, filled with the luxury of natural light. After a lifetime living in back-to-back terraces, where the homes of other slum-dwellers crowded in on almost all sides, it was the daylight in her new home which she loved most. The electric cooker was a godsend, but the sun in the morning was worth more to her than anything. That morning the sun had not yet risen and under the glow of her electric lights she'd prepared a family breakfast, making three different kinds of eggs, just the way each Baum liked them, and making coffee on the hob with a hissing contraption Albert had introduced her to. When Mary had first succeeded in making breakfast for her family in their new home she had allowed herself to feel rather smug that she was a successful wife and mother straight out to bat, and even if she was on the young side and from a rather less-educated background than Albert, she had succeeded. The feeling of elation had not lasted long. She had married at Easter, and now it was nearly Christmas and the real gaps in her ability were beginning to become apparent.

Mary wrung her hands. She had a long morning ahead of her and she knew it. Albert would be going out to work at the Mackintosh's toffee factory, Maximillian would be at school, and her sister Bess would be running errands for Mrs Starbeck. Mary would be alone with the little girl who had the fiercest temper she had ever known – and Mary had long thought that she herself held that crown.

The trouble for the newly minted Baum family was that they were required by the local school board to teach little Greta to speak English before she was permitted to enrol in any of their infant schools. Mary had thought it seemed a reasonable enough request for the board to make until she had attempted to teach Greta. It had not gone down well. Mary had no German, and Greta refused to reveal whether or not she had any English. Mary had begun by pointing at items around the house and repeating the names for them in the hope that Greta would follow along, but the child only ran away to play with her Mickey Mouse puppet theatre.

Mary tried taking Greta's puppets away and asking Max to explain in German that she would get them back when she had finished her English lesson, but this had caused a tantrum so violent that Mary had been genuinely afraid that Greta would make herself ill. Mary had then attempted – at her sister Bess's recommendation – a system of rewards involving a jar of sweets, but even that hadn't tempted the little girl.

'Did she go to school in Germany?' Bess had asked one day when she'd been minding the children for Mary.

'No.' Mary didn't like to think about the life the children had had before they came to England. 'They couldn't go to school. It wasn't safe. They stayed at home in their apartment, and went for a walk in the park with their aunt once a day if she could find someone to go with them all.' It was little wonder that Greta stubbornly clung to the things she knew; the dog-eared Minnie Mouse puppet, the eggs fried in a slice of bread, the language of the aunt who had not yet been given permission to leave Germany and join them.

Mary reappeared from the kitchen carrying her own cup of tea by way of an excuse for having risen from the table. The scene was no calmer for her absence. A glass of milk had been spilt and Albert mopped at it with a napkin while Max remonstrated with his sister in German.

'That is enough now, Max.' Albert looked around him for somewhere to put the sodden napkin and decided to leave it in his own plate; there was no time to eat the rest of his breakfast now. 'If it is necessary to speak with firmness to Greta that is for your mother and I to do. Please to remember this. Now it is time for school, young man. Do you have your books?'

Maximillian stood to attention beside his dining chair and said, 'Yes, sir.'

'Then we shall leave together. First you may give your mother a kiss.' Albert smiled at Mary as she lowered her face to receive a peck on the cheek from her relentlessly obedient stepson. 'It is today that you visit the library with Greta, yes?' Albert kissed his wife's other cheek and then smoothed down his hair as he walked out to the hall to fetch his hat and coat. Mary followed him to the front door and answered, 'The library and then the market for tonight's tea.' Mary wanted to suggest that she might give Greta a day off from her lessons because she herself was already exhausted and the day had barely begun. Mary couldn't even face the thought of traipsing through town for food, let alone wrestling a recalcitrant Prussian five-year-old on and off buses while carrying an armload of books, but she didn't want to appear indolent to her industrious new husband.

'I am sure that you will make good progress today.' Albert gave his young wife a reassuring smile. 'And you, young lady,' he said, crouching down to Greta's height, 'please be good and work hard for your mother.'

Greta scowled. The men of the house went on their way and Mary was left alone in the comfortable semi-detached villa with the angriest child in the world.

Mary thought it would be easier, in a way, if she disliked or resented Greta, if she had no patience with her stubbornness, and if she could meet the little girl's anger with anger of her own. But it wasn't a simple battle of wills, because Mary felt that she understood a fraction of the pain and fear her stepdaughter suffered, recognising it from her own childhood. Something unexpected had happened when they first met; Mary had realised, with a suddenness and a ferocity which had taken her breath away, that she loved this little girl to distraction and that she would do anything for her.

Mary wished she could take away little Greta's anger the way her own had been taken away by forging friendships in the factory, but Greta couldn't make friends in Halifax until she learnt to speak to the other children, and that was the seemingly insurmountable problem.

'Come along, Greta. It's time to clear the dining table for your lesson.'

'*Ich bin nicht Greta,*' the little girl muttered, kicking up the carpet with her tiny red slippers. '*Ich bin Mina Maus.*'

'How about this: if you're good and learn your alphabet I will give you a lollipop to eat after supper tonight. Does that sound nice?' Mary gathered up the plates of half-eaten breakfast and passed them through the serving hatch into the kitchen to wash up when Greta had her nap; first was the English lesson and she wasn't going to let herself put it off. Mary fetched the books they'd been working from and piled them up along with a crisp new exercise book for Greta, and a freshly sharpened pencil. Her next job was her least favourite – she knew that she would have to catch Greta and probably have to carry her kicking and writhing to the table. There were no enticements which worked on the child, save one. Mary, too tired to wrestle, decided to use her emergency bargaining chip: the Minnie Mouse puppet.

'Greta,' Mary called out coaxingly as she retrieved the puppet from the place where she had hidden it behind the radiogram, 'I have Minnie Mouse for you.'

Greta ran to the table and sat down without hesitation, holding out her arms for the favourite doll in desperation, but Mary handed over the pencil instead and pointed to the exercise book saying, 'You can have her back when you have finished today's lesson.' And carefully tucked the puppet behind her back where she sat on the dining chair.

Greta, angry and frustrated by what she felt to be a cruel trick, stabbed the freshly sharpened end of the pencil down on the table, just in time to catch the back of Mary's hand as she moved in to stop her damaging the woodwork. It happened very quickly, but Mary did not miss the look of fear and distress on the little girl's face as she realised what she had done, and saw the blood swell to the surface. Greta screamed in genuine fright and Mary howled in pain. She stared at the wound, hoping that she wouldn't need to see a doctor, but she would, and he would have more to tell her than she could ever have feared.

Chapter Eighteen

'The public shame!' Mrs Hunter's voice rang out, uncharacteristically shrill and with a passion Diana hadn't heard in it before. Judging by the direction of the sound she was behind the study door, and as Diana and the housemaid exchanged looks of worry and astonishment, it was clear that neither of them intended to approach.

'Perhaps I should wait in the morning room, Patterson.' Diana took off her gloves and placed them on the hall table with her hat, eyeing the study door all the while in case the lady of the house should come out. Raised voices, indecipherable, indicated that Mr Hunter was also there.

'We must suffer it for the children!' Diana heard him bellow, and wondered if she dared stay in the house to continue her mission.

Diana had intended to collect a parcel of clothes which were castoffs from one of the Hunter lads. Her plan to leave the country relied on her being able to dress Gracie as a little boy for part of their journey, but of course the Hunters didn't know that – she had told them she was collecting for a charity case. Time, Diana supposed, was not such a pressing factor – the ship didn't sail until the new year – she could come back when all was quiet again.

'I've never known them like this.' Patterson must have thought that she was doing the right and honourable thing by her employers in excusing their behaviour because she was a naturally loyal employee.

'Nor have I,' Diana said quietly and decided to press a little further; what had she to lose? 'I've heard they plan to send the children to Canada.'

Patterson shook her long head sorrowfully. 'It's an 'orrible decision to have to make. Mrs Hunter's cousins are in New Brunswick, but they're elderly, they can't take on mor'an two of 'em. Having to decide which to send and which to keep.'

'They won't go with the children?'

'You know what they're like. Everyone else first and 'emselves last. The master's got his company and all them hundreds of workers' livelihoods depending on him staying and keeping it all going, then there's the mistress's charities and her refugees – so many poor folks as would die in Spain if she didn't stay and keep at it. No, they'll stay, war or no war, for the good of all the people who rely on them.'

They *were* good people, the best people. Diana admired them, respected them, loved them. Even the thought that she was going to betray them by stealing their adopted child made her stomach lurch, but didn't this mean she might save another? If Diana took her Gracie to safety in America didn't it leave one more place open for another of their children to go to safety with the Canadian cousins?

'When do you think they'll send them?'

Patterson pulled her chin back into her neck and huffed. 'Your guess is as good as mine. Now all these letters from France have started . . .'

'From France, or from French Canada?' Diana hoped the housemaid knew enough to understand the distinction, but little enough not to be reticent about spilling the beans.

'No, the French stuff's got nothing to do with Canada! The cousins are all in the English-speaking bit. This is stuff from across the channel. And there's been all sorts of visitors – at all hours too!' Patterson became a little breathless with anxiety and looked around her to make certain that she wasn't within earshot of cook and whispered, 'Cook said that she heard someone say that he's got,' Patterson gulped, and her pulse beating visibly hard in her neck she leant closer to Diana and mouthed almost silently, 'got a *son*! In *France*!'

Diana wanted to ask more, but hurried footsteps down the hall told her that someone was coming out of the study. Diana moved quickly to the morning room to keep out of the way, but Mrs Hunter was retreating in the same direction, and they almost collided.

'Have I come at a bad time?' Diana stepped back from the doorway to allow Lydia Hunter to barge past to her desk and begin rapidly opening and closing drawers.

'Diana, I wasn't expecting you!' Mrs Hunter took a deep breath and swallowed hard, 'I'm ashamed to say you've caught me all of a fluster. Were you due to call? I don't remember.' Lydia Hunter was clearly more than flustered; Diana thought she was distraught. She couldn't tell whether the older woman was worried, disappointed, or confused, but she could see that she was desperately searching through old sheafs of papers in her desk and not truly seeing what was written on any of them. Like a schoolboy cramming for an exam at the door to the examination room, Mrs Hunter had anxiously unseeing eyes and a sense of urgency to her chaotic search.

'No, not today.' Diana's tone was calm and dignified as always, though she knew in her heart of hearts that she felt as overwrought as the other woman looked, for Diana had come to steal a disguise with the intention of doing this kind woman a grievous wrong. 'I came to collect the parcel of old clothes you mentioned; the ones you thought might do for my friend's children.'

'Of course, of course.' Mrs Hunter put on an unconvincingly businesslike air of capability but the catch in her breath was still there.

'Is there something I can help you with?' Diana took a half-step further into the other woman's morning room. 'Have you lost something I might have filed for you?'

Mrs Hunter stepped between Diana and the papers on her desk, screening them from view. 'It's nothing to do with our work, Diana, it's a family matter.' Mrs Hunter then seemed to chastise herself inwardly and said earnestly, 'You know that we all think of you as one of our family, don't you, Diana?' She swallowed back some rising emotion and added, 'In these two brief years I feel that you have become a daughter to me.'

Diana was taken by surprise, but she was also saved the necessity of responding immediately by the appearance of the maid, Patterson, who wanted to tell Mrs Hunter that the magistrate and solicitor had arrived and had been shown into Mr Hunter's study.

Diana couldn't know that the meetings in the Hunter house were about the last war, not the new one.

Chapter Nineteen

'Irene Calder, why am I hearing you've been upturning the work in my husband's kitchen?' Mary stood with her hands on her hips at the door to the old factory stable, a woollen bobble hat clutched in one hand like a weapon, the pompom twitching ominously.

'I didn't mean to, it was all an accident!'

'What, did you just stumble accidentally down the corridor to the kitchen and in through the door?'

'Well, no . . .' Reenie had to admit that she hadn't really gone to the kitchen by accident. 'I thought we'd call in on your Albert and pass the time o' day. Ada – that's the cousin of my new supervisor – she's new and she's feeling right down in the dumps and she doesn't like Mack's all that much so I thought I'd show her the best departments.'

'Albert says he left the kitchen locked. He always leaves the kitchen locked.'

'He wants to get that lock seen to. All you have to do is lift the door up half an inch by the handle and then give it a good shove with your shoulder and it pops open.'

'And so after you'd broken in, what possessed you to turn the place upside down and break open a sack of sugar with a spatula?'

Reenie took a deep breath. 'Would you believe me if I told you that it was bees?'

'Not at this time of year, no.'

Mary's sister Bess, who had come to visit them for the dinner hour, poked her grinning face round the frame of the door and asked, 'Why not at this time of year?'

'Never mind,' Mary was impatient, 'I want you to promise me, Reenie, that you'll stay away from Albert's kitchen, otherwise I'll tell Diana.'

Reenie blanched at this. 'Does Diana not know yet about the bee incident?'

'No.' Mary let herself into the stable stall with Bess in tow and plonked herself down on one of the hay bales. 'Albert and I decided that as you're on your final warning this could be the straw what breaks the camel's back. We'll give you one more chance, but you've got to knuckle down in this new job and stay out of trouble.'

Reenie surprised herself by feeling a little hurt at the way Mary referred to 'Albert and I'. Reenie knew that Mary didn't mean anything by it, but it felt as though she really had slipped away a little more, was a different person now to the old Mary, now she was a wife and mother and only at the factory on a temporary basis. Reenie felt that a bond had been severed to build that new one with her new family, and although she didn't resent it – quite the reverse, she rejoiced in her friend's new life – she did feel a little lonely and missed the old Mary sometimes. 'Bess,' Reenie asked, 'if you're here with us, who's looking after Mary's children?'

'Oh, don't worry about that.' Bess settled down and unwrapped her plump packet of sandwiches. 'Max is at school and Greta has gone to play at a neighbour's house for a bit. Encourage her to speak English, like.'

Reenie looked to Mary with concern. 'Is she still not speaking it?'

Mary shook her head. 'We don't know if she can't speak it, or *won't*. Albert thinks she's learnt a lot but won't try, and I think it's a bit o' both. I've tried learning some German and I can't make head nor tail of it, so I can only imagine what it's like for her.'

'I think she does all right in German,' Bess shrugged. 'We get along all right. She points at the things she wants, and I mime what I want her to do, like putting her shoes on, and she does it, like.'

Reenie thought she'd pay good money to see Bess the miming nanny in action, and suspected that Greta was sharp enough to make the most of this entertainment. 'What does Albert say about it?'

'He's wound up like a top, worrying over his sister who's still stuck in Germany, and when he's worried he gets formal. He's very, very formal about Greta's education.' Mary unwrapped a slice of fruitcake and said, 'But I'm tired of talking to people about it, and I notice you haven't answered my question: do you promise not to go near Albert's kitchen again?'

'Yes, I promise – but I did have a very good reason for going there, and if he had let me explain properly then he'd have—'

'I don't want to hear it!' Mary said, holding up her hand to silence her friend.

'Oh, I do,' Bess said.

'All right, then I'll tell Bess.' Reenie shuffled in her hay bale seat the better to begin. 'I have come up with a plan to impress my new manager into recommending me to be reinstated in my old—'

'No!' Mary cried. 'Please! Not more plans!'

'This one is sanctioned by Diana.' Reenie noted the look of suspicion on Mary's face and proceeded. 'I am going to impress my manager by taking his cousin under my wing and help her make friends and settle in to the factory. She doesn't seem to like working at Mack's, and I can't understand it because everyone loves working at Mack's.'

'Do they?' Mary raised an eyebrow.

'Well, I do,' Reenie shrugged. 'I love it because it gives me a sense of purpose, I know I'm being useful.'

'That's debatable, but go on.'

'I know that *you* love working here because when you're working on the line it's the only time you're not worrying. And I've always reckoned Diana loves it because she's the independent type, and earning her own money makes her more independent.'

'I think you're overthinking it, Reenie. Most people want to work here so they can earn fifteen bob a week.'

'Well, yes, there's that too, and there's the girls what just want the social opportunities like the dances and outings – I think Ada's friend is one of those.'

'She already has a friend! So you don't have to befriend her, you can just leave well alone.'

'No, her cousin Harry asked me to befriend her and I really think she's lonely. Besides, I just think it's sad to see someone get a job which could be the making of them, and be miserable in it.'

'I could make friends with her,' Bess volunteered.

'You don't work here anymore, but it's a nice offer.' Reenie thought for a moment and then said, 'Hang about, do you still have any of your old overalls from when you were on the factory floor, Bess?'

'Probably; do you want me to come back?'

'No, but if I could give your overalls to Ada it might help her feel a bit more at home. Hers are far too big because she got them to match her friend so that if her friend was ever short of an overall she could borrow Ada's. I don't know how she can get any work done, she's swamped in cotton.'

'Why don't you take her to stores and choose new ones,' Mary suggested. 'You must know someone down there. A beekeeper perhaps? Or the circus-load of tap-dancing hippopotamuses you took into the confectioner's kitchen when you last visited.'

'You're right,' Reenie was already formulating a plan. 'If I can get her new uniforms which fit, at a time when everyone is short of materials, that will definitely make her feel more welcome, make her job more enjoyable because she won't be fighting her own clothing with every step. And it will impress her cousin because it shows ingenuity. Just you wait and see, I'm going to be back in my old job in no time.'

Chapter Twenty

'You've let yourself go, sis.' Tommo Cartwright was sitting in the kitchen of Diana's boarding house with his feet on the rough table, waiting for his stepsister in the dark. 'You'll never get yourself an 'usband dressed like that; you look like an undertaker's bookkeeper.'

Diana stopped in the doorway, her finger on the tip of the light switch, caught in indecision; to run, or fight, or wait. 'What do you want, Tommo? I'm not giving you money, if that's what you're here for.'

'That's a nice welcome, I must say.' He said it quietly as he looked her in the eye, his words dripping out evenly, like clicks on a slowed metronome, his menace growing in the silence and the gloom.

When Diana had heard that her stepbrother had been released from prison on parole her first thought was of the broken locks on the back door of her boarding house. The door had a modern latch key, but the original bolts top and bottom had long since rusted solid. Neither Diana, nor her former landlady, had ever worried about intruders to the property because it was such a busy one with plenty of tenants to ward off intruders.

Tommo wouldn't be warded off, though. He was a brazen little horror. He'd robbed the toffee factory blind and done it all under the noses of the unsuspecting workers. He was that type; the type to take chances and to take his arrogance to the bank. Why should he tolerate the inconvenience of ringing the bell and waiting in the cold when he could just break in? Tommo, Diana hoped, was there because he was expecting to take his place as lord and master. That was, of course, her best-case scenario; she didn't dare allow herself to think about what would happen if he decided he wanted revenge. It was her evidence, after all, which had sent him to prison. But what else could she have done in the circumstances? If she hadn't turned King's Witness she might have been prosecuted as an accessory and then she would have lost Gracie for certain.

Gracie. He'd want to see Gracie now that he'd been released. Whether his professions of family feeling were real or theatrics Diana had never been able to tell, but Tommo had been insistent when she had visited him after the trial that he would try to rescue Gracie from wherever Diana had placed her, and return the child to the bosom of her dysfunctional and fractured family.

'Are you breaching your parole being here, Tommo?'

'Not if they don't catch me.'

Diana stood up a little straighter, flicked on the light switch, and then called up the stairs behind her, 'I'm going to make a pot of tea, Cynthia. Do come down and join me.' Her fellow boarder responded that she'd be down in a couple of minutes and Diana walked briskly to the range, throwing her coat over the back of a chair as she did so. 'I'm going to boil the kettle because I want a cup of tea, Tommo. I also want you to be gone before it whistles.'

Tommo took his feet off the table and gave the chair next to him a sharp kick. 'You think you're so bloody clever, don't you? Well, you've been pretty bloody stupid this time. You went to one of my pals to book them passages to America. Did you think I wouldn't find out? If you try to take Gracie away it's kidnap, and don't think I don't know where she is and just how things stand with the family what adopted her. If you take her from them, you take her from me and I'll shop you to the cops so's you can't get off the boat at the other end. I know you booked Gracie under a boy's name to cover your tracks, and I know what name too.'

'What do you care where I take Gracie? Really, Tommo, what is any of this to you?'

'We're family. Family matters.'

Diana gave her stepbrother a withering look.

'It's the only reason you're still standing after what you did to me,' he said.

She met his eye. 'You brought it on yourself.'

'I came here to warn you. Leave Gracie where she is.'

Diana felt a chill run down her spine. 'Why?'

'You know why.'

Diana feared she did. If Gracie stayed in one place it would be easier for Tommo himself to snatch her away and reunite his family on his own terms. Diana thought it highly unlikely that he wanted her to stay with the Hunter family in the interests of her own safety; he'd always talked about removing her from her adopted home and she entertained no illusions that he'd changed in prison.

The kettle began to whistle on the range and Diana could hear footsteps on the floorboards above the kitchen; Cynthia Starbeck was on her way. 'You can show yourself out.'

At first – for a moment – Tommo showed no sign of moving, but her threat was implicit, *leave or I will have a witness that you broke your parole and came to Halifax where you have known associates*. Diana continued to make the tea, deliberately ignoring her brother in an act of bravado. Cutting it fine, Tommo huffed, shoved the chair over behind him, and slunk off toward the back door.

Diana didn't wait to drink her tea. She snatched up the Halifax Directory and began looking for locksmiths who could change the locks immediately. She couldn't risk another unannounced visit. She scribbled down a couple of telephone numbers, then called up to Cynthia, 'It's in the pot!' before rushing out.

The hurried trip to a public telephone box reminded her of what she was missing out on that evening. The streets were thronged with young people dressed to the nines beneath their winter coats, going out to factory dances, their faces alight with the glow of anticipation at a night of excitement.

Diana had no wish to dance; she'd had her reckless youth and now all her time and energy was needed to maintain the life she had built around her daughter. She didn't ever think about letting her hair down and enjoying a night of music and dancing; the constant worry of losing her daughter was exhausting.

Diana waited outside the public telephone box, a queue of two other women ahead of her. The night was crisp, and they hugged their coats to themselves and stamped their feet on the granite grey cobbles to keep their toes from going numb. Diana was caught up in her worries about her brother when she became aware of accusatory looks from her fellow callers and was brought back to her immediate surroundings.

'You not got yours yet, then?' the first woman asked, pulling a bobbly black wool shawl a little tighter around her chin in place of a coat and scarf. Diana must have looked confused by the question because the second woman held up a carton and waved it saying: 'Your mask? Have you not got your mask fitted yet?'

Diana suddenly noticed the gas mask cartons hanging over the other women's shoulders on strings and blanched at the realisation that she'd forgotten to bring hers with her. It was treated as somewhere between a social faux pas and an act of aggression to be seen out without your mask. Some people had legitimate reasons for not carrying them – those who hadn't had a chance to be fitted yet – but for a growing number of people the act of refusing a gas mask was a political statement, and Diana realised that the two women were trying to size up whether she fell into that latter camp and make their displeasure felt.

Diana hated all this added hostility around the war preparations; they had troubles enough to face without turning on one another. If this was how life felt before war had been declared, what would it be like once they were really truly fighting the enemy? What would it be like six months into the war? What if the war lasted a year? Or eighteen months? What would life be like in Halifax by then? What would life be like in Halifax for little Gracie faced with gas attacks, air raids, neighbours at each other's throats over which side they took in one of the innumerable factions who wanted to police people's words, thoughts, and actions now that there were so many sides to take. What if, among all that awfulness, another threat lurked too: Diana's stepbrother.

Standing in the queue for the telephone box, waiting to call out a locksmith, Diana made her decision. She'd speak to Lydia Hunter and try to persuade her to send

Gracie away. This town wasn't safe for her daughter anymore. The safest thing for Gracie was to give her up all over again – this time forever.

Chapter Twenty-One

'Kathleen! Just the person!' Reenie burst into the kitchen of her parents' farmhouse with a little more spring in her step than she'd displayed of late. 'I've got a project on and I want to know what you think.'

Kathleen and her mother raised an eyebrow each in unison. 'This isn't you trying to impress that manager again, is it? Because I think you're on to a great big heap of "no" with that one.'

'It's not what you think. He's asked me to take his cousin under my wing, and all I have to do is help her make some friends and settle her in, like. If I manage that he's bound to be impressed and recommend me to be sent back to my old job.'

Reenie's mother warmed to the scheme, but Kathleen had her reservations. 'Why would he recommend you to be sent back to your old department if he's shorthanded in his department? Wouldn't he be more likely to let you go if you were more trouble than you're worth?'

'I can't risk doing anything that might cause trouble, because then I'll be sacked once and for all. Besides, he's already said that he'll be impressed if I can cheer his cousin up, and if anyone can manage that, then I can.'

'Do you have time for all this? I'm not being funny or anything, but you've already got a full-time job, plus helping out on the farm. If you got your old job back you'd be doing even more work than before. Wouldn't you be better off just staying as you are and not impressing anyone?'

'When I said I wanted your advice this wasn't really what I had in mind. I've been thinking about this poor lass who's wretched at Mack's, and I thought that if I got her a nice gang of mates they'd rally round and she'd be all the better for it – you know what a waste it is to have a job at Mack's but not enjoy it!'

'All right, then, what's this plan? Out with it.'

'So far I'm just taking her around places in the factory she wouldn't normally see and letting her get a feel for the whole place, like.'

'How's that going?'

'Well,' Reenie didn't dwell on details, 'it's all right, but I think I should really be concentrating on encouraging the other girls on her shift to make friends with her.'

'No.' Kathleen shook her head like an old hand watching a greenhorn error. 'Whatever you do, don't try to make anyone feel obliged to enter into a friendship with anyone else, that's worse than nothing. Instead, try to show the girls on her shift just how popular she already is, and how many friends she has in other departments. Then, when they see that she's already popular, they'll want to make friends with her too to find out what they're missing.'

Reenie pouted her lips in thought. 'I like it, but I'm not sure how to make her shift mates see her in this new light short of taking her to lunch each day which might get tedious.'

'Your best bet is to leave her notes and presents beside her coat peg. Notes thanking her for coming on outings and notes asking if she'll be free to walk home after work. Try leaving a jar of mother's rosehip syrup for her, or summat.'

'Rosehip syrup's not all that special. It needs to be something that's a bit more fancy; something that will really make the other girls jealous.'

Mrs Calder piped up, 'I've got a couple of jars of pickled calves' tongues that I swapped with next door for walnut ketchup. I don't mind sacrificing a jar in a good cause.'

Reenie demurred. 'I think she's a vegetarian, Mother. She wouldn't get much use out of pickled calves' tongues.'

'All the better.' Kathleen was fond of a bit of tongue in a sandwich. 'She can receive it, which shows she's popular, then she can give it away as a gift to one of the other girls to win someone else over. I think pickled tongue is the ideal gift for every occasion.'

'That's settled, then.' Mrs Calder beamed and got to work. 'I'll find a nice ribbon to tie round the jar.'

With their mother safely out of the way looking through her collection of loose haberdashery, Kathleen asked, 'How are you finding this new manager? Is he giving you any trouble?'

Reenie didn't meet her sister's eye. 'Oh, he's a bit grumpy but he's no bother.'

'I've heard he's handsome. Is he handsome?' Kathleen asked casually enough, but with just a whiff of insinuation.

'I don't know.' Reenie matched Kathleen's degree of casualness, and then raised it. 'I can't say as I've noticed.'

'Well, if you do,' Kathleen said, pointedly, 'tell Diana and get yourself moved. I smell trouble.'

Chapter Twenty-Two

'I just knew that you and Sidney would hit it off.' Caroline took another slurp of her ice-cream float, stirring the remaining blob of vanilla into the cloudy cream soda with her straw. 'You are my two favourite people in the whole world and I'm as happy as could be.'

Ada sat opposite Caroline at their café table in the Prince's Arcade. Caroline would rather have met in the park in the open, and Ada would rather have met in the reassuring old-world antiquity of one of the Victorian department stores, but Caroline had offered an unexpected compromise and suggested they meet in the daring deco shopping parade which Ada was convinced still smelled of new paint and whose smattering of unnecessary chrome details had an air of not quite being paid off yet.

The café had booths with pale-pink leather upholstered banquettes in the stylised shape of seashells, and Caroline had invited Sidney Otter to sit next to her so that he could have a better view of Ada's new dress which she herself had picked out for her friend. The two of them sat very close together, which Ada supposed was only natural if they'd known each other since they were children although Caroline had said they hadn't become really close until recently. They'd be more like siblings, perhaps. But what was that Caroline had been saying about, 'when I met Sidney'?

'Don't you just love Ada's dress, Sidney?' Caroline's enthusiasm rolled over the little company like a wave, compelling them to enter into her version of the world. 'Ada always looks pretty, but I think this dress makes her look extra nice because it's green like her eyes. Don't you think she has lovely green eyes, Sidney?' Caroline's hand slipped below the table and Sidney Otter grinned.

'Oh, yes, nice dress. Both of you, nice dresses.' Sidney grinned around the room, but didn't ever meet Ada's eyes for long enough for her to find out what colour they were. 'This café's a bit all right, isn't it? You two lasses come here all the time when you're not at Mack's?'

'Oh yes,' Caroline enthused, and Ada thought she could see in her face that her friend really did believe what she was saying. 'We practically live here. We're not your usual factory girls, we're very sophisticated.'

Sidney's hand dropped below the table, 'I can see that. I don't know why you don't pack up there and come and work at Crossley's. They have late Saturday working at Crossley's so's you can earn more, and they've only got half as many overlookers so you can get away with murder.'

'I just *adore* Mackintosh's,' Caroline pronounced her employer's name in full, giving the impression of a closer association with the firm than a mere couple of weeks in wrapping and packing. 'It's the most wonderful place to work, and the dances are the biggest in town,' another slurp of her cream-soda float, 'but I don't feel like I've really made any friends at Mackintosh's, and perhaps I'd be better off at Crossley's.'

Ada's chest constricted at the thought of being left in the noisy confusion of Mack's without even her best friend to turn to. Caroline might have been easily distracted by new acquaintanceships, and she might have a rather patchy relationship with the truth sometimes, but when all was said and done, Ada was certain that Caroline was a good soul and always had her friend's best interests at heart. The dances were torture, but that was because Ada herself was being awkward and not giving them a chance; it was her own fault she didn't enjoy them, not Caroline's. And the work itself wasn't nearly so bad as it could have been, and there were hundreds of girls who thrived on it so it must be Ada's own fault that she wasn't. She desperately hoped Caroline wasn't really going to leave.

The problem was that Ada knew she didn't try hard enough, and she realised that this young man was an opportunity to try. He was not handsome in a classical way, but looks weren't everything. He had a bulbous sort of nose and a low forehead, but he had a good head of hair and that was something the other girls might envy if she walked out with him. His thin lips and narrow eyes managed to look pleased with themselves and as though they were enjoying a private joke all the while, but Ada supposed that given how hard he must have worked to have risen to the ranks of buyer at Crossley's, he had every right to look pleased with himself. He wasn't tall – as Caroline had promised – in fact, he was about an inch shorter than Caroline herself, but Ada didn't mind that and she was a little put out that Caroline would have thought she was the type to care enough that she would fudge the facts. He didn't look like Basil Rathbone either, and his hair was a light ash blond, not the dark shade Caroline had insisted he was, but these things were superficial and Ada only cared about getting to know the man within.

'What sort of wool is Crossley's buying at the moment?' Ada asked with earnest interest.

Sidney gave an amused smirk to Caroline and then shrugged. 'The kind you get off sheep.'

Ada flushed with embarrassment. Of course this man wasn't going to discuss wool buying with someone who knew nothing about wool, that was presumptuous. She might have a genuine interest, but presumably everyone had a genuine interest when they heard what he did and asked him the same question. He was probably heartily sick of having to explain the rudimentary elements of his work to amateurs. Besides, wouldn't the precise nature of Crossley's purchasing arrangements be trade secrets? It was a stupid question, and she would have to try harder. What did other girls ask young men in these situations? What would one of her Heyer heroine's ask?

'I hear the king has been visiting Bradford this week,' Ada said with dignity.

Caroline nearly choked on her ice-cream float. 'Has he? That's nice.' Her hand dropped below the table again. 'Sidney, do you like Ada's hair? I styled it for her this morning. She suits it away from her face, doesn't she.' Caroline launched into a warm and compelling story about how she had always thought that her hair would fall out if she didn't brush it one hundred times before she went to bed – as her Sunday School teacher had told her – and then one day had discovered that some days her brothers didn't brush their hair at all and they were quite all right and she realised what a fool she had been. Caroline carried the conversation along without effort because Caroline carried every conversation along whether people wanted her to or not. Wherever Caroline was, the room would light up with her anecdotes and her compliments and her fierce encouragement; the Christmas lights in the window of the café were as nothing to the sparkle of Caroline Caffrey. She glowed, and she told Sid how much he liked Ada, and she was so pleased that he would take Ada to the next dance so that Ada could learn how to enjoy herself. She said that it would be a special favour to her, and Ada resolved to try very hard to like Sid, because next day Caroline told her how much he liked her and she wanted to believe that it was true that someone did.

Chapter Twenty-Three

It was the eleventh of November and the public bar of the Old Cock and Oak had never been so crowded or so quiet. The landlady had an entertainment licence and used it to play the wireless sometimes, but this night was not an entertainment.

'There's nothing on Radio Paris,' a spotty youth called up from the radio set where he was crouching with an intent look, 'it's just music.'

'Try Radio Madrid!' Someone called out from the back of the packed bar, 'We know they've got news on Radio Madrid!' A general rumble of agreement hummed through the waiting punters, and the name of the station was repeated in a far-off room.

The landlady, who seemed protective of her expert radio operator, called out in his defence, 'He can't get that, we've tried it. It's too far off. Stockholm's the farthest it'll pick up.' This prompted muttered arguments about the distance to Madrid as the crow flies, and why war-torn Spain hadn't invested in a better transmitter.

'I don't understand,' one elderly woman piped up, 'why we can't hear any of this on the BBC.' And she shook her copy of the *Daily Mirror* in frustration.

The reader of the *Mirror* was not the only patron to carry a paper with her, some people had arrived with clutches of different titles hoping to piece together the reports of what was happening across Europe. The *Manchester Guardian* talked of 'Wreckage In Streets'; 'Germany's Day of Wrecking and Looting'; 'Synagogues Burned Down in Many Cities'. The *Daily Mirror* led with a front page story of 'Nazi Day of Hate'. The BBC gave a brief account in their daily news bulletin, but it was maddeningly brief. If the newspapers were anything to go by – and some of them were running photographs – all the Nazi-occupied countries of Europe were in the grip of a frenzied pogrom against their own Jewish citizens, all while the authorities looked on, but made no move to intervene. Mobs were demolishing homes with sledgehammers; synagogues and Jewish schools were on fire; shops and other properties were being smashed and vandalised; and some reports said that as many as 10,000 Jewish men had been arrested and sent to concentration camps. And then there were the reports of suicides . . .

A man with a copy of the *Daily Worker* tucked under his arm made to leave, apparently in disgust at the inadequacy of the pub's domestic radio. 'It's an orgy of violence, that's what it is.' He said, 'An orgy of violence.'

'Who's gonna' stop 'em?' an elderly matron asked of no one in particular.

'Hush!' several people called out at once, insisting that the young wizard of the airwaves be given quiet to at least try to find something out.

'I will not be hushed! I'm eighty-seven and I've seen a score of wars, and I tell you we're getting another one before Christmas.'

Donna the landlady tried to pacify her customers, 'This is bad, but we'll not go to war over it. Mr Chamberlain got his agreement signed. We've been promised peace.'

The air in the pub was heavy with tobacco smoke, and heavier with frustration. One by one the patrons who had come in seeking some confirmation of what they'd read were giving up and going home to worry about their hard-won peace, or about people in faraway lands of whom they knew nothing, or sometimes of both. Diana Moore sat on a bench by the door, her old colleague Heather Rogers and a few other faces from Mack's taking up the remaining places around her. She thought of Mr Baum and his sister and his children. She thought of her own child. The world had lost its mind and sometimes she felt that only she was sane.

The assassination of one diplomat in Paris by a Polish kid had led to reprisals so brutal and terrifying that it was hard to believe that England wouldn't be at war by morning. If there had been anyone left in England who had doubted the need to stop the Nazi war machine; to offer safe-haven to the Jewish people; to prepare for war, then surely this would be an end of all their doubts.

The radio hissed through stations from Oslo and Milan, but the lad who seemed to know so much about radio sets was coming up against a determined silence. The landlady took the mood of the room and announced with reluctance, 'I'm sorry, I've got to close up—' Groans and entreaties rippled through the remaining patrons, while others gave up their wait and cleared out. 'I can't risk my licence. I can lock a few of you in to keep trying if you think you'll get somewhere, but the rest of you will have to go home. The *Courier* has a radio and they'll be printing extra editions, no doubt.'

Diana turned to her colleagues. 'I've got a radiogram at my boarding house. We might as well all go to mine.'

'Can you get Madrid?' one of them asked.

'I doubt it, but we can try.'

Arrangements were made to get messages to wives and mothers that they wouldn't be coming home, and a few said they'd come to the boarding house by and by. It was all the same to Diana. She'd stay up and listen either way; she had no kids at home to worry about waking. But she had to stay up and listen, even if she learned nothing new. She had to know how near the danger was. She had her plan and she had her savings, but she wasn't ready to put it into action yet. She couldn't afford for the war to come today.

Chapter Twenty-Four

'They're calling it the worst pogrom in living memory!' Old Mr Pardew mopped up his fried egg yolk with a slice of white buttered bread and jabbed a finger in the air for emphasis before saying, 'And you can't tell me it wasn't all planned a'forehand! They've got evil intentions that lot!'

'Well, we've known that since '34 at least,' Norton sniffed. 'When they had their Night of the Long Knives they showed their true colours. Awful what they're doin', awful!'

Reenie arrived at the staff canteen just in time to find her colleagues from the Engineering Maintenance Department pushing away their breakfast plates and gulping back their cups of tea. Reenie sidled onto the end of the bench at the far end of their table as quietly and as inconspicuously as possible. Her previous overtures of friendship having been rebuffed by her grumpier colleagues, she thought it best to keep herself to herself and wait until they moved to start their shift.

Mr Pardew wasn't ready to let the topic go just yet. 'You've got folks like Oswald Mosley banging their drum about how fascism has the trains running on time and everyone gets to dress up nice, but what use is all that if there's beatin's in the streets and sacred places aflame?'

'Oswald Mosley can go to hell. He wants lockin' up.' Norton leant over his greasy plate and looked directly at Reenie for the first time since her arrival in their department. 'How's your friends? They all right?'

'My friends?' Reenie was so taken aback by the change in attitude towards her that she didn't know what to make of the question.

'*Jewish* friends.' Pardew said. 'Your friend married that Jewish chap from the kitchens, didn't she?'

'Oh, yes, Mary!' Reenie tried not to say too much or too little, hoping that this crack in the ice was the beginning of a great thaw. 'She married the head confectioner, Mr Baum. He brought his two children here from Germany.'

'Rotten business.' Norton sniffed again and growled, 'Rotten, stinking business. You tell your friends they're welcome in Halifax.' Norton drained his teacup and plonked it down defiantly. 'You tell 'em Mosley doesn't speak for everyone round here. Britain won't go down to fascism without a fight.'

The other grumpy old men growled in acknowledgement, and one or two slapped Reenie on the back as they rose from their places on the bench to head toward their first job of the day. Reenie stayed where she was, wondering if this pat on the back was a change in their attitude to her at last, or if their attitude had never changed, and she'd just been wrong about it all along.

The first job of the day was a problem, and it was set up in the maintenance workshop down by the stables. A machine which Reenie knew well enough waited among the sawdust and engine grease of the brightly lit lean-to.

'Ever worked with this one, Reenie?' Harry Swallow lifted the hood on the foil and band machine which Reenie herself had adapted from a cigarette wrapper to the most reliable machine on the Caramel Cup line.

'It's not conked out already, has it?' Reenie supposed she oughtn't to be surprised if it had, it would be all of a piece with her luck these days. The machine she thought was solid as a rock had turned out to be nothing of the sort.

Harry shook his head and walked around the old beast. 'It doesn't need fixing. There's a problem with a machine setup. It needs a new safety hood which protects the workers' hands, but also doesn't stop them moving round the machine easily.' Harry led Reenie to the machine, folded his arms, and nodded in its direction. 'Go on then, work your magic, now's your chance.'

Reenie looked at him suspiciously; she wasn't sure if this was a taunt or a trick. She wanted to think the best of everyone, but she also knew that he'd been so strict with her in the past and that this must be a test to see if she'd try to do something more elaborate. 'I know I've got to leave it be. I won't interfere.'

Harry sighed. 'This isn't a trick question. I know I said I didn't want you going off and doing daft things on your own, or trying to improve everything for the sake of it, but that's because I don't want you thinking you have to prove yourself anew every morning. You've got the job, you're here, now just solve the problems that actually need solving. Like this one. There's a time and a place for your sort of fancy footwork, and it's not when you're on your own and you've got no one to help if it goes wrong. This time you've got me to tell you where you might run into trouble, and you've got the rest of the team to help pick up the pieces if it all goes horribly wrong. This is the time and the place for your sort of problem solving, so I'm giving you your chance. Take a look at this hood and tell me where you think it should be refitted.'

It was another unexpected turn of events. Perhaps she had misjudged her new colleagues entirely. They had been gruff when she'd arrived, but perhaps they weren't annoyed that she'd been sent to them – perhaps they were annoyed that she was the *only* help that had been sent to them. They had got off on the wrong foot when they had all been out of sorts, and Reenie was starting to wonder if Harry really did value the contribution she made. He certainly seemed happy with her work as she busied herself all afternoon with her new project.

*

Reenie stepped out into the yard beyond the workshop, a glow of satisfaction from a job well done warming her against the bite of the November air.

'Is that snow?' Harry Swallow was close behind her, pulling his coat collar up as he set out for home at the end of their shift.

'I think it might be.' Reenie looked hopefully at the sky, willing this to be the first day of a better season at Mack's now that her colleagues seemed to be accepting her. 'If it keeps on this cold I wouldn't be surprised if we had a white Christmas.'

'Yep,' Harry drew closer, 'not long now and the Christmas lights'll be up.' He paused, and Reenie could smell the engine oil on his overalls and a whisper of bay rum still lingering from his morning shave. She felt a little electric shiver run down her back.

'You did well, today, lass. I want you to know that I'm not hard on you because you're no good, I'm hard on you because you've got potential. You're a value to the company, if only you'd stick to what you're supposed to be doing. Machines aren't the only things what can burn out, you know?'

'Did I honestly do well? Have I helped?'

'You have. I'll tell you true, I've been impressed by the way you've took this demotion on the chin and just knuckled down to the work. I don't think it's fair you've been demoted for something that were an accident, none of us lot do – and if I'd been in charge I'd have done things differently – but I was told to keep an eye on you and make sure you didn't get into trouble, so that's what I've done. I'm glad to have you on the team to tackle the problems we might ordinarily struggle with for longer if you wasn't here.'

Reenie blushed almost as red as her hair. 'I thought you thought that I was a nuisance.'

'Aye, you are, lass; you are. But you're *our* nuisance now.' He looked up at the sky which was dusting a fine powdery snow onto the factory yard. 'How's about you come and be a nuisance round town with me this Friday after work? The town corporation are putting up the Christmas lights and we could see them lighted, if you've a mind to it.' The look he gave her was direct, a cheeky smile playing across his parted lips.

Reenie's breath caught in her throat and she felt for a moment that she understood why so many of the factory girls fell for Harry Swallow. His long brown eyelashes batted lazily over hazel eyes which seemed to promise much, but care little. He always made her thoughts run to the same thing – that he was everything Peter was not; older, worldly-wise, more than a little rough around the edges, and thrillingly dangerous. Reenie's face lit up and she opened her mouth to agree, but he turned away for a moment, and in that moment she hesitated, and in her hesitation she thought more about Peter. Good, honest, gentlemanly Peter whom she had hurt so that she could keep this job. He would be coming back to Halifax some time before Christmas to visit the Major, and what would he think if he heard that she was already walking out with someone else and putting her job in jeopardy? Reenie cared enough not to treat what she and Peter had had so lightly.

'I'm sorry, I'm busy on Friday,' she said, 'I need to get home. My mother will be wondering where I am.'

Harry shrugged and Reenie scurried off toward the stables hoping against hope that a cold snap wasn't coming to the Engineering Maintenance Department.

Chapter Twenty-Five

Mary had no choice but to take Greta with her to Dr Arnold's surgery. The dressing on her hand which he had applied after the pencil stabbing incident was due to be changed and the doctor had said that he wanted to keep a close eye on it to guard against any possibility of infection. 'In your condition,' Dr Arnold had gone on, 'we can't be too careful.'

Mary had worried about those words ever since. What condition? She felt run down, that was certain, and she knew she had all the signs of anaemia because her sister Bess had suffered in just the same way not two years before. Mary had tried to eat an orange a day and get plenty of fresh air, but it didn't seem to be working. She was exhausted to her very bones and she felt herself on the verge of tears constantly.

'My wife will see to your daughter while we take a

look at that hand.' The doctor's kindly manner would usually have put Mary at her ease as it put so many other patients at theirs, but there was a problem which she felt ashamed to have to mention.

Mary looked around the surgery's comfortable waiting room. Someone, presumably Mrs Arnold, had decked out the ceiling with paper chains of primary colours in honour of the season, and a generous coal fire crackled behind a stout fireguard. A wicker basket of cheerfully painted wooden toys had been tucked away in a corner for the benefit of visiting children. The walls were adorned with restful prints of rolling Yorkshire countryside, and the few informative posters from the Ministry of Health gave encouraging messages about the benefits of eating this vegetable or that. It was a welcoming place, and these were welcoming people, but Mary couldn't leave her little girl there. It was a terrible thing to feel both ashamed of a child's behaviour, and fearful for them too. Mary knew that Greta would likely give the nice doctor's wife trouble, but she also felt that it would only be a natural response in Greta's situation. To be left in a strange place with a stranger, no matter how kind, would be terrifying to an already terrified child.

'I'm sorry,' Mary looked apologetically from the doctor to his wife, 'she doesn't speak any English yet, and I don't know how to tell her to wait nicely.' Mary held Greta's hand a little tighter as she could see that her stepdaughter was looking anxious, and the warning signs of a tantrum were brewing. 'She speaks German.'

To give the doctor's wife due credit she didn't show a hint of surprise that a young woman should walk into her husband's surgery with a daughter to whom she could not speak. Mrs Arnold's eyes lit up. 'Oh how wonderful! I haven't spoken German in years. What a treat!' She knelt down to Greta's height and said earnestly, '*Guten Morgen. Mein Name ist Florence. Welchen Namen hast du?*'

Greta's gasp of astonishment was priceless, and her relief at meeting someone with a language she understood was made evident when she lunged at the doctor's wife to hug her fiercely and cry, '*Greta! Mein Name ist Greta!*'

'There now,' Mrs Arnold said to Mary, as though having a second language under her belt was all in a day's work as a doctor's wife, 'I think Greta and I shall get along famously.' Mrs Arnold pointed to the basket of toys and said something to Greta which the child seemed happy about, and they entered into lively conversation in which Mary recognised the words 'Mina Maus'.

'If you'd like to step this way, Mrs Baum?' Dr Arnold ushered Mary towards the door of his consulting room. 'Today is our day for Nurse Carlisle's midwifery clinic. I thought you might like to have a checkup with her while you're here and took the liberty of reserving you an appointment. There will be no extra charge on this occasion.'

Mary had no time to disguise her look of shock before the door to the consulting room clicked closed behind her.

The journey home by the number eighteen bus passed in a haze of anxiety. Mary had an easier time of things on the way home as Greta was in a better mood. The child had obviously enjoyed the freedom of a playtime with a German speaker, and Mary felt even more guilty that she hadn't succeeded in teaching the child English. Greta was clearly a good girl at heart, and it was only the language which was a barrier to her happiness in her new home. Of all the things which Mary thought she ought to be able to teach a child, the language that she had spoken herself for more than twenty years ought to be the easiest.

The crowded bus swayed and Mary, standing in the aisle and holding onto the leather strap overhead, swayed into an elderly lady with pince-nez who was sitting reading the *Racing Post*. 'I'm very sorry,' Mary said, steadying herself and looking around for a seat.

'Seats upstairs,' the conductor called out as he went up himself to check passengers' tickets.

Mary remained below, gazing out into the darkening street at the illuminated shop windows which glided softly by. The doctor had been right, of course. Mary herself hadn't noticed, she'd put it all down to anaemia and exhaustion, but the doctor was a professional and to him it had been as plain as the nose on her face. At her last appointment he had made that discreet reference to it – he was an expensive doctor by Mary's standards and she wasn't used to middle-class manners – and he had arranged a discreet midwife's examination for her following visit. Mary's look of panic when they confirmed the news had not appeared to surprise him, or the midwife; she supposed they saw all sorts.

'There's a war coming,' Mary had said. The doctor had understood. 'Your baby will be here by the summer,' he'd told her, 'your husband will help you.'

But Mary didn't want Albert to have to help her; he had been through enough. Mary wanted to be a help to him, to help his children – *their* children now. A war was certainly coming, and with it a near-certain invasion. They would be one of the families most at risk, and they would need to be ready to flee, to America if they could get the permits. A pregnancy would make all of that impossible. What if they couldn't get abroad and had to go into hiding? How would they hide with a baby? She was already so exhausted by all the responsibility she had taken on, she couldn't take on any more, it was too much, it was all far too much.

The bus lurched around a corner and a handful of people tried to squeeze past Mary and Greta to alight.

'I told you there's more seats upstairs.' The conductor had returned and seemed to be making Mary's move compulsory. 'Don't block the gangway unless you're getting off at the next stop. Are you getting off at the next stop?'

Mary shook her head.

'Then go on upstairs.'

'I can't,' Mary said, her voice cracking. 'I'm expecting

a baby and I'm worried about slipping and falling down them and—'

The elderly lady with the *Racing Post* leapt up with the alacrity of a woman half her age and pressed Mary into her seat with gusto. 'Oh, my dear, you cannot be too careful. Trust me when I say that you cannot be too careful.' The faces of other concerned women turned to Mary now, and Greta was being placed on a seat beside her, and her basket of shopping was slipped off her arm to be lifted into the luggage stand.

Mary felt the tears coming again now, hot and fast down her cheeks. 'I'm so frightened,' she gasped. 'My baby's coming, and the war is coming, and I'm so frightened.'

Chapter Twenty-Six

'What was so urgent that you had to send a messenger girl? I was in the middle of my weekly accounts.' Diana Moore didn't come down to the stables much, but she conceded that when they needed to talk privately it was useful to have them at their disposal.

'We can't talk here.' Mary nodded in the direction of the stable stall and Diana walked over and peered inside.

'Hullo, who are you?'

A girl who Diana dimly recognised from her dinner-plate eyes sat nervously on the edge of a hay bale beside the long-suffering Ruffian.

'I'm Ada Helliwell. Reenie Calder told me I could come and eat my lunch with her. This is her horse.'

In unison Diana and Mary said, 'We know.' Ada sneezed twice, and then the horse sneezed and then a sort of relay of sneezes ricocheted back and forth between the two.

'I think you're allergic to the hay,' Diana said. 'Perhaps you should come out into the yard.'

'Oh, I don't mind it,' Ada said, resigning herself to needless discomfort.

'Suit yourself.'

'You're both here! I *am* pleased!' Reenie turned the corner into the yard and saw her two friends before her waiting visitor.

'I think Mary and I ought to go back to my office.' Diana didn't look in the direction of Ada because although she was blunt, she wasn't rude.

'No!' Mary blurted out quickly, and gave Diana a look which said that they couldn't speak freely in her office. 'I need to tell—'

'Ada!' Reenie called into the stable. 'Come out and meet my friends, Mary and Diana.' Then to the friends who were quite evidently not in the mood for social introductions, 'Mary, Diana; this is Ada, the cousin of my supervisor. She's new, but she's not really found her place. I thought we could make her feel at home, all girls together. We've got the factory dance coming up, and I'm thinking of getting a lipstick. What do you reckon?'

Ruffian snorted loudly and Ada gave another sneeze. Diana attempted to ask questions of Mary with looks, and Reenie – intent on her plan to get her job back by impressing her manager – ploughed on with her oblivious and determined small talk. 'I've never bothered with lipstick, I've always thought you can be a bit too young

171

to pull it off, if you know what I mean, but I was eighteen the other week and I think I might push the boat out.'

Mary ignored Reenie and persevered – in guarded terms – with Diana. 'If someone on my line was planning to hand in their notice . . .'

'Then they can give it to you. You're an overlooker now, it's part of the job. Let Hiring know you want someone new to fill the position and induct them. There's no need to summon me down from my office to tell me that in a stable yard with cloak and dagger.'

'Will you be wearing lipstick to the dance, Ada?' Reenie asked.

Ada looked as though she were about to sneeze, but the moment passed. 'I'm not sure if I want to go or not. It's a bit difficult to decide, you see.'

'But if the person who was handing in their notice thought that they might be about to be dismissed if the truth about them were discovered, and they were holding back their notice to hang on as long as they could to help the war effort, but wanted to give fair warning – off the record – that a replacement for them would need to be found . . .'

'Then reassure them that I don't care what the truth about anyone is so long as they clock in on time and only steal items of value under one shilling. We want all the help we can get right now, and that's why I've put you in charge of that section; you pick the right girls for the right job and keep output high, and you don't stand for any nonsense. If I didn't have you on that line there'd be a lot fewer gas masks heading out to the good people of Halifax. I trust you to keep an eye on them all and sack them if they want sacking, but for God's sake hang on to them until the last possible moment if they're a good worker.'

Mary threw a glance in the direction of their surprise visitor and then back to Diana. There was more, there was evidently more, and Mary was bursting with it.

Diana rolled her eyes. 'You can either tell me here, or you can tell me in my office, but I'm not traipsing all over town looking for the ideal conditions for Mary Baum to unburden her soul of whatever is worrying her this week.'

'Can you two pack it in?' Reenie called up from the hay bale she had now settled herself comfortably on. 'I thought we could have nice natter together while we eat these scones my mother made, and welcome Ada into our little group. We could talk about what normal girls talk about: dresses and lads and that.'

'You'll get no talk of lads from me, I've gone off them, and Mary's got married—' Diana stopped abruptly and looked at Mary as if seeing her anew. A realisation was dawning and this made Mary look more anxious than ever.

'What are you going to wear to the factory dance, Ada?'

'I don't know. My friend Caroline always lends me a dress. But I don't know if I want to go this time.'

'Why wouldn't you want to go to a dance?' Reenie asked. 'It's one of the great perks of working at Mack's.'

'I'm a bit worried about it. There's this lad who my friend says wants to take me to the dance, and she says I ought to be right pleased he wants to take me, but I just don't know—' Ada's tentative confidence was cut short by a groaning wail. The air raid siren was off again, and another air raid drill – at least, they hoped it was a drill, but they supposed there would be no notice if it wasn't – cut short their dinner hour. They scrambled for their gas mask cartons which were always at hand now, and scurried off as quickly as they could towards the shelters, each worried about entirely different things.

Chapter Twenty-Seven

The noise was suffocating, and so was Sidney Otter. He had arrived to collect Ada from her family home at seven o'clock that evening, smelling of beer, spirits, and a scent Caroline sometimes wore. It had probably rubbed off Caroline as she walked him round to Warley Street, something she said she'd done as a favour to Ada to make certain he found the place all right. Caroline had badgered Sidney into linking arms with both of them, and the three of them had walked companionably together. Sidney didn't pay Ada much attention, but how could he be expected to when Caroline was around monopolising the conversation?

Caroline said that she had managed to find a couple of young men to dance with later on, so they wouldn't need to worry about her. She just wanted Sidney and Ada – her two favourite people in the world – to have fun and make the most of the evening. And then she encouraged them to go down to the bike sheds to shelter from the cold while they waited for the dance to open and said that she'd see them on the dance floor once she'd found her first partner. Caroline had winked at Ada and whispered in her ear, 'I've told him he has to show you a good time so let yourself go and enjoy it.'

The wait in the bike sheds alone with Sidney had been a confusing mix of disappointment and distress. Ada had always thought that her first kiss would be magical, a romantic apogee worthy of Georgette Heyer, a gentle expression of courtly love. The reality had been an affection grudgingly given, roughly taken, and she'd been left with the uncomfortable suspicion that Sidney would rather have had Caroline and was making do with her.

The dance – when they got there – was over-subscribed, but they only saw Caroline with one dance partner. One ever-present and very attentive dance partner. Sidney seethed with a resentment and anger which Ada didn't know how to manage.

'What's Caroline doing with him? Who is he? *You're* her friend, *you* ought to know.'

Ada was at a loss. The young man Caroline was dancing with was just as new to her as Sidney Otter had been a week before, but she knew that Caroline had a lot of friends. 'I've never seen him before,' she said, wishing that she had and could explain all this away and make Sidney calm again. 'Is he perhaps one of the friends from Bridlington? Do you recognise him from your summers together there?'

Sidney snapped impatiently, 'What summers in Bridlington? I've never been to Bridlington.'

'Aren't your parents old friends of Caroline's parents? From their many years holidaying together at Bridlington?'

'I've already told you, I've never been to Bridlington, and I don't care to. I met Caroline at a dance three weeks back and I wish I never had.'

Sidney barged his way through the dancers to have it out with Caroline about her choice of partner and Ada, more miserable than ever, slunk away to join the queue for the ladies' lavatories where she could hide away. In the brightly lit, cool corridor, lined with gleaming white glazed bricks, the conversation of the other young women in the queue was animated.

Ada recognised a few of the girls from her own line – girls who had been so kind and attentive when she had cut her hand – and she wished she had the courage to ask for their kindness now. Ada was unhappy, but more than that, she didn't know if she had a right to be. Ada felt she ought to be trying harder with Sidney, and she wondered if she was very self-centred for feeling that she disliked him sometimes. Her father would probably tell her that her standards were too high and that she ought to put more of an effort in to see the good points in the young man. Sidney did have his good points. He was honest and trustworthy (Caroline would not have introduced them if he weren't); he had good job prospects and was a steady worker (Crossley's wouldn't have promoted him if he weren't); and he evidently liked Ada and wanted to spend more time courting her (he wouldn't have kissed her before the dance if he weren't seriously interested in her). All in all there was no good reason not to like him, and she ought to feel fortunate to have this chance. If only she could ask those nice other girls what she ought to do for the best.

'But shouldn't we do something to help?' one of them was saying to her gaggle of friends. 'All those Jewish people in Germany and Austria who have lost their homes; shouldn't we do something?'

Dolly Dunkley, that notorious member of the BUF, was ahead of them in the queue and butted in to offer her two penn'orth. 'If I were you I'd be watching your own backs. There's dangers here in Halifax and the Jews in Germany aren't the only people who've seen violence.' Dolly tucked in her chin and her nostrils gave a little twitch. 'I've heard there's been some girls attacked on their way home from dances. Properly attacked. I've got an uncle who's very high up in the police and he says there's a dangerous man on the loose but they can't publicise it because there's national security implications.'

A new girl, who had not learnt first-hand to take Dolly's 'uncles' with a pinch of salt, asked with ill-concealed awe, 'What's a security implication?'

'It's when you think there might be spies.' Dolly was evidently enjoying the horror she was creating. 'I was walking home from work one night and I saw him. He didn't get a chance to lay hands on me because I run so fast no one could ever keep up with me, but he chased me for a bit and he came close. I think you ought to be asking what you can do to help yourselves, more than anything. The thing in Germany's finished now, but you're still in danger.'

Ada wondered if she could nip outside for some air, claim that she'd been chased by the phantom attacker and say that she had to go home, but then Caroline appeared.

Caroline looked flustered and wilted, beads of perspiration collecting on her upper lip, and a dark smudge of Tangee mascara casting a shadow thinly under each eye. She found Ada quickly enough and pulled her out of the queue to 'have a quiet word'. At which point she sighed and said, with exaggerated patience, 'I'm not angry with you, Ada, but I do feel rather frustrated that you aren't doing your best. You've been neglecting Sidney so much that he felt he needed to come and bother me. This wasn't the act of a good friend, Ada. A good friend would have put the effort in to fascinate Sidney so that he had eyes for no one else.'

'I'm sorry.' And Ada felt a stab of guilt that she had been so complacent and thoughtless and made everything go wrong. 'I just didn't know what to do.'

Caroline tilted her head on one side and gave Ada that smile that told her Caroline would tolerate all her friend's shortcomings because she loved her, and she would guide her through this as she had guided her through their first day at the factory. 'It's all right, he still likes you, but there are a few things you'll need to start doing to please him if you want him to walk out with you. You'll need to spend a bit more of your wages on dresses because he's really not going to want to be seen out with you if you don't try.' She said it not unkindly, and with an air of a caring mother to her child. 'We'll also need to work on your hair and your face make-up as a regular thing; oh, and don't get upset about this because I don't have time for you to make a fuss, but he will want you to shave your legs and under your arms. It's nothing to get het up about, it's very easy and I'll explain how to do it, but he likes girls to have that Hollywood-starlet look. You've got to remember that you're in the real world now and not one of your novels, so a husband isn't just going to fall into your lap, you have to work at it.'

Ada wiped a tear from her cheek. She didn't want to get het up, but she couldn't help the tears.

'You know you're lucky; Sidney's quite a catch but he's been willing to overlook some of these little things while you've been getting to know each other and not many lads would be that patient. But the most important thing is that you do your best to flatter him, fascinate him, and keep all his attention on you so that he can think of nothing else. Be a little bit mean to him sometimes, then flattering and attentive, then mean again. Keep him on his toes so that he never knows what to expect.'

Ada nodded and twisted her lips together to hold back more tears, because she'd been told not to get upset, and she knew deep down that it was wicked of her to let herself.

Caroline gave another patient sigh. 'Just forget this ever happened, Ada, and we'll start again. Go and dry your eyes and then come out to the dance floor. I've agreed to dance the next two dances with Sidney, so you've got until then to take some deep breaths and put your best foot forward, all right?' Caroline gave her friend a warm, enveloping hug and then returned to the dancing while Ada waited in the bright corridor and folded her arms tightly, twisting her lips together again, willing herself to be a better friend who didn't make a fuss.

A door at the end of the corridor banged open and closed, sending a draught up the queue of women, and giving Ada a glimpse of the fire escape beyond. The din of the dancehall awaited her and Ada felt half-delirious with misery and confusion so instead of waiting in the queue of women, she made for the fire escape.

Perhaps it would be better if she left and didn't come back? Surely Sidney would be better off with another girl who wasn't so much to put up with, and who didn't have to work so hard to be like everyone else? The cold night air caught Ada unawares and she began to shake and sob simultaneously. She had left her coat in the cloakroom and Caroline's flimsy borrowed dress offered no warmth.

She headed for the bike sheds which were dark and deserted, and Ada found herself desperately wishing Dolly Dunkley's phantom were there so that he could put Ada out of her misery. She slumped down next to a roof post and knocked over a bicycle in the process, spilling the contents of its unfastened pannier bag on the floor. *Stupid, stupid, stupid!* Her shoulders shuddered with cold as she tried to right the bicycle and put back the things she had spilled on the floor. Someone had brought their shaving tackle to work with them, and as she scooped up the soap and brush she was reminded of Caroline's injunction to shave under her arms and felt ashamed and embarrassed that she hadn't already done all that and had had to be told, and more desperate than ever to escape another dance with Sidney Otter. She saw the paper packet of new razor blades and a desperate thought occurred to her. She could get out of all this, get some time to think. Before she knew what she was doing, Ada had stolen one of the absent cyclist's razor blades and was tearing at her borrowed dress with it. She nicked her forearm just enough to draw some blood and threw the spent blade into the gutter. Then, within earshot of the factory dance, Ada screamed blue murder.

Chapter Twenty-Eight

Sergeant Metcalf was one of the first policemen to arrive at the scene of the attack at the Mackintosh's toffee factory. The factory watchmen – who had telephoned direct to the station – had arrived on the scene too late to catch the assailant, but they were confident that he must have made away on foot over one of the perimeter fences because no suspicious characters had passed their gate cabins since the girl had raised the alarm.

The girl was awaiting questioning in the factory sick bay where two matron ladies were mothering her with strong, sweet tea. She had been wrapped in a pair of wool blankets by someone, but still she shivered. Metcalf had been led to understand that the assailant had attempted to cut her clothes off her, however he would reserve judgement until he had uncovered all of the facts. Uncovering all of the facts might prove challenging because the Halifax constabulary had no women police constables, not even Specials. The decision, then, had been made to send for a woman doctor from the Infirmary and to wait for her arrival before asking to see the girl's clothes and wounds. How long that would take, heaven only knew because the Halifax constabulary had a shortage of bicycles and only one car.

'Good evening, miss. My name is Sergeant Metcalf and I'm from the Halifax police,' he said quietly. 'Now don't you worry, you're not in any trouble, but I would like to talk to you about what happened to you tonight, when you feel quite ready. Shall we start with your name?'

The shaking beneath the blankets intensified. 'I'm Ada; Ada Helliwell.'

'And what brought you to Mack's tonight, Miss Helliwell?'

A look of panic, almost as though she thought she'd been caught out doing something wrong.

'You don't need to worry, I'm not here to tell your parents you've been out to a dance, that's no crime. Was it the dance you came out for?'

'Yes.'

'And did you come alone?'

Again that look of fear. And terrified silence. Was she reliving what had just happened to her?

'Did you come to the dance alone, Ada?'

'Yes.' Then suddenly she blurted out, 'No! I came with my friend Caroline, and her friend Sidney. Caroline likes the dances.'

'And did you arrive together?'

'Yes.'

'At what time?'

'About half past seven.'

'And how did you pass the time between half past seven and now?'

She blushed. 'Could we forget about it? I'd just like to leave it, please.'

'What would you like to leave, Ada?'

'I don't want to talk about it. I just want to leave it and go home.'

'The watchmen told me you'd been attacked and someone had cut your clothes and your arm. Would you like us to catch the person who did this, Ada?'

A pained silence.

'We want to make sure that whoever he is doesn't do this to any other girls. If you give us a description of him we can keep a watch for anyone who looks like him and see if we can prevent this happening again.'

At this stage in the investigation it seemed that their only hope was a clear description and a miracle. They had found absolutely no evidence at the scene whatsoever, not even a smudge of a fingerprint to hang their helmets on. Not that a fingerprint would have helped as much as the public thought; fingerprints were time-consuming to identify and the process of checking them required hours of focussed work among reams and reams of card police files. Police cars weren't the only thing the local constabulary were short of – they needed good officers to do all the leg work.

'Do you just want to know what he looks like so that if you see him you can know him?'

'That would help us a lot, Ada.'

Ada appeared lost in thought and fear. Finally she said, 'He was tall and dark and he had bright buckles on his shoes.'

'Did you notice anything else? What else did he wear? Was he someone who you would recognise again?'

But Ada was sobbing now, and there was no more information to be had for the moment. Little could Ada and the sergeant know that before long, the attacker would be given a name – and that he would strike again.

Chapter Twenty-Nine

The makeshift factory dancehall was noisy and disordered in an entirely new way. The bright overhead lights illuminated worried faces and frustrated feet. There were now a few more policemen on the scene, including an inspector who advised the factory manager on what they must do next.

Reenie had pressed her way through the crowd of people to reach her own manager, who was talking intently to a group of colleagues.

'Harry,' Reenie said urgently, 'have you heard it's Ada?'

Harry nodded gravely and stepped aside to talk to her alone. 'She's been attacked. Someone came out of the darkness and slashed her with a razor blade and then ran off. She's alive, but they've got her in the sick bay and the police wouldn't let me in to see her.'

'But don't they know you're family?'

'The only family they're letting in is her dad, and they've sent a car to get him.'

'Is she in a very bad way?'

'I don't know. They said she wasn't badly hurt, but what does that mean? How badly is badly?'

'She's alive and that's the main thing.'

Harry ground his teeth and appeared to be mastering strong emotion. 'I hope they find whoever did this and lock him up, because as God is my witness if I ever got my hands on him I don't know what I'd do, I really don't.' Harry's instinct to protect his younger cousin was natural, but stronger than Reenie could have anticipated. It made her feel ashamed for thinking him uncaring when she'd first met him; he was anything but uncaring.

Reenie looked around her for something to say. What could you say when something so awful had happened? 'Who did she come with? Did she come on her own?'

'No.' Harry had a thunderous look as he said it. 'She came with Caroline Caffrey. I've always thought she was a bit on the troublesome side, but this is a lot even for Caroline.'

'You can't blame some flighty girl for this; she can't have let Ada get attacked deliberately.'

'No, but she must have left her alone, and Ada should never have been left alone. You know what she's like, she can't look after herself.' Harry ran his hands through his hair, his fingers splayed on either side of his temples, his fingers trembling with anger, or shock, or both. 'It's my fault. I got her the job here. I knew I should have spent more time with her myself, but I was busy. I thought Caroline was a necessary inconvenience to get Ada to come and work at Mack's. I thought she'd settle in quick enough, make some more friends, find her way. If I'd taken more care of her she wouldn't have been on her own tonight and whoever this attacker was would have had to deal with me.'

Reenie didn't like the direction this was taking. 'Do you blame me? You asked me to make friends with your cousin, but I wasn't with her when she was attacked. Do you blame me?'

Harry looked horror-struck, 'No, Reenie, I never meant—'

'Well, you've started banging on about how she shouldn't have been left alone, and how she should have had friends with her, but you and I both know that I'm the one who you specifically asked to befriend her and I wasn't there either.' Reenie felt the colour rising in her cheeks as her voice followed. This wasn't her; she never stood up for herself like this, she never stood her ground by raising her voice, or confronting people but the tension of the night had frayed her nerves and suddenly she was angry. It wasn't a childish anger at a childish injustice, this was a fury which had been a long time coming; Harry's dismissive treatment of her, the stifling feeling of being made to behave and stay out of trouble, and do as she was told, and sit back and watch everyone else stumbling into war when she knew that there was so much more that could be done and they weren't even trying to do it. She was sick and tired of being treated like a child and she was damned if she was going to take the blame for Ada's attack. 'I don't want to hear about who should have been there to prevent it. People shouldn't do things that need preventing. If you want to get angry with someone, get angry with her attacker, but leave me out of it!' And with that Reenie stormed out of the dancehall, intent on finding her horse and going home.

Chapter Thirty

It was the morning after the dance and the good people of Halifax had woken to the news that a young girl had been attacked in the street and that the man who attacked her was still at large. The factory had been thrown into chaos; extra policemen had been brought in to interview the hundreds of teenaged girls who insisted they were witnesses, and the production lines they had abandoned were forced to limp along with a skeleton staff.

For the first time in months the threat of war was pushed off the front page of the *Halifax Courier*, and the only topic of conversation in the town was the attack. Speculation was rife, and more than one girl wondered aloud about the safety of walking home alone. Fear gripped many hearts, but Dolly Dunkley had the solution: it was flags.

'If you're carrying a British Union flag then whoever he is will know not to mess about with you. Everyone knows that the British Union look after their own. He might not be frightened of the factory watchmen, but you'll soon see he's frightened of Oswald Mosley.'

The girls who mingled outside the factory gate waiting to be admitted were willing to listen if it passed the time, and some of them even entertained the notion that they might try Dolly's suggestion. 'But what if he doesn't see your flag?' one girl in brown box-maker's overalls asked. 'What if he just bursts out of the darkness without looking at what I'm carrying?'

'Oh, he'd see it all right.' Dolly acted as though she had expertise in this subject, and little did she know that she truly did. She had inspired the creation of this fictitious attacker, and it was her imagination which was shaping him. Dolly straightened her shoulders like a pigeon shaking out its feathers. She did look a lot like a pigeon. 'I've got an uncle who's very high up in the militia and he says they know who he is and he's watching for local girls with fair hair. He's a foreigner, they've said. If he's stopping to look at your hair colour he'll see your flag.'

A girl with light brown hair looked worried. 'But what if he can't see in the dark what colour your hair is? I might get "got" by mistake!'

'What does he want with fair-haired girls anyway?' An apprentice from the Joiners' Department, who wasn't quite old enough to grow facial hair, but who had had time to cultivate a healthy disdain for the opposite sex looked out from under the lowered peak of his flat cap and made a face which suggested that girls as a species were no good for anything. 'If he's a foreign agent, why isn't he attacking lads who could go off to fight? What's the use of girls to anyone?'

'He's trying to kidnap them,' an older lady chipped in, 'that's obvious. It happened often enough when I was your age. You'd see a girl at work every day of your life and then suddenly – poof! – she's gone; taken in the night and never seen again. White slavers, it was. They're about; they've never gone away.'

'I reckon it's all these immigrants,' the lad of fourteen said with a knowing nonchalance. 'The place is swamped with 'em; Spanish, Jewish, Russian. What do they get up to all day and night, that's what I want to know?'

Dolly couldn't agree more. 'Who knows what they get up to behind closed doors. And what have they all got in common? They're all anti-fascist. Don't forget Halifax has got one of the strongest branches of the British Union in the country. I reckon it's revenge for their riots the other week.'

'Is that what they're calling it?' the lad with the flat cap asked. 'Just riots? It was a bit more than riots.'

'Yes, but what I want to know is what they're calling everything we've been through?' Dolly flailed around for an example which explained her own feelings of unease. 'We've had attacks on women – don't think this is the first one, this is just the first one you've heard about – then we've had our parks taken off us to turn into air raid shelters of all things; where are we meant to go for exercise? And we've been terrorised into carrying gas masks and doing endless air raid drills. And that's before you even start on what it's like to be a working man or woman who has to earn their own living, when folks from Spain get to come over and have everything handed to them on a plate. The Liberals are up in arms about what the rich Jews have gone through with a few broken windows; but what about us? Not all of us can even afford houses with windows!'

A few of the girls who were feeling particularly hard done by muttered in agreement, though none of them stopped to ask themselves if they really knew anyone in Halifax so poor that they had to live in a brick box with no windows.

'I'm just glad that I've got the British Union to look out for me, because I just don't dare think about what it would have been like if I hadn't joined.'

Dolly claimed to have a lot of friends in the BUF, but where were they? She went to meetings, but she was never seen in cafés or on cinema trips like the other girls. Perhaps even these British Fascists could see Dolly for what she was, someone congenitally dishonest. What Dolly needed was a friend who didn't value truthfulness the way other people did. Someone who thought of honesty as an obstacle to the otherwise smooth-running of their life, a nuisance to be got round with more lies and half-truths and outrageous demands. Dolly needed a friend who viewed all things in life as negotiable, even facts. But above all, Dolly needed a friend.

At that moment a cloud of golden hair pushed its way through the crowd of workers. 'Is this the right place to be to talk to the police? You have no idea how much I have to tell them! This has been just *awful*. I almost don't know where to begin. You don't mind if I push in front of you, do you? It's just all been so *shocking!*'

The waiting workers welcomed the newcomer. *All that fair hair,* they thought, *she might well be next.* And they weren't wrong.

Chapter Thirty-One

'Do me a favour and mind some girls for me.' Diana Moore caught her friend in the overlookers' office and marched her in the direction of the factory gymnasium where the trouble was.

'Which line?' Mary sounded unenthusiastic, but that didn't mean she wouldn't do it.

'They're not on a line, they're waiting to be interviewed by the police. There's scores of them; all convinced they saw the Slasher and some of them even think he touched them with his blade.' Diana's voice almost faltered on that last word. Her stepbrother used to call himself 'The Blade'; he was Tommo 'The Blade' Cartwright and he had just come out of prison. She had wondered to herself what he'd meant when he told her to leave Gracie where she was. Was he trying to throw her off the scent of his real plan? Was he planning revenge for what he knew she'd done? Had he been waiting to attack her?

No, Diana chastised herself, why would this be all about her? The girl bore no resemblance to her whatsoever, and why would Tommo have lurked in the bike sheds for Diana? But the girl had been cut with a blade, and the blade was more than Tommo's weapon, it was a name for himself. A chill went down Diana's spine and she shivered.

'You all right?' Mary frowned at her, one of the few people who was as stubborn in the face of trouble as she was.

'There's a draught coming from somewhere. Anyway, all you've got to do is mind them, you don't have to do anything. You can sit down and stay rested.'

Mary looked affronted. 'Why would I need to sit down and be rested?'

Diana raised an eyebrow.

'How do you know already? I haven't told you yet!'

'Summoning me down to the stables for a private conference and then refusing to speak even if we went back to the offices? A bit obvious. How long do you plan to stay?'

Mary stopped outside the door to the gymnasium where even now she could hear the voices of scores of girls gossiping as they waited for the police to interview them. 'As long as I can. I don't want to leave this place, you know that.'

Diana nodded and looked on the verge of sharing something, but then seemed to change tack. 'You'll have

to move on eventually. I know this place has been the making of you, Mary, but now it's time for you to be the making of your kids. Start thinking about letting this place go. They need you, and we'll manage somehow.'
We, she thought. She was speaking for the factory, but would she herself be there much longer?

Chapter Thirty-Two

Rows of chairs had been set out hurriedly in the factory gymnasium in the manner usually reserved for lectures or prize giving ceremonies. The girls who waited in these rows to be interviewed by the harassed-looking policemen were mostly young, but one or two older women sat impatiently among them.

The hall was noisy with animated chatter and in one corner the chairs had been turned round to better allow one girl to regale a large group with the scandalous inside details of the attack which was already being described as the act of a 'Slasher'.

'Well, she's my best friend, so I know *everything*,' Caroline told her newly-acquired intimates. 'Honestly, it was so embarrassing, I just didn't know where to put myself. I'd been that worried about Ada because she's been shut up at home for years nursing her poor mother, and I thought when her mother died that would be it, she'd be free and she'd come and paint the town red – after a week or so for mourning, of course, because they were close, like, she didn't want her mother to die or owt. Anyway, months go by and still not a hint that she's thinking of getting herself out there to catch a husband, so I said to her cousin, I said, "Look, get us jobs at Mack's, she'll come and work at Mack's if it's with me. There'll be dances, there'll be outings, there'll be eligible lads with good steady jobs." I'd have to give up my own job – I was personal secretary to a man who sent shipments of nourishing food to war orphans and he begged me not to leave, but I had to, because when your best friend needs you, you do what has to be done.'

The girls listened and nodded. This, they agreed, was the mark of true friendship.

'So I left my job and brought us both here. I settled her in, and I got her a chance with a lad I'd met at another dance and *he* said he thought she needed someone to show her a good time and we were meant to be going to the dance together that night, the three of us, but then all of a sudden she says she wants to go off to the bike sheds with him before the dance starts and I didn't know where to look! I just felt *such* a gooseberry! So I went on into the dance and she went off with him and I had to go and make friends with a girl in the queue for the ladies and tell her everything that was happening because I felt *so* embarrassed, I just needed someone to confide in! This lad, Sid, he'd already told me what he planned to get up to with her, so I knew what they were doing, you see, and I just—'

'What were they doing?' butted in Dolly Dunkley, who Caroline had asked to sit beside her on account of them having met before.

One of the other girls rolled her eyes and said, 'I think we all know what they were doing.' And urged Caroline to go on with her story.

'Well, he came back in to find me in the dance later and he hadn't liked her much, he preferred me and he told me so in front of this other lad I was dancing with, and this other lad got stroppy, and the whole thing got so *dramatic*! I mean, honestly, it was like an opera. I thought they were going to fight right there on the dance floor, so I had to tell Sid the truth, I said to him, "Sid, Ada's in love with you. She told me herself, she's loved you since the moment you met. I've got to think of Ada."'

'And what did he say?' The girls all leaned in closer to hear the answer.

'Well, little did I know that Ada had gone back to the bike sheds and told Sid that she'd be there waiting for him – oh, yes, that was why she'd gone down there! She'd gone to wait for Sid. I just couldn't believe her behaviour, and I was going to say something to her, but what can you say when it's your best friend and you've known them forever? I would never say anything to hurt her, so I just had to watch and hope she didn't get herself into any trouble. I mean, she's a grown woman so she knows what she's doing. Anyway, she went out to the bike sheds to wait for Sid – but Sid was with me all the while – did I say that Sid was with me behind the bandstand? I had to promise that he could kiss me so that he would go back to Ada for a bit. So she waits for Sid and then the next thing I heard the dance is off, the lights are up, the police are coming, and Ada's in the sick bay because she's been attacked by some man!'

'Did she give you a description of him?'

'No, I still haven't been allowed to see her yet. Look, don't tell Ada I told you any of this, but I just had to talk to someone because I'm so worried about her, and no one understands what it's like when your friend is in danger, and what if it's someone who was looking for her in particular and they try to get her at home? Or what if it wasn't her and they thought she was me? She was wearing my dress, after all, and so it could be me the Slasher is after. In fact, I think it is me! There wouldn't be anyone who would want to get Ada – she's a mouse.' Caroline flicked back her golden tresses and tried to assume a look of sainted martyrdom.

'I just don't know what to do for the best with Ada. I mean, she said that she doesn't want me to tell anyone anything about her and Sid, but what if that's only making it all worse? I'm sure it's only making it worse and it's better for me to talk about it and find a way to help her and get advice. And what about me? If it's me he's after then I'll need to get the police to protect me, won't I? And I can't do that if I don't tell them, and I can't talk to the police until after I've got advice from my friends about whether or not I ought to tell them what happened.'

The gaggle of girls all agreed that she should ask their advice before talking to the police, who were making them all wait anyway; it was the only responsible thing to do.

'What would you do if you were in my place? Do you think I ought to be worried about walking home from work? Should I ask one or two of the young men at the factory if they'll walk me home? I ought to, just to be on the safe side because there's simply no knowing what will happen next. I suppose I could ask one of Ada's older brothers—'

A shout reached them from the street outside, it was a news seller calling out the headline of an extra edition. Ada's attacker now had a name, and he had made his second attack on a local girl.

'Slasher!' the boy called. 'Slasher strikes again!'

Chapter Thirty-Three

'Is that a *second* attack?' The director of production took the newspaper extra edition from his colleague and scanned the contents.

'No, it's a third, and on a man too. He was leaving his job at the Co-operative stores when the Slasher appeared out of nowhere, but he fought back. Seems he sustained some nasty injuries.'

'And what are the police doing? Any suspects?'

'None as yet, and they're not likely to at this rate. They're following him about on bicycles because they've only got one motorcar for the whole Halifax constabulary.'

'Lend them one of ours from the pool; we can't have a madman on the loose preventing us from meeting our Christmas orders.'

'About that . . .'

'Don't tell me they're planning to shut the factory down because there's a lunatic on the loose?'

'No, it's not that bad, but it *is* going to be a problem. They're proposing to have a curfew. Townwide and beginning tonight until he's caught.'

'That's no good, it could interfere with our nightshift workers.'

'I fear it will interfere with *all* our workers; they're suggesting it should begin at dusk.'

'Well, how on earth would that work? It's November in Halifax so it's dusk for most of the day. How do they propose *any* businesses keep going?'

'Early closing has been suggested.'

'That's all very well for a greengrocer on the King Cross road, but don't they realise that we're making seven million sweets a day here? We've got a workforce of ten thousand, and a contract with the government to assemble vital war preparation apparatus. We can't simply close early, it isn't possible. This is not a quiet time of year, and this is not a year in which *any* time would be convenient.'

'The local Boy Scouts Association has volunteered to provide chaperones so that groups of employees can travel home together and this will be permitted under the curfew. It is lone travelling which will not be permitted without special dispensation.'

'This sounds as though it has the potential for chaos. Who is issuing this permission, and who is checking it? And what constitutes grounds for special permission? I don't like the sound of this, Mortimer, I don't like the sound of this at all. They need to find this man and lock him up quickly; Halifax can't possibly function while this carries on. We're a factory town and we cannot suspend production. Perhaps we ought to offer a reward for any information leading to the arrest of this person?'

'There is a reward already, sir, and it's not helping matters. Groups of people have formed vigilante clubs intending to sweep the streets together and the chief constable doesn't like it one bit.'

Chapter Thirty-Four

'Now then, ladies, if you'd like to form an orderly queue we've got some nice young lads waiting here to escort you home.' The factory watchman, addressing the massing crowd from atop a stepladder and through a megaphone, thought the whole thing was madness. The crush of women workers leaving the factory at that time of day was already a jostling ocean, but to try to release them in dribs and drabs to waiting chaperones would take all night. The Scouts had volunteered first – didn't they always? – and so lads who would be utterly useless against an armed attacker were queuing in uniform with the intention of taking women in groups depending on where they lived.

'The first lot to leave are . . .' the watchman turned to the Scout leader and consulted with him, then announced, 'King Cross! Anyone walking back to King

Cross can leave in the first group. Raise your hand if you're walking to King Cross!' Various women, dotted about at various distances through the crowd raised their hands, and it would take forever to wait for them to squeeze their way through to the front. Then there were the women at the back who couldn't hear, the men who wanted to get past the waiting women, the women who needed to hurry up to get home to the kids, the women who had fathers, brothers, husbands, or sons waiting to collect them (and who were themselves obstructing the passage of all the people trying to leave), and the women who wanted to take their chances and be let out, for the love of God. The special constables had all got the day off work to put their uniforms on, and the town was suddenly teeming with people who had been endowed with authority or status who wanted to hunt the Slasher, or guard his potential victims.

'How do we know none of them're the Slasher?' a girl in a messenger's uniform hollered in the direction of the watchman. She had a point; whoever the Slasher was he had a home and a job somewhere – although if it were obvious that he was the Slasher he'd have been more easily caught.

'You've got to take your chances,' the watchman called back. The Scout leader was affronted and began to object in the strongest possible terms, while several people in the crowd objected to being held up, and more than one asked for a precise estimate of how long they'd be held up. One person said they'd be there all night at this rate and within moments the word that they were being told to wait all night was round the crowd and had reached even the ones at the back who couldn't hear the watchman. A rumbling of complaint and jeers roiled up like a surging sea and the watchman thought about organising the Women's Employment Department to call order. Diana Moore could give them all 'the look' and they'd get on with it. He was saved having to make that call by a scream, a horrified shriek of a scream, and then shouts.

'Hey! Hey! He was here! He's getting away! He's in the crowd! She's been slashed! For God's sake open the gates and let us out! She's been slashed and we're all trapped in here with him!'

Chapter Thirty-Five

'I thought you might like some toffees to share with all your visitors.' Reenie held out the largest tin of Quality Street she had been able to obtain at short notice. It was possibly a tin for the wholesale trade as it didn't have a weight on it and looked large enough to bath a baby in. At the time of picking it up it seemed like a good idea, but now that she was at the Helliwell house and saw that there were no visitors she started to feel she might have overdone it.

'Thanks,' Ada muttered, rising from her place on the settee by the fire to take it.

'No, don't you get up, you're recuperating. I'll just put it down here for you on the sideboard and you can get it when you're ready.' Reenie stood for a bit, bobbing about awkwardly, then darted for a nearby chair and sat in it abruptly. 'So . . .' she began, not knowing what to say to a girl who had been through something so unimaginably terrible, '. . . are you keeping warm?'

Ada looked at the blanket on her lap and then nodded while taking in a quick breath. 'Yes.'

'That's good.' Reenie nodded too and looked around the room for something to comment on. 'I see you've got lots of library books. Any good ones?'

'*These Old Shades*,' Ada nodded and said in a mumble, 'but I've read it before.'

Now Reenie nodded again, an unstoppable tick which seemed to hold the conversation together, the nod being passed between the two of them like a pass-the-parcel of awkwardness. 'I like the drawing on the cover. It looks a lot like the couple on the Quality Street tin.' They compared the two and agreed that there was a distinct similarity. 'You know there's an art department at Mack's where they design all the tins and cartons? When you're back at work I could take you to meet the artists one dinnertime. You'd like meeting artists.'

Ada shrank back into the settee. 'I don't want to go back to Mack's.'

Reenie resumed her nodding. 'Of course not, you've had a terrible fright and you won't want to go back to Albion Mills again. But I've been thinking: if I talk to your cousin, and we talk to the right people, we might be able to get you moved to the Queens Road factory so as you don't have to give up your job, but you don't have to see the place where it happened, neither.'

Ada shook her head. 'It isn't just that. I discovered this morning that my friend Caroline has – has shared confidences of mine with the other girls, and now I couldn't face going back to Mack's. I would be humiliated.'

Reenie didn't think much to this Caroline and wondered why Ada put up with her. No wonder Harry had wanted Ada to befriend his cousin. 'Perhaps we could find you somewhere new to work, where you don't know anyone, someplace nice and quiet. Or better still, what about working where you *do* know someone? You could work in our department. Your cousin Harry could do with a hand with all his papers; he's got rotas and purchase requisitions coming out of his ears. You're clever with books, you'd probably pick it all up in no time.'

Ada nodded, but didn't say anything, which meant that Reenie resumed her nodding to fill in the silence. They nodded and nodded and avoided each other's gaze as though it would be bad-mannered to look at the person who you were expressly there to see and who had been speaking directly to you not moments ago. They both looked around the ceiling and inspected its corners, then to the top of the flex which held the light fitting. Finally the door frame.

'Do you like the area?'

'Which area?' Ada looked anxious.

'Just, you know, the area round the house here. The street. Good neighbours are they, all this lot round here?'

'Yes,' Ada nodded.

Reenie began to regret her visit. After all the time she had spent with Ada she had wanted to check in on the girl and make sure that she knew she was in the Calder family's thoughts, but now she was almost wishing she had sent a card.

'Can I—' Ada stopped herself and looked toward the kitchen door, which was closed. 'Can I ask you something?'

'Yes, anything.' At this point Reenie thought she'd be willing to tell her the colour of her undergarments if she'd just have a conversation.

'Has there really been another attack like – like the one on me?'

'Yes.' Reenie was now a little speechless with surprise. 'Did you not know?'

'My dad didn't want anyone upsetting me, so I haven't heard anything except once, but then everyone hushed up quick.'

'Well, the first one was down near Clough Mills—'

'The *first* one? You mean there's been more than one?'

'I'm afraid there has. We're on five now.' Reenie hastened to reassure the girl who was pulling her blanket tighter around her. 'They are all all right! No serious injuries. Just very shaken, and their clothes cut like yours. They're calling him the Halifax Slasher and we're having curfews and not being allowed to walk home alone.'

Ada's face drained of what colour it had and her eyes glazed. 'I don't understand,' she said. 'That's just not possible. How could someone be doing that?'

'Did you think it was someone who was just out to get you and not anyone else? Do you think you have some enemies or summat might want to give you a scare?'

'No, nothing like that. I just . . . Oh, I don't know what I thought.' And then Ada pursed her lips and folded her arms as though she was angry with herself and said, 'I think I just didn't really think about it enough. I only thought about myself. I should have thought about other people.'

'There now,' Reenie reassured her, 'don't be so hard on yourseln', it's not your fault, you didn't ask for this to happen. What would your mother say if she were here, eh?'

And Ada seemed to listen to this, and to think about it – and it seemed to worry her even more.

Chapter Thirty-Six

'Is it just us two then today?' Reenie didn't mind the extra work, but she felt rather awkward about working alone with Harry Swallow so soon after she'd turned him down; so soon after she'd let down him and his cousin; so soon after everything. The maintenance and repair workshop was echoey without the bustle of her other colleagues to bring it to life.

'Just us.' Harry didn't look up from the tin-cutting machine he was stripping down.

Reenie bit her lip. She couldn't tell if Harry was treating her casually because he was occupied with his work, or because he was annoyed with her for storming out of the factory dance after they had both lost their tempers. She'd given this a great deal of thought – far too much perhaps – and she wondered if she ought to say something to explain herself. Reenie often felt that she needed to explain herself. 'Is there . . .' Reenie hesitated, searching for just the right words, 'something wrong?'

'Yes.' Harry wiped the engine grease off his hands and nodded toward the rotor cuff, 'We didn't replace the bearings when we should and it's worn through.'

Reenie felt that this answer made her feel even more anxious and as she went to work on unscrewing the damaged part of the machine she felt the air between them tighten with all the unsaid things she was holding in. The morning dragged on interminably, and the afternoon too. They exchanged functional words, drank necessary tea, and ate a unceremonious lunch. It wasn't until their afternoon break, the time of day when the last of the winter sun reached the skylight on the roof and gave the workshop a peachy glow, that Harry finally asked Reenie what was troubling her.

'Do you mean about the machines, or more general, like?' Reenie was beginning to hope that it was a strictly work-related problem which had prompted the question.

'More general, like. You can't fool me, Reenie, you've got something on your mind.'

Reenie took a slurp of tea and frowned. This was a bad business. She hadn't asked Harry to ask her to go on the town with him, and she'd not been uncivil to him when he'd asked, so why should she now have to be in the doghouse for turning him down? It seemed unfair, but if he knew her reasons perhaps he might understand? 'I was just worried that you might have thought that I thought that if . . . no, I mean . . . I didn't want to be rude to you when you asked me to go to see the lights with you t'other day, it's just that—'

'Oh, that?' Harry seemed genuinely to have forgotten all about it. 'You mustn't fuss over that, lass, I certainly don't. I think the town's got bigger problems today, to be honest.'

'It's just that I didn't want you to think I don't think highly of you, it's that I was only recently engaged to be married.'

Harry nodded, not giving any indication whether he knew about Peter or not.

'I was engaged, but I didn't really want to be, it just sort of went that way. I couldn't say no because I didn't want to hurt him, but I didn't want to say yes as soon as I did. Then I hastened the wedding on because I thought it would get him out of some trouble he was in—'

'Why couldn't he get himself out of this trouble? Wasn't he a grown man?'

'It was complicated. It felt at the time like I was the only one who could help, and you should always try to help people who need help, shouldn't you?'

Harry raised an eyebrow. 'I'd draw the line at marrying them, but that's just me.'

'I called it off at the altar.' Reenie looked down at her hands, rough from factory work. How ungrateful and blind had she been to throw all that love away? Peter had never complained that she ruined her hands with hard work, or met him in her overalls. There was many a lad as wouldn't put up with that.

'You cut it fine.' He showed no indication of either approval or disapproval, leaving Reenie to her own pessimistic interpretation. 'What made you do it?'

'I didn't want to be married. I didn't want to give up my job doing something I loved and was good at to spend all my days washing pots, cooking supper, and hanging out wet laundry. Peter was a good man – he *is* a good man – but he wanted a different life, he wanted to get down to being all domestic, and I wanted to reach for the sky. Am I wrong, do you think? Is it selfish of me?'

He paused to think and squinted toward the middle distance, a mote of dust falling in a shaft of sunlight catching his attention for a moment as it sparkled and fell. He didn't answer her question, but offered a confidence of his own.

'When I asked Delia Crispin to marry me I was trying to make her happy.' He put down his teacup, folded his arms, leaned back, and sighed. He was going over ancient history. 'She'd had some hard luck in the years before we met; her father had died, she'd been in a motorcar accident and still had a lot of pain, and her little mending shop had run out of money and closed. Everything had gone wrong for her, but when she smiled I caught a glimpse of the person she could be. I was sure that if things went right for her for a while she'd flourish. Do you know what I mean by flourish?'

Reenie nodded earnestly, but didn't dare interrupt something which seemed important.

'I worked hard; I did a good bit of overtime to help clear a debt she had so that she could redeem her sewing machine from the pawnbroker and start up work mending again. I went round each day to help do those bits of hard work that she and her mother were too sickly to manage. I sat up late into the night listening to the family nursing the injustices they felt life had heaped upon them, and I told messen' they'd get over it all with time, and I could look forward to the day in the not-too-distant future when we'd all sit round the fire laughing, forgetting all the bad times. Having something to look forward to and to work toward helped me, and so I thought having a wedding to save for and hope for would raise Delia's spirits. I bought her a ring and took her to Filey and asked her to make me the happiest man in the world, and I honestly believed I would be. I kidded myself for a long time.'

Reenie waited while Harry gazed ahead of him, lost in his memories, then finally she prompted him. 'Did she say yes?'

'Aye, she said yes, but one day I realised that we both wanted more. Delia wanted me to buy her presents I couldn't really afford, she wanted to spend everything we had now, and borrow money on top. She wanted us to live with her mother and settle down to the life she knew; a life of weekly trips to the pawnbroker and grumbles about the landlord.

'I wanted to work hard to save for the future and put us on a steady footing for our life together, but there was more than that; I loved my work. I feel sorry for these people who are trapped in work they hate, I really do. It must be awful to spend your weekends dreading Monday, and to have no escape. Me, I got lucky with my job at Mack's and I know it. I'm not tied to a desk, I get to use me hands, I get to go see different places – even factories in different cities – I get to feel like I've made an improvement to something, I've solved a problem. There are people in the factory who have an easier day on the line because I fixed their machine; who wouldn't want to do that?'

Reenie could understand the love of factory life, the passion for problem-solving.

'I wanted a different life to Delia. I wanted to travel and see other places; I wanted to see where the job could take me and if I had it in me to try for foreman; I wanted to strive for better even if it meant making sacrifices along the way. We were pulling in different directions and I knew it, but I loved her all the same. How could I not? She was my Delia; my kind, thoughtful, generous Delia who could flourish if only I did more.' Harry picked up his teacup again and looked into it as though the answer to all his unasked questions might be found there. 'It was the hardest decision of my life, and I didn't take it lightly. I agonised over it for a month or more. I thought about what I would be losing, and if she didn't have the right idea after all. I wondered if

I'd become miserly, and if her philosophy of living for today wasn't the better one. But then I realised that it wasn't about one of us being in the right and one of us being in the wrong, it was about whether we were a pair. My granda always used to say to me, "Do not go unequally yoked." He was a farmer and he knew how important it is to have a good pair of animals to pull a plough together: you couldn't have one stronger than the other, or one bigger than the other, you had to have them pull the same weight over the same distance for the same time. Delia and me, we pulled in different directions.' He pulled himself up and carried his cup over to the tea tray on the bench. 'Don't ask yoursen' if you did the wrong thing, or the right thing. Ask yoursen' if you were pulling in the same direction. If you were you wouldn't be in different places now. And don't mind me, lass. I understand; better than anyone else, I understand.'

Reenie watched Harry go out into the yard to light his cigarette, his tousled hair taking on copper lights in the sunset. Reenie wondered why he took so many girls out to dances just once, and never courted them again. Was he still in love with his Delia? Or were all those girls wrong about him? Did they go along to dances hoping for a bad lad and fail to disguise their disappointment when they discovered that he was a good man?

Reenie wasn't disappointed. At last she had found someone who understood.

Chapter Thirty-Seven

Diana took a sip of water from a glass which the solicitor had placed in front of her. The water was cold, but that wasn't why she shivered. Diana had been summoned to a conference at the Hunter family home with Mr and Mrs Hunter, their solicitor, and his clerk and she thought she had an idea what it might be about. All these months George Hunter had known that she was the natural mother of his adopted daughter Gracie, and all these months his behaviour had been strange. Now, as she saw the solicitor laying out a series of papers before him on the mahogany table of the Hunters' spacious dining room, she realised he must be about to issue her with some sort of restraining order; a notice instructing her to quit Halifax and never attempt communication with her daughter again. Perhaps it was because she had asked about sending the children to Canada; perhaps it was because she'd pressed them to let her take Gracie to have her gas mask fitted; perhaps it was because they had heard that her stepbrother had been released from prison. In truth, it could have been anything, and there was no point now turning over all the ways in which she had failed to remain invisible.

Diana had thought Mrs Hunter her friend, but now that she caught her eye she saw nothing but disappointment and hurt. How could these people be so pitiless? Of course she was Gracie's mother; why else would anyone so willingly sit through even the dullest of their fundraising concert parties, the noisiest of their dinners for aldermen's wives, their never-ending committee meetings for charitable causes which went on late into the night? Diana had never resented helping those worse off than she was, but had the Hunters never thought to ask themselves why a young woman with good prospects would agree to do all of this to the exclusion of all else, even sometimes sleep? Why else would she look so like the little girl they had fed, clothed, and nursed to health?

A smart rap at the door told her that someone else was waiting to pile recriminations on her head, and Mr Hunter called them in. 'Justice Llewelyn,' he said, as though this newcomer was who they had all been waiting for, 'this is Miss Diana Moore.'

'A pleasure to meet you.' The Welshman bowed slightly and took her hand to shake it once, respectfully. He was tall, old, and carried himself with a benign confidence;

and he treated her as though she were doing them all some great favour simply by being in attendance. His manner was totally unexpected and Diana began to wonder if this wasn't the meeting she had thought it was going to be.

'You know my wife, Lydia,' George Hunter said to the judge as he stumbled through the remaining introductions, and Diana wondered if she had imagined a slight hesitation – or was it embarrassment – over the word 'wife'. Surely there couldn't have been anything in the ridiculous rumours about the Hunter family, could there?

The solicitor nodded to his clerk and then addressed the room with a warm professionalism. 'We'll begin, shall we? Mr Hunter, would you like to . . . ?' His voice trailed off as he refrained from mentioning the unmentionable.

'Yes.' George Hunter sat up a little straighter and exchanged a glance with Lydia Hunter who gave his hand a reassuring squeeze. 'Yes, I think I'd like to thank you all for coming, but most especially Diana. I know that you have been most understanding and most discreet at this . . .' He flushed in embarrassment and tried to begin again on a different tack. 'I shall come to the point: you have likely heard some rumours, Diana, about a change in our family circumstances. This much is true; I was married once before I married Lydia. I was a young ambulance driver at the front in 1915 and I met and fell in love with a nurse who was French. We married in haste – the war was indescribable and many did as we did.' He looked again to Lydia Hunter and it was a look of apology. 'Her name was Isabelle.' He paused, looking for a way to tell his story without reliving it. 'Our hospital, such as it was, took a direct hit.

'I had reason to believe that I had seen Isabelle killed outright and she had been given information – clearly incorrect information – which led her to believe I had abandoned her. She did not write to my family because she was too proud. I did not write to her family because she'd told me she had none.

'Isabelle had a baby soon afterward and lived for another twenty years. When she died two winters ago her baby – now a young man called Jean Marc – decided to go in search of his grandparents, my parents. He did what any practically minded Frenchman would do and he wrote to the Mayor at the Town Hall to ask where he would find the family of George Hunter, late of the Friends Ambulance Unit, Flanders.'

There was a silence as every heart in the room beat a little heavier. Diana could not imagine what any of this had to do with her, but she could see now why Mrs Hunter had been so withdrawn. It had nothing to do with Diana and everything to do with Lydia Hunter's world collapsing around her.

'I have met Jean Marc, but I have met him twenty-one years too late.' George carried a greater weight of sadness in those words than Diana could imagine. He could evidently see that she didn't understand what he was trying to tell her, and so he said, 'You understand that

I did not know that my first wife was still living when I entered into marriage with Lydia?'

Diana frowned in confusion. 'Of course. I would never suspect . . .' For once Diana didn't know what to say or how to say it. She had questions, of course, but she was far too considerate to ask them.

The solicitor smiled encouragingly in the direction of the Welshman who had nodded along sagely with the whole sorry account. 'Mr Justice Lewellyn is here to reassure you, not as a friend of the Hunter family, but as a legal authority, that this is not a criminal matter. The Director of Public Prosecutions has agreed that it would not be in the public interest to pursue this in the courts and so we are all here today to work together to do the work necessary to repair the situation as best we can.'

Diana looked to each of them in turn for a clue as to why she, of all people, had been summoned to hear about this very private matter. 'I don't understand . . .' Her voice had lost its usual confidence.

George Hunter cleared his throat and then said the one word which no one else dared to say aloud for his sake, 'Bigamy. They are talking about bigamy, Diana. When I married Lydia I committed – without knowing it – a criminal offence. Not only is my marriage to Lydia not legally recognised, but none of the contracts we have entered into since then have any legal standing. The bank accounts, the purchase of the house, not even the children's birth certificates. My first wife is dead and it is a tragedy, but it does mean that I am free to . . .' His voice faltered, then, 'I am free to remarry Lydia quietly, and we can draw up all these contracts afresh and . . .' George Hunter didn't finish his sentence, his eyes giving away that his mind had slipped away to another place, perhaps another time.

Diana began to understand. 'Is Gracie's adoption still legally recognised?' she asked the solicitor directly and he responded with kind efficiency.

'No. This is one of the only circumstances in English law where an adoption would be declared invalid. The Hunters adopted the child as a married couple, you see – a single legal entity, not two separate persons – so the law no longer recognises the adoption.' He handed a sheaf of papers to Diana. 'Parental responsibility reverts to her natural mother and the child will need to be signed over for adoption a second time after the marriage has taken place. Then the Hunters will go through the motions of adopting Grace Cartwright at the same time as Mr Hunter formerly adopts his other children. We've taken the liberty of preparing all the necessary paper-work for signature, which Mr Justice Llewelyn can witness privately so that there is no necessity to attend court.'

Diana looked at the papers before her. She didn't dare to believe that any of it could be true. Gracie was hers again. She looked to Mr Hunter. 'This has to be signed by Gracie's mother . . .'

Lydia Hunter cleared her throat. 'It's all right Diana.

I know it's you. I've always known. I'm not blind, my dear.'

They held each other's gaze for a moment and Diana saw in the other woman's eyes some of the love and pain she felt for Gracie. Diana hoped her own eyes didn't betray what she was thinking, or planning to do.

Chapter Thirty-Eight

'I don't suppose any of you are going to be walking anywhere near town tonight, are you?' Reenie had been waiting in the engineering maintenance office after her shift, hoping that she might find a chaperone to walk with her.

'Why, where do you need to be?' Harry asked.

Reenie had been hoping one of the older men would offer, but now that Harry had responded in front of everyone she felt that she had to screw up her courage and say, 'I'm just going up to Howard Lane. I wanted to see old Major Fergusson to take him a Christmas card and he said not to come while seven.'

'I don't mind walkin' you.' Harry picked up his jacket, and unwound a scarf from the hatstand. 'I was off to have a pint in the pub with some mates not far from there. I can walk you round then come and get you after an hour if you like. It's no trouble.'

Reenie privately thought that it might be trouble if her sister Kathleen saw her, but with any luck Kathleen would be safely under curfew at home, and her brusque and businesslike walk with her manager to the Major's house would never come to light.

On arrival at the Major's house Reenie realised her troubles that evening had only just begun. The house itself was right enough; a solid Victorian place with a smart face, rather like the Major himself. It looked out onto People's Park in a grand sort of way for a terraced house, and the bay windows top and bottom glowed with warm light from the inside. It was a place which had always felt welcoming, but as she approached Reenie saw, illuminated in the drawing room, that she was not the only person the Major had invited for a Christmas visit; Peter MacKenzie was there too, and there was a girl with him. A girl with sable-coloured hair and a slender figure. A girl who hung on his arm.

'Reenie!' The Major called in delight as his housekeeper showed her into the drawing room. 'I'm so glad you came. You see that our old friend has called; a surprise visit, but a welcome one.' He did not emphasise the word 'surprise' but he caught Reenie's eye as he said it so that she might know that he hadn't planned an ambush. 'And he has brought his fiancée Clare with him. Clare, have you met Irene Calder?'

Reenie turned to shake the hand of the girl she hadn't known existed but who now seemed able to wring her heart right out of her chest with her delicate, porcelain fingers.

Clare gave her a winning smile. 'Oh, Peter's told me so much about you. You're very clever to work on all those machines.' This other girl reached up to her throat to absent-mindedly straighten her choker of pearls between a thumb and forefinger. Little bright beads as neatly symmetrical as her bright, white teeth, and her bright, neat accent. 'Peter says you were in Norwich not so long ago. It's such a shame I missed you, however I was away in Switzerland to be finished, but I'm back in Norwich now for good.' She beamed up at Peter, lovingly.

'I-I don't know if I mentioned Clare to you, Reenie,' Peter stammered out. 'She and I were at school together . . .'

The plush red rug in the centre of the drawing room gaped like an open mouth, and failed to swallow her up. 'Congratulations on your engagement.' Reenie said it kindly, but without her usual enthusiasm. 'Have you been engaged long?'

'Only a month.' Clare was cheery; perhaps she didn't know how recently Peter had been engaged to someone else and that that someone else was Reenie. 'But we've known each other for so many years that it feels longer. Now,' she said, opening up her ostrich-leather clutch and taking out an engagements diary, 'we must get a date in the diary for you to come to us for dinner.' Clare led Reenie gently by the elbow to the settee where they could sit side by side.

'In Halifax?' She looked to the Major to save her, but he was already deep in conversation with Peter. *Her* Peter.

'No,' Clare's pearly teeth gleamed, 'in Norwich, silly. I've already booked out the whole of the next twelve months with the dinner parties that we're going to host in our new home.' She leafed through the pages which were crammed with invitations and plans. Norwich evidently did a lively trade in dinner parties if you were of that sort. Clare must have seen Reenie's eyebrows rise and said, 'It's important to keep organised when you've got such a busy calendar. My father is a military man and I get it from him.'

Reenie nodded as she watched Clare trying to select the best possible dinner party to tack Reenie onto as a single guest. The Major was still listening intently to something Peter was telling him on the other side of the room and she tried to think of something to say to this girl who she wished had stayed in Switzerland. 'Major Fergusson told me that Peter's been doing well in his new work.'

'Oh, yes, he's got an officer's commission in the army but they aren't training him to fight just yet, they're using his knowledge of factory machines and production lines. He's travelling around the country a lot. They couldn't pack him off fast enough! I think he's been a godsend. There are a lot of factories they'll need to convert to munitions and other war work, but someone has to look at them and say whether or not they'll be suitable. He was in York last week. Did you know they've got a factory building there which was specially built to withstand a dust explosion? It's a risk, apparently; Smarties – that's their newest sweet – is covered in flour and sugar, but the flour can ignite and blow up a building. When the war comes they've agreed to stop making Smarties and turn the whole thing over to making fuses for bombs, and all because Peter told them to. Isn't he clever?'

Reenie found it hard to hear this other girl, a girl she had known nothing about until a moment ago, tell her so much that she didn't know about her Peter. It stung and she did her best not to show it. 'It must be hard for you not seeing him if he's away all the time.'

'It is, but it's not for much longer, though.' Clare scrunched up her nose in a pleased way as she confided to Reenie that she was soon to have her own way. 'Daddy is pulling strings to get him a desk job close to home. No fighting or travelling for my Peter, he'll have a nice quiet war at home with me.'

'But does he want that?' Reenie thought she knew Peter, and what he'd wanted was to make a difference.

'Oh, men don't know what they want until they get it. Better to have a desk job than be blown to bits!'

Reenie said nothing, but waited to be told when she was going to be summoned to Norwich to eat and drink with strangers, one of whom appeared to be her former fiancé.

Chapter Thirty-Nine

'How was it?' Harry asked as he collected Reenie an hour later from the door of the Major's house.

Reenie shrugged. She was usually talkative even at the worst of times, but she didn't feel that she could trust her voice until they were a good few streets away from the site of her heartache.

Harry persevered, 'Well, I won a pair of socks in a Christmas raffle at the pub, so I'm happy.'

They walked on a little further in silence, their strides falling into sync and then out again with irritating frequency. 'You don't have to talk to me, I'm just the man who agreed to cut his night short to come and pick you up and walk you home so that you wouldn't get eaten by the bogeyman.'

Reenie relented. 'I'm sorry. I didn't mean to be rude.

It's just that Peter – my fiancé, as was – he was there unexpectedly.'

'Ah.' Harry caught pace with Reenie's stride and their journey seemed to go a little easier. 'And did he try to rekindle anything?'

'No.' Reenie felt guilty for wishing he had, even though she'd have turned him down all over again; hurt him all over again. 'He was with his new fiancée.'

Harry whistled. 'Did you know that he'd got engaged again?'

'No.'

'And was there a scene?'

'No. She was very nice and she's planned out the rest of his life from breakfast till supper on his dying day and she's invited me to be at one of their dinner parties, but she says they need to fit me in soon because they're hoping to be married in the next three months and then have a baby by this time next year, and then another one the year after that.'

Harry did not whistle this time. This was a blow he could understand. 'Do you need a stiff drink? We can stop somewhere. I know a friendly place round the corner.'

Reenie shook her head.

'I could walk you back to Mack's and you could burn out the motor on a machine; I'd not tell on you. We'd fix it in the morning.'

'Not tonight, thanks.'

This gave Harry pause. 'Well, things are bad if you don't want to mess about with a machine.' He shoved his hands deep into his coat pockets and looked about him in thought before finally announcing, 'You know what you need? Christmas lights. Have you seen them yet this year in town?' Reenie didn't answer and so he carried on, 'The Corporation have outdone themselves. Three colours of lights, they've got. And the Town Hall looks like a Christmas tree. Best thing is there are so few people about with the town being on curfew that we can largely have the place to ourselves. Come on, Reenie, come and see the Christmas lights.'

'You know Advent doesn't begin until next Sunday, they're far too early.'

'Well, you can write a letter of complaint to the Corporation once you've thoroughly investigated it.'

Harry walked half a pace ahead, and Reenie followed. He didn't link her arm, or hold her hand, but she felt that he was leading her all the same. There was a companionable feeling to being bossed around by this wistful young man who wasn't going to fall in love with her, and who understood why she wasn't going to fall in love with him. But for all that there was a frisson of something; an electric charge; a tightness in her chest; a not-quite-placeable tension, and Reenie tried to pretend that her sister was wrong and that all of her own intentions were innocent.

The night was crisp, and clear, and quiet. The air smelled of coal fires, damp leaves, and the bay rum

Harry splashed on his face when he shaved. There were other people out running errands or travelling to and from shifts, but they were in pairs or groups, and they moved hurriedly, keen to get inside. Harry seemed unconcerned that they might encounter a dangerous attacker, and Reenie pointed out as much.

'I doubt whoever he is is going to jump on a pair of factory engineers under the blazing light of the Halifax Corporation Christmas decorations, do you? He'll be hiding away down the back of some terrace, waiting for a lass who's putting her washing out.'

'Oh, don't,' Reenie shivered. 'I don't like to think of him out there, waiting. I don't like to think of him getting anyone else.'

Harry could see that he'd upset her and did his best to take her mind off the reason that he had to escort her through the streets to her horse that waited in the factory stables. 'Let's not think about him, then. Let's think about Christmas. It'll be here before you know it, and I bet you've got a present for that horse of yours.'

'Of course I haven't got a present for me horse!' Reenie said as she followed along, knowing full well that she had crocheted Ruffian a blanket and it had taken her the best part of a year. They turned down Silver Street and slowed their pace as they gazed up at the red and white lights which spanned from one shop rooftop to the other. Someone with a head for heights had hung garlands of evergreens from the crenellations of the solicitor's, and everywhere they looked the symbols of the season were decked out and illuminated with scores and scores of twinkling lights. They carried on down Crown Street, Princess Street, and finally on to Crossley Street where their object – the Halifax Town Hall – sparkled with electric bulbs in red, green, and yellow, a spectacle so bright and unexpected that it quite took Reenie's breath away. The majestic sandstone palace, busy with arcades, columns, arches, and carved people looked like something from fairyland, with climbing Christmas lights turning all 180 feet of the steeple into a giant Christmas tree. Reenie gasped in awe at the sight and, unthinkingly, slipped her hand into Harry's. They stood still for a moment, neither willing to move, neither knowing what to think of the gesture.

Then Reenie let go gently and turned quickly in the direction of Commercial Street, plunging her hands firmly into her pockets where they could do no more to betray her.

'Wait for me, I'm meant to be chaperone, remember?'

Reenie turned to look in Harry's direction, but didn't stop walking. 'Come on, we've seen the lights and they'll be turning them off soon it's that late. Besides, I've got me horse to feed, he's not had his supper yet.'

They were coming up on Barnett's Hardware Stores and Reenie had to slow her pace to get round the zinc baths, Christmas trees tied up with string, and other goods which had been allowed to spill out onto the dark pavement that night.

'Stop here a minute,' Harry said, pulling her into a doorway that Barnett's didn't use. He'd intended to say something about the moment she'd reached for his hand, something clear, and measured, and professional. But then he knocked his head on something and realised that the disused doorway he'd pulled them into was hung with bushels and bushels of mistletoe, and Reenie saw it too, and before she knew what she was doing she had stepped forward and kissed him.

A shriek like a strangled puffin made them turn and see the world beyond their doorway. Dolly Dunkley, leading a group of girls carrying small flags, had seen them and was outraged.

Reenie could tell that her indiscretion would be all round the factory by morning.

Chapter Forty

'I just can't help feeling a little bit jealous, that's all.' Caroline jabbed at the scoop of ice cream atop her soda float with a straw and looked around the café with the air of a patient martyr. 'Sid's like a brother to me, we're very, very close. He's the closest friend I have, so it's hard for me to see him with someone else.'

The café was busy with Christmas shoppers who, laden with parcels they had saved for all year and were squirrelling away below their seats, were stopping for a well-earned cup of tea. The tang of Assam and Darjeeling in the air mingled with the aroma of ginger iced buns and rain-soaked winter coats. The place should have had a cosy, reassuring feeling, but to Ada it just reminded her of the day she'd met Sid, and the beginning of this awful mess she was in.

'And now you've been in the *Courier*!' Caroline said it breathlessly with a pained sort of awe, then with a flick of light resentment, 'You know I would *love* to be in the *Courier* and I just can't help feeling that it isn't fair.'

Ada's stomach churned and her own cup of tea sat untouched in its saucer going cold. Caroline made her feel as though she ought to apologise for having gone to the dance with Sidney Otter and for not having shared some of the sympathy she'd received of late. Ada told herself she could have tried harder to tell people that Caroline had been with her at the dance and had suffered too through worry, and that would have given Caroline the attention she craved. But there was still the matter of Dolly Dunkley. Ada was convinced that she was right to feel hurt and betrayed that Caroline had shared so many private details of Ada's own life with this virtual stranger.

'I wish you hadn't told people what had happened in the bike sheds before the dance. You said that if I went off with him that would be a secret between us and you'd never tell a living soul.'

Outraged that she should be reminded of this transgression, Caroline threw down her straw, folded her arms, and slumped back in her seat. 'And you had to go and tell everyone that I promised that! Now everyone thinks *I'm* the villain of the piece. Thanks very much, Ada, now everyone's selling me up the river!'

Ada's own sense of injustice spurred her on with a mite more courage than usual to correct her friend. 'You're not being sold up the river, that would mean that you were being very, very seriously betrayed and you're not being betrayed you're just being found out and having to face the consequences of your actions – which is the complete opposite.' Ada stopped short of demanding an apology for herself because she felt that was implicit in the statement.

'And who's the one doing the betraying? My best friend, Ada! My own best friend is betraying me at work among my new friends, at the dream job I've been trying to get for years. How do you think that makes me feel?' Caroline flicked a golden curl back from her brow to emphasise the tears welling in her eyes. 'How am I meant to go back to the job I love and the people I love when you've done this to me, and I have to see people every day treating you like you're famous now? How do you expect me to sit back and watch you with Sid, knowing how I feel about him?'

Ada stared. Caroline had listened only to the words in Ada's comment which she wanted to hear, and had disregarded the meaning wholesale. This was typical Caroline, and it had always been easy in the past to forget this side of her, or pretend it away. In the intervals of kindness and patience and affection Caroline had lavished on her, Ada used to forget that her friend could be like this. Then whenever Caroline's web of lies caught up with her and she tried to blame everyone else for the consequences of her own actions, Ada would remember, with a sudden jolt, that Caroline was often like this, and now it was happening again. Ada's strategy had always been to defend herself only so far, and then to privately admit defeat, be conciliatory, make herself smaller, and try to smooth everything over by losing face herself. Keep her only friend.

'I'm sorry about Sid,' Ada offered as her first move in the difficult chess game of helping Caroline regain her own position on the board so that the game didn't have to end. 'If I'd known that you liked him I'd never have—'

'I *told* you I liked him. I told you that the moment I met him in September I knew we were going to be special to one another.'

'Do you mean this September just gone? I thought you said you'd known him for years?'

'No.' Caroline picked up her straw and gave Ada a look which showed the offence she felt that her friend hadn't listened to her, 'I said I *felt* like I'd known him for years. The moment we met we felt like we were soulmates and we just knew that we'd been twins in a past life because we were so close we were like twins.'

Ada looked at her cup of tea and wondered if she could take a sip without her stomach heaving. Her mouth was dry and the misery of her situation was making her nauseous. 'Then why did you want me to go to that dance with him?'

'I wanted us all to go to the dance *together*. Don't you remember? The *three* of us, walking along arm in arm? I thought it would be nice for you to come along with us two and I didn't want you feeling left out. I thought you were just doing me a kindness by dancing with him while I got rid of Roland who I'd promised a couple of dances to, but . . .'

Ada didn't hear the rest. There was a ringing in her ears and she thought the room would spin her out into the street if she didn't hold on tight to the edge of her seat. It was all becoming clearer now; Caroline had been stringing along two young men and had seen a way to keep them both on a hook if she used Ada to keep one of them busy while she made her mind up. Perhaps she hadn't wanted to keep them both, perhaps she'd wanted to palm Sidney off onto Ada permanently and had just changed her mind because something had come a cropper with this Roland. Whatever her motives Ada knew with absolute clarity that it was useless to try to reason with Caroline because she created her own memories, and they flickered and died to be replaced with perfectly formed new ones the moment her conscience or convenience needed them. If Ada had been hoping that Caroline would be a sympathetic, or even a wise person to confide her current problems in, she was clearly mistaken. Ada was in a horrible situation of her own making, and she had nowhere to turn.

Chapter Forty-One

'And do you have anything to say for yourself, or do you have the grace to simply blush and show remorse?' Diana did not occupy herself with any of the work of the office on this occasion, she simply folded her arms, leant back in her chair, and waited for Reenie to begin babbling.

The room was empty but for the two of them; Mrs Wilkes's office door stood ajar, and Reenie could see that her desk calendar had not been turned over for some days. She too had deserted her post. Perhaps Mrs Wilkes was coming back in a day or so, or perhaps she wasn't. It all felt the same to Reenie. Seemingly everyone was leaving Mack's and nothing would ever be the same again. Was it really worth staying if it wasn't the place she loved anymore? If all her friends were gone?

The plush office didn't have its familiar cosy feeling. Something was not right. The dark oak doors with their carved acorns and monogrammed 'M's gleamed with recently buffed furniture polish, the thick carpet gave its usual spring underfoot, and the clock ticked with the reliability of Diana herself. But then it gave a half-click and its rhythm slipped, and Reenie realised it had run itself nearly two hours ahead of where it ought to be. If Diana had so much work to do that she didn't have time to mend her own office clock then they were in worse trouble than she'd ever thought they were.

'It's not what you think it is.' Reenie blushed as she tried to sink through the floor on the other side of the desk.

'You don't know what I think it is, Reenie Calder, you don't know the half of it. You have no conception of how difficult it is to be a woman who chooses work over marriage in the twentieth century.'

'I might be young, but I do know a thing or two. I gave up my wedding day to stay on.'

'You've been working at Mack's for nearly two years and all of that time you've been sheltered from the realities of working life. You've had your parents to fall back on if you lose your job; you've had managers who championed you when you didn't fit in; you've had friends who rallied round when you needed help, but you won't always be lucky enough to have those things. I won't always be here to get you out of trouble, and this time you've got yourself into three different kinds of trouble. Allow me to enumerate them for you; first, you've got involved in a flirtation with your own manager which puts your employment in jeopardy, you do understand that, don't you? Managers who knock off their direct reports don't keep those direct reports in post when they've finished with them. It gets uncomfortable and the girl is out on her ear—'

'Harry's not like that.'

'They're *all* like that, Reenie. Even if he's good and kind and does nice things for his mother he'll still want you out of his way when it all fizzles out. He may very well show compassion as he shows you the door, but he'll show you the door all the same. He'd be a bad manager to allow anything which might interfere with the efficient running of his department – and an old flame would do that.' At this Reenie tried to argue for Harry, but Diana wasn't finished by any means. 'And, secondly, you allowed yourselves to get caught, which brings me to the accusations of favouritism. You were seen by – and God help me, I don't know how you could be so stupid and so unlucky at the same time – Dolly Dunkley, who has made a formal complaint that you are in a job beyond your years and experience because you've been having a fling with a manager, and she thinks it isn't fair and the girls she was with will back her up!'

'It wasn't a fling!' Reenie burst out, tired of being told what she thought and felt. 'It wasn't a fling, it was something which happened out of the blue and I hadn't meant for it to happen, not really—'

'And that's the third thing, because I thought you of

all people would be more wary of what a flirtation with *any* man can lead to. Even if he weren't your manager; even if he didn't work at Mack's; even if he were more chivalrous than all the knights of the round table put together and only wanted to walk you to and from church on Sundays, you of all people know that it has to be leading somewhere. You either risk breaking his heart, or going down a road you can't walk back up again. I told you once before, Reenie, that being a woman means making hard choices. You told me that you'd made yours and you want the job, not married life, so now you need to show me you meant it. Don't be the lass who has to "go and visit her aunt in the country" and spends the rest of her days crying over the secret baby she had to give away; don't be the lass who managers won't take seriously because she's got one foot in the factory and one in a fairy tale – and don't waste everyone's time hanging on here if what you want is a husband.' The steel-banded irises of Diana's eyes sparkled, and Reenie knew that it must be anger because Diana was constitutionally incapable of shedding a tear.

'I'm sorry if I've caused you more work by letting something happen which I hadn't intended,' Reenie said, trying to hold in some of her breath, some of her need to pour out all her confidences at Diana's feet. 'Are you sacking me, or can I stay if I promise it won't happen again?'

'It's out of my hands now,' Diana sighed. 'My manager has to decide what to do about you. Her opposite number in Men's Employment will deal with Harry Swallow.'

'No! He can't!' Reenie blurted out, 'Harry shouldn't get into any trouble, he's not done anything wrong. They won't dismiss him, will they? Tell them they have to let him keep his job, they have to.'

'Reenie, I don't know what frustrates me more about this situation, the fact that you let a manager carry on a flirtation with you and you didn't come and see me about being moved elsewhere, or that you don't see the inequality in your situations. You're sticking up for a man who knew that—' She stopped and rose from her seat to walk to the window. 'You know what? Never mind. It's not worth me even trying to explain. You can go back to work until you're told otherwise.' Diana dismissed Reenie with a wave of her hand, but then seemed to change her mind. 'No! You *do* need to understand. Harry Swallow was your manager, and he's older than you; he knows very well that he is in a position of power over you in more ways than one; he has to take more than half the responsibility for what has happened here because no matter how innocent it might seem to you, he has taken advantage of a situation when he should have shown restraint. I don't ever want to hear you taking responsibility for a man's action or inaction again; you were not put on this earth to save a man from himself.

'And that man doesn't have even half the talent and promise that you do. All right, he's good at his job, he's a valuable worker, but not anywhere near as valuable as you. If you stay on at Mack's you'll be able to shape the future of the whole company. You're behaving as though his job is more important than yours – as though his need to earn a crust means more than yours. If you put your mind to it you have the potential to improve the working lives of hundreds, if not thousands of other employees by redesigning the way they work. You can't keep demanding that we all treat you as if you matter, but then behave like you don't. And listen to me now when I say this, because it's very, *very* important: I'm not always going to be here. You need to find somewhere you can slot in and do the work and not need a champion all the time.'

Reenie frowned. 'Why won't you be here?'

'I'm going away.'

'Where?' Reenie asked, taken aback by the very thing she knew she'd been told before and had ignored. 'When?'

'I don't know.' Diana turned to look out of the window. 'I think I'm going to America.'

Chapter Forty-Two

Caroline was wearing crisp, new white overalls over the top of one of her favourite work-wear frocks. The new overall was not one of Ada's – Caroline had gone through all of those already. As agreed, Caroline had started wearing Ada's when her own began to look grubby, and Ada had inherited Caroline's seconds. Ada couldn't understand how her friend managed to spoil clothes so quickly; if it wasn't an ink stain on the cuff it was a grass stain on the hem, and if the hem wasn't torn, the pockets were out of shape from being over-filled with heavy items she shouldn't have been carrying in the first place. Caroline gave the impression to strangers of being a bright blaze of goodness, but those who knew her well knew that she was also careless with things: things she owned, things she borrowed, things she stole . . .

'I don't think you should have done that, Caroline.' Ada pursed her lips and deliberately didn't meet her eye as she said it; she didn't think she could have borne seeing the look of astonished injury turn to outrage on Caroline's face.

'Done what?' Caroline put away her compact mirror – factory floor contraband – into the pocket of the overalls she had just helped herself to from someone else's peg in the cloakroom. 'I don't know what you're talking about, Ada, I really don't.'

'The girl who owns that overall might get into trouble when she comes to put it on and finds it missing. She won't be able to go on the line until she gets a replacement. She might even lose out on earning money because she has to wait for an overall before she can start shift.'

Caroline rolled her eyes with a good-natured, indulgent expression, 'Oh, you do fuss, Ada. I pick up an overall because I've forgotten my own and the way you tell it you'd think I'd been stealing the food out of the mouths of fatherless babes. It's only an overall. Whoever's it is will get another one from stores and it will be fine.' Ada said nothing and Caroline filled out the silence. 'Besides, I thought you wanted me here with you on your first day back? I can't very well come and give you moral support if I've got no overalls, because they won't let me on the production line. It's one or the other, Ada – you've got to decide which.'

But it wasn't one or the other; these were not the only two possibilities to choose from, and Caroline was not working on the line that day purely to give Ada moral support, she was doing it because it was her job too and she was due on shift too, and she needed to be at her post. Ada felt again the heavy futility of arguing with Caroline when she was only capable of hearing the things she wanted to hear.

'Ada, we're glad to have you back.' The overlooker for their section had come to meet them fifteen minutes after the start of their shift as agreed. Ada was going to face questions from the other girls, but they could at least spare her the clamour of the cloakroom on her first day back. 'How are you feeling, precious?' The kindly overlooker squeezed her hand, and Ada's heart squeezed with guilt.

'I just want to be back at work and pretend nothing's happened.'

The return to the factory floor was even harder than Ada had anticipated. There were no questions at first, only looks, and then the well-wishes started. The first was from a girl at least three years older than Ada who said – with a pained expression – 'I think you're very brave.' Next was the turn of a porter taking away a wheeled cage of finished cartons. 'You ever need to walk home or 'owt just let us know and me or one o' the lads can make sure you get home safe.' An older woman from the next section checked with Caroline to see if Ada was all right, not asking Ada directly, but speaking clearly enough that Ada knew she was being checked on. Everyone was being so kind and thoughtful and attentive, and the guilt at the thought of illegitimately receiving all this care made her guts twist.

'Have you heard?' Jessica Pullman cooed across the line to her colleagues, 'there's been another attack just this afternoon.'

'How did you hear that while you've been standing here all the while?' Phyllis Furnell asked.

'I've just heard one of the porters telling Noreen's section. Can you see him? Over there with Noreen. What's his name? Is he Tom?'

'Looks like Tom.' Phyllis called him over. 'Tom! Did we hear you say there's been another attack?'

Tom appeared to be about to launch into an astonished and salacious account, but then caught sight of Ada who was in the middle of the row, picking up empty cartons from another cage and carrying them over to the line to put at the elbows of the wrappers. Caroline saw where his glance went and said, 'Don't worry about Ada, she doesn't mind you talking about the Slasher. In fact,' Caroline reassured them with confidence, 'Ada said she wanted to be told as soon as there was any news – good or bad.'

Ada said nothing. She did not challenge her friend to tell her precisely when she'd said such a thing. With Caroline the sands of fact and truth and decency would shift beneath you so fast when you put your foot down that it didn't always feel safe to try.

'Well,' Tom leant in to be better heard by the women over the noise of the production hall, 'I picked this up not ten minutes ago when I went down to the landing stage.' He pulled a rolled up extra from the *Halifax*

Courier from his pocket. 'The Slasher's struck again, but this time up by Bankfield. Says here it was another man this time.'

Ada shivered with remorse.

'How is he? Did he survive?'

'He survived all right, but the Slasher took half his coat in his fist as he fled. The police found it a good distance away, cut to ribbons with a razor. Same attacker by all accounts. Same description.'

'What kind of man wakes up of a morning and decides to do a thing like this? Hasn't he got daughters, or sisters, or a mother?'

'You know I think I saw him.' Caroline confided in the company, a little breathless and hushed, but eyes shining. 'I went home from work the other night on my own and just as I was getting back near our house a man stepped out of the dark with a razor held aloft like so,' and she arched one arm over her head, as though the man's arm had been a streetlamp and the razor a bulb, 'and I noticed the bright buckles on his shoes the other girls said they saw, and I screamed and I ran, and I heard his steps behind me but I got to my house just in time, and then he was gone.'

'Well, you had a lucky escape, my girl. Why weren't you with a chaperone?'

Caroline didn't appear to need to think about her answer. 'I got separated from the party I was walking with.'

Ada knew herself to be of that party and she distinctly remembered seeing Caroline to the door. A despicable thought about Caroline crossed Ada's mind, but she then reminded herself that Caroline wasn't the only liar here, and if anyone was the more guilty for starting the whole bally circus in the first place, it was she herself. A few other women chipped in that their sisters, or brothers, or cousins had been unlucky enough to have identical experiences to Caroline's, and they all agreed that he seemed to follow a pattern, and Ada wondered if they were *all* making this up. But could that really be? The newspaper said the victims of this Slasher were cut in the same way Ada had been at the start. Could all of these good people really be inventing it out of some desperation as Ada had done? Were there really so many desperate people in the world these days? Surely some of them must really have been attacked. But then if they had, was it Ada's fault? Had she put the idea into someone's head to start with?

Ada broke out of her reverie with a snap. The line had stopped and two overlookers were standing either side of Caroline and an angry-looking girl was saying, 'It *is* mine, I know it's mine. Just look in the collar and you'll see where I've sewn my nametape.'

Caroline appeared confused and a little hurt. 'I don't know what you mean.'

'Is that your overall?' the first overlooker asked Caroline.

'Well, of course it is.'

'Then you won't mind taking it off and showing us the inside collar.'

Caroline coloured and took off the overall with an overdone nonchalance. She appeared to be deliberately not looking at the collar, while attempting to look casual about it. The collar revealed its owner.

'Where did you get this?'

Caroline cultivated the innocence of a tiny wounded bird. 'I found it in the cloakroom, it was just lying around.'

'But you knew it wasn't yours?' the overlooker pressed.

Caroline gave a helpless shrug and looked on the verge of tears. 'I forgot mine and I asked my friend Ada if the spare overalls in the cloakroom were for anyone to borrow, and she said yes they were. I'm new, I didn't know, I just didn't want to hold up work by making a fuss.' Caroline looked earnestly and apologetically to Ada. 'I'm sorry, I had to tell them.' And Ada didn't know which was worse with Caroline; the deception when she was there, or the loneliness when they were apart. Ada's life was so very lonely now that her mother was gone, and Caroline was her only friend, and she loved her for all her faults, and she knew that Caroline loved her too. And she couldn't blame her, she was Caroline, and this was the way she had always been.

Chapter Forty-Three

Chester 'Sleepless' Parvin was sitting beside the window of the newsroom looking out. The view from the offices of the *Halifax Courier* had changed so much in these last few years that he almost felt he didn't know the town any more. Barrage balloons, air raid shelters, trenches in the parks, first aid stations on the corners of shopping streets, and now curfews to prevent more attacks by this Halifax Slasher. At first the community spirit had been strong and local clubs and sporting associations had banded together to patrol the streets and chaperone women to and from their places of work, but now the mood had turned sour. Ever since the announcement of a reward on the Slasher's head, vigilante groups had begun hunting the streets in packs and there had been a few wrongful arrests of innocent bystanders accosted purely on account of being on foot alone at night.

Sleepless heard a commotion down in the street and opened the window so that he could lean out and get a better look at what was happening. The streets were dark, but the streetlamps illuminated a mob of about seven men chasing one frightened man into a blind alley.

Sleepless leapt from his seat, not pausing to shut the window or pick up his notebook. He ran headlong down two flights of stairs, along a corridor and out into the street in the direction of the mob.

There, at the end of the snickelway, he saw the mob piling in on the man who was now barely visible. Sleepless's footsteps must have alerted them to his presence because some of the men turned round and it looked as though he might be next. 'No, stop!' Sleepless called out, fumbling for his card. 'I'm a reporter for the *Courier*, I'm not the Slasher!'

'A course you're not,' one of the men said, 'We've just caught the Slasher and we're taking him to the police for our reward.' The man turned back and spoke into the mob, 'Bring him out and show him to the reporter.'

The man who was supposed to be the Slasher was brought forward, his eye already beginning to swell and his face bloody from an indiscriminate punch.

'I did that,' one of the mob said proudly. 'I slowed him down when I saw him prowling around alone. That's how we caught him. C'mon you, we're taking you to the authorities and they're gonna hang you out to dry.'

'No, wait a minute, we've lost Arthur and Bob. Let 'em catch up so's they know where we've gone.'

'I'm Arthur!' The injured man cowering on the ground cried out. 'I'm—'

'Shut up, you!' The self-appointed leader gave him a sharp kick in the ribs for good measure.

'No, hang about, he's wearing Arthur's neckerchief. Where'd you get that from?'

'I *am* Arthur! I got separated from you! I told you, I'm not the Slasher!'

A scuffle behind them on the cobbles put every man on high alert again, and the missing Bob was almost attacked himself as a potential Slasher, but someone recognised him in time and potentially saved his life.

'What happened to Arthur?' he asked. 'Did the Slasher get him?'

'No, we saw him alone and we knew only the Slasher would be out on his own so we went for him.'

Parvin shook his head. He didn't need to take notes. He'd remember this for a very long time.

Chapter Forty-Four

It was with a shock that Diana Moore found her step-brother waiting on her doorstep when she arrived home. He leant against the letterbox, smoking a cheap, stubby roll-up, his coat collar turned up against his neck because he didn't have a scarf.

Diana had forgotten about Tommo. The news from the Hunters had been too momentous for her to hold anything else in her mind. She had so many troubles to manage at this moment that she felt like one of those music hall acts who spin plates on sticks and keep them all in the air simultaneously. Diana had to keep spinning out her friendship with the Hunter family and make certain it didn't drop; she had to keep spinning her plans to flee to America because she wanted to take Gracie to safety and there was still so much work to be done; she had to spin the difficult characters who lived in the boarding house she managed for other, absent owners; she had to spin out her job at Mackintosh's – not only because she would need to save every penny of that salary to take to America, but because she wanted to leave her friends there well enough provided for with safe jobs after she was gone and couldn't protect them anymore. Add to that her own fears and grief at the thought of war, the grief of recent personal losses and her own sleeplessness, and the last thing she needed was to have to manage another of her brother's moods.

Tommo took a long drag on his cigarette, threw it to the kerb and exhaled. 'Where you been, sis? I've been waiting.'

There was no cunning smile on his frog-like mouth and Diana thought she saw that other Tommo, the brother who was there, buried deep down under all the arrogance and resentment he showed the world. There was a Tommo – a Tommo who had been more in evidence when her father was alive – who would sometimes emerge in their conversations late at night when they sat by the fire, a boy with a sense of right, and wrong, and the spaces between. Their father would complain about the government, or the state of the air they breathed, or whatever else he'd read about in the paper after supper, and Tommo would play devil's advocate trying to offer him a reason for optimism, and their father would be glad of it and would come around.

But that was a long time ago. What she wouldn't give to talk to her father now. Or perhaps not her father, because she was ashamed of what she was planning to do with Gracie and that ticket to America, and it was better her father would never – could never – know. Perhaps the best person, the only person she could talk to now, was the Tommo of old. But was he there to be found when she needed him, or was it wishful thinking? Diana took a chance. 'You can come in for a spell, but I've a house full of boarders – if you're trying anything . . .'

Tommo waved his hand and the thought away. 'Gimme a chance. I just wanna talk. I've got a proposal might solve both our troubles.'

Diana cast her eyes disdainfully up and down him, looking for a weapon or a trace of the boy he'd once been, then unlocked the door and let him follow to the kitchen.

'I'll get straight to the point,' he said, carefully taking off his hat. 'You and me, we've both got a problem; I'm out of my usual line of work, and when conscription starts – which could be any day, let's face it – I'll be just the right age to be stuck with some sandbag-filling duty in the south, and that's not my cup of tea. You, me darlin', are all set to go to New York with Gracie, but you've got all the same problems you've always had: money and the need for help. You need to earn enough money to keep the pair of you, and more on top of that to pay someone to care for her while you work to earn that money. And let's not forget you've got to get work without references because you're going to be in hiding for the rest of your life.'

'Did you come here to lecture me, or do you have a better idea?'

'Yes, I do.' The old, almost-honest, Tommo looked her in the eyes and she was tempted, for a fleeting second, to believe that this was the real him, that she'd exaggerated his other faults and, given the right conditions, he could be like this all the time. 'We'll go together,' he said.

'You'd have to get false papers. They'd not take you in America with a criminal record, Tommo. And I suppose you think you can fall in with the criminal gangs in New York and we can go back to the kind of life we had in Halifax before you went away. No thank you.'

'I don't suggest we go to America. I suggest we go to Spain.'

'Are you mad? Do you have any idea how dangerous it is there? Have you any conception of what it's like?'

'But it's the last place anyone would look for you, and it's the easiest place in the world to disappear in, and start making a new life. We sail to Portugal then cross the border on foot. If anyone asks we're artists, poets, whatever; plenty of English arty types over there so no one will question it. Tell everyone we came over to Spain before the war, had to leave our farm because soldiers took it. No one is gonna' care what we say when they've all got worse problems of their own. Then we find a nice little village to earn our bed and board until the fighting stops – about two months, I reckon, by what I've read in't papers, if that – then settle in a town for the long haul. By then everyone around us will be in the same boat and we won't stand out as newcomers. I provide for you and the kid like we did before I went away, and we're a family again.'

So this was what all this was about. He was chasing his happy fantasy of the family life they'd had. Where was his mother in all this? Presumably she'd gone to ground as soon as she was released from prison herself, and he'd not managed to track her down.

'You're utterly mad! You could go to Australia, South Africa, Canada, America, even Hong Kong – but no, you have to be clever and come up with a country where you don't speak the language and the government drop bombs on their own people.'

'I didn't say it wasn't risky, but it's better than your plan of dressing the kid up and getting on a boat to sail to the most obvious place in the world. There aren't many places where you can disappear with her, and I doubt there are many people offering work to keep the pair of you.'

Diana cursed herself for believing, even for a heartbeat, that Tommo was anything more than what she knew him to be. The disappointment was bitter, and it stung. 'I would never, ever risk Gracie in a place like that. The whole purpose of this – the *only* purpose – is to get her to safety away from any war.'

'If all you wanted was for her to be safe then you'd leave her where she is. We're not at war, and when we are there'll be time enough to get away, her rich parents'll see to that.'

'There wasn't time enough in September, was there? There wasn't time enough when the BBC stopped everything to broadcast prayers from the Archbishop of Canterbury, and messages from the Admiralty.'

'What are you talking about? What prayers? What broadcast? If this is the Munich thing I missed it. I was inside, wasn't I? No wireless, no papers. We got a bit o' news, but you don't get details.'

Diana was struck by the thought of what it must be like to emerge from prison after two years and see barrage balloons floating over towns like inflated elephants, and a labyrinth of deeply dug trenches in public parks for the nation to cower in. The shock must be incredible, and now it didn't seem so out of character that Tommo's first instinct would be to charge into the heat of the worst battleground and let it do its worst to him, rather than wait and watch from afar as danger inched nearer.

'We didn't get any warning,' Diana said, her tone resigned now. 'You've no notion of how bad it was; how terrifying. Hitler invaded Sudetenland, and that was it, everyone knew war would be declared within hours if we didn't get a miracle. The BBC changed all their broadcasts; ARP men told everyone to wear warm clothes if we went out because they thought the enemy attack would start straight away, and people in cities would just have to walk out to the countryside in whatever they stood up in. They told us not to take our pets with us when we fled our homes. They announced that all the poisonous snakes and dangerous animals in zoos were being killed to prevent danger if they escaped in the chaos of an invasion. Everyone found a wireless somewhere and sat by it. Chamberlain had flown to Munich to negotiate with Hitler, but no one honestly believed anything would come of it. There were people packing bags ready to go, but they didn't know where. We waited and waited, and then gone midnight the news came that he'd signed a peace treaty. Beyond the eleventh hour. We'd thought the first of October would be the day of war, but it was the first full day of peace. It was so sudden. There was no warning. It'll be like that next time. There'll be no warning.'

'Then why haven't you already left?'

'Money. I worked out exactly how much I'd need to keep me and Gracie for six weeks, and I worked out how much longer I'd need to stay on at Mack's to save it.'

'You'll need more than you think you will. If you're smuggling her out by boat you'll need money for bribes everywhere or the people what adopted her'll catch up with you in no time, and then it's prison for you.'

'No, it's not like that anymore. Something's happened. It's complicated, but it means I could take her and they couldn't come after me.'

'Do you mean you've got something on them?' Tommo's eyes brightened. This was more like his way of doing things.

'Something like that.'

'If I could get my hands on some money I could get us away sooner—'

'No. I'm still not sure I'm going through with it.'

'Why not? There's nothing stopping you now.'

Nothing that would stop you, certainly. But so much was staying Diana's hand. 'She's already lost one mother, and I don't want her to lose another one. I want her to have everything I can't give her, and if there's still a chance that they can keep her safe . . .' And above all, thought Diana, I don't want to be like you. Seeing her brother, seeing his approval of her plan to steal back her daughter; his selfishness at planning to take her somewhere even more dangerous to serve his own whims; to use unspecified devious means to prevent Gracie's good adoptive parents coming after her; to take so lightly all the heartache this would cause for Gracie? No, Diana was sure now, she didn't want that. She didn't know what she wanted, but she didn't want that.

Chapter Forty-Five

'Slasher attack!' A lad on a bicycle screeched his brakes to a halt on the pavement beside the Borough Market gates and dumped two heavy bundles of newspapers onto the cobbles. 'Get your *Halifax Courier*! Latest attack! Police baffled! Curfews for women!'

This corner of the market was evidently a prime location for news sellers, and a lad sprinting to the same spot on foot with a single bundle saw that he'd been pipped to the post and reluctantly turned down Russell Street instead. The remaining lad, artfully leaning against his bicycle like a shooting stick, while holding it steady with one knee bent, turned out evening papers with a steady rapidity.

Mary had no hands free to take a paper even if she wanted one. She had emerged from the market with Greta, Max, and a basket full of groceries. She hadn't told Albert yet about the new baby – there hadn't been a good time. He'd come home from work the day the doctor had told her to another letter from the Home Office contradicting themselves over the permission he sought for his sister to come to safety in England. Her life in Germany was becoming more frightening by the day and Albert didn't need one more family member to worry about.

'Mother,' Max called out in an accent which was quickly adopting a Yorkshire intonation. 'Greta's bag is not correct.'

Mary looked down to see that the bag of oranges she had given Greta to hold were being dragged along the ground, their zest grating on the pavement. 'All right, Greta, you give that one to me.' Attempting to lift an extra bag, and herd the five-year-old in the right direction caused a muscle to twinge in Mary's back and she gave a little yelp of pain. She wondered suddenly if carrying things might be bad for the baby; she didn't know, her mother had never told her about the facts of life. Mary tried to move out of the way of a stout, red-faced man who was marching toward the news vendor. He scowled at Mary.

'You ought not be out on the streets!' he said. 'There's a Slasher loose and you're wandering around with kiddies! They ought to be at home! What sort of a mother are you?'

Mary felt that accusation hit its mark. What sort of a mother was she? Evidently a careless one. She was careless of the safety of these children she had, and she felt the conception of the child she carried must also be due to her own carelessness too. Greta was still angry, Max was still suspicious of her, and Mary hadn't even thought about the danger that this Slasher might pose to them in the middle of town in broad daylight. But then it wasn't broad daylight anymore, it was November and the night mists were drawing in. Halifax was at the bottom of a valley and the sun vanished behind the steep moorland with a suddenness she always forgot would come.

'Come along you two.' Mary tried to rearrange her parcels of shopping to give her a free hand to steer Greta round the corner, down Albion Street and King Edward Street beyond it, weaving through crowds of unaccommodating shoppers. 'We must go to the nearest bus stop and go straight home.'

Max reached for his sister's hand to lead her, always the little grown-up, but his question held the fear of a child. 'Is this Slasher a Nazi? Does he look for Jewish boys and girls?'

'No, no, it's not that,' Mary tried to reassure him, while emphasising the seriousness of the situation, 'this isn't Germany, it's not—' Mary was taken by surprise as the bottom of the bag holding the oranges split, spilling the bright fruit and sending them rolling into the gutter. At that same moment a break in the traffic at the crossroads ahead of them allowed Greta to see the bright lights of the cinema on the other side of

Commercial Street and the five-year-old girl let go her brother's hand and darted out between the vehicles, vanishing from Mary's view.

Maximillian was caught in panic, not knowing whether to pick up the oranges his sister had caused to be spilled, or to run after her. Mary acted decisively, dropping all her parcels on the floor, snatching up Max's hand and pulling him quickly across the road. Her heart was in her mouth as her eyes searched the street for the tiny girl, but then she saw her, and a wave of nausea made her sway to the point she thought she'd faint. Mary steadied herself and walked over to the cinema, Max shaking by her side. He had evidently been as afraid as Mary herself had been, and the relief at finding Greta standing with her nose pressed against a movie poster was overwhelming for both of them.

'Mina Maus!' Greta cried out with vehemence as she pointed to the cartoon characters who almost leapt out of the poster to greet her. '*Sie haben Mina Maus!*'

The drama which the little girl had caused in the road had not gone unnoticed, and a mix of bystanders, waiting cinemagoers, and an usherette gathered around to help Mary. The parcels she had dropped on the other side of the road were brought to her and pressed into her hand, Greta was given a ticking off in broad Yorkshire by a woman who had children of her own, and the usherette offered Mary a sit down.

'I need to telephone my husband,' Mary said tearfully. 'Is there a 'phone box near here?

Mary was shown a kiosk just inside the door and, surrounded by bruised oranges, parcels of food she felt too sick to eat or cook, and two children she thought she didn't understand, she telephoned the Mackintosh's factory switchboard and asked to be put through to the kitchen of the head confectioner. When Albert's reassuring voice answered she sobbed, 'Albert . . . Albert, I'm having a baby.'

'Oh my darling, that – that is wonderful news!' he stammered in shock, trying to understand the call. 'But are you well, is the baby well? You are distressed, what has happened to you?'

'I took the children out when there was a Slasher and I dropped all the oranges in the gutter and then Greta ran to the cinema and I thought she'd been knocked down and she wasn't but people had to help me and I think I'm a b-bad mother because even the doctor's wife speaks German and I can only say Mina Maus and *nein*.'

'Where are you?'

'I'm at the National Cinema on Commercial Street in their phone kiosk.'

'Stay there. I will arrive presently.'

Mary, exhausted physically, mentally, and emotionally, paid for their three tickets and allowed herself to be dragged into the noisy auditorium where the sound of children's laughter was too raucous for anyone to notice her heavily blowing her nose. Mary, Max and Greta settled into three soft, comfortable bucket seats at the back, and Mary saw to it that she was on the outside of the row so there would be no darting off from Greta. She needn't have worried; Greta was immediately captivated by the brightly coloured images which flicked over the screen, showing a Mickey Mouse cartoon in which Mickey and Goofy were taking a caravan up a mountain. Goofy was singing a happy song, and Daffy Duck had just made his entrance. Wild horses couldn't have dragged Greta from her seat.

Mary watched the chaos of the caravan and wondered if they would have to live like that when the invasion came; driving around the country, hiding on hillsides. How would she cope when the baby came? Bess was already helping her with the children on the days she worked at the factory, but would they have to move her into their home? What would Bess say to that? Or Albert, come to that?

The cinema was warm and the seats allowed Mary to slump back and rest her weary head. She would just close her eyes for a moment, just until this swell of nausea passed. Just until Albert arrived. She wouldn't go to sleep.

Mary's hand flopped off her lap and down to her side. An ill-used orange escaped and rolled under the seat with a thud, but the sound didn't wake her. Nothing would wake her until Albert arrived.

Chapter Forty-Six

'Well, don't let Mother know whatever you do.' Kathleen eyed Reenie over the top of the book she was reading, but showed no sign of intending to put it down.

'I reckon she's used to me being "almost sacked" by now. She won't be that fussed.'

'Yes, but that's when you've been "almost sacked" for a misunderstanding, or for trying to help. This time it's kissing a manager in a shop doorway on a busy Christmas shopping day, which is quite something even for you.'

Reenie's face coloured. 'Well. I'm a woman now; she can't be shocked if I kiss a young man. Not six months ago she was hastening me to the altar, so as far as kissing is concerned that horse has bolted and she can't tell me off for it.'

At this Kathleen really did put down her book. 'But in a public street, Reenie, of all places. It's a reflection on her and the way she raised you, you must see that. She'll think that *other people* will think that she raised you to be fast and loose in public, and not fast and loose in the dark of a mid-priced cinema like respectable folk. And she'll think that this means *my* reputation will be tarnished by association. It's not a simple matter of kissing, Reenie, it's breach of social etiquette with far-reaching ramifications for every member of the household. Also, you didn't keep her abreast of the details. You should at the very least have given her all the scandalous details of your shocking romance with a manager over a pot of tea at the kitchen table. You go on about being eighteen and a woman, but you don't even know how to get round your own mother.'

'I don't want to "get round" my own mother. Mothers are not there to be "got round"; they're not the constabulary.' Reenie sighed and picked up the cat who was occupying her chair. 'I didn't mean for any of it to happen, honestly I didn't.'

'Of course not. You just decided to go for a nice purposeless stroll through the town during a curfew with a handsome young man who has a reputation for being the Casanova of Calderdale. You were perfectly innocent.'

Reenie harrumphed as she plonked herself down at the table and clumsily released the marmalade cat which had coiled itself like a spring in her arms and now kicked its back legs to be free. It leapt forth and scampered away across the stone flags of the kitchen floor in search of a warm patch or an entertainment. Reenie watched the cat go with more than a little irritability. She knew that Kathleen was right, but she didn't want to admit it. Her own behaviour around Harry was something she felt embarrassed and perplexed by. In truth, Reenie had felt very lonely since Easter. Peter had left town, Mary had devoted more time to her new family, Bess had left the factory, and Diana had become ever more distant. Reenie had friends in every department, and seemingly in every street, but these weren't the same as the friendships she'd forged with her closest circle, friendships on the precipice of adulthood, full of the meaning and importance of youth. Reenie wondered if her situation was a paradox; she had felt lonely without her friends and had filled the hole in her heart with a dangerous flirtation, but now that it had gone wrong she wanted the absent friends to console and advise her, but she just found herself right back where she'd started at loneliness. No, Reenie thought to herself, it wasn't a paradox, it was something else. Diana would have known what it was called, but she couldn't talk to Diana because she was the one she'd angered most. There really was nowhere to turn.

'I can hear you thinking and it's putting me off my book,' Kathleen said, irritably.

'Well, excuse me for being in emotional and professional turmoil.'

'What are you in emotional turmoil for? Have you fallen for Casanova already?'

Reenie pulled a face in thought. 'No, not really.' Harry

held certain attractions for her, but it wasn't love, and it wasn't the same as she'd had with Peter. It was something more complicated and she didn't want to think about it overmuch.

'Do you still love your job?'

'No, not really.'

'So what have you got to lose? He can't break your heart if you haven't given it him, and losing your job can't hurt overmuch if you're not that fussed about it anymore. Do as you please and, if they sack you, just get another job.'

'What happened to the breach of social etiquette with far-reaching ramifications for every member of the family?'

'That's not my problem, that's Mother's. I say try and find what will make you happy. It's unusual for you to be unhappy, so there must be something badly wrong. Work out what is it and fix it, that's my advice. Once it's all fixed then you can tell Mother.'

'But how can anyone be happy when the world is in this state? We're making gas masks at work and every time I find a way to look on the bright side, an air raid siren goes off. And then I remember that things are only going to get worse. No matter how bad things feel now, they'll be worse when we're at war and everyone gets called up. Mary's beside herself; she's not only got Bess to worry about, but a Jewish family and a baby on the way. And there's me throwing away all my chances to help anyone by getting demoted from the job where I can do the most good, then getting dismissed from the one where I wasn't doing—'

'You're over-thinking it.' Kathleen said, snapping her book closed with a clap which shocked the cat. 'You're the sort of person who's ecstatically happy if the weather is fine enough to hang out washing; you don't need to look for a grand purpose or knight in shining armour, so just look for the thing which is making you unhappy, knock it on the head, and then go back to waxing lyrical about how brilliant it is that nuts and bolts come in so many different sizes.' Kathleen now took her turn to harrumph. 'Look, it's not my business, but ask yourself why you're not walking away from this Harry fella without a second glance. Why didn't you go straight to Diana and ask her to move you when you thought he might want to walk you out? You could have steered clear very easily, and even now you could be running a mile, but you're not. What is it about this Harry fella that's made you get caught up with him? You're a toffee on the conveyor belt; you'd usually sail past him and he'd be forgotten before you reached twist-wrapping. Your conveyor is stuck and you're sitting here looking at him and you're getting snared up so's you can't easily float away. If you want my opinion it's probably because you've seen a way you can help him; that's how you usually get yoursen' in trouble.'

Kathleen diplomatically returned to her book, leaving only the marmalade cat to reproach Reenie with a look. For herself, Reenie shifted awkwardly in her chair. There was more in what Kathleen had said than she liked to admit. She wanted to help Harry's cousin Ada, that was obvious, but when she thought about it she knew that she wanted to help Harry recover from his broken heart, because *her* heart was broken, and if his could be mended, then maybe there was hope for her own.

Chapter Forty-Seven

When Mary awoke in the cinema, Albert was in the seat beside her squeezing her arm. 'The cartoons are over,' he said gently and quietly as she pulled herself back into the familiar world and out of the dream where she'd been making fudge in a barrel and had built a factory by hand. 'They're about to show the main picture.'

The house lights were up, and the grown-ups who had come to see *Fire Over England* before going home for their supper were squeezing past each other to get to better seats. Paper bags of sweets rustled everywhere and the smell of the stale and sticky carpet caught Mary off-guard and she fought down a lurch of nausea.

'Are you feeling unwell?' Albert asked, taking the temperature of her forehead with the back of his hand. Its coolness was refreshing after her deep sleep.

Mary shook her head. 'I'm all right. I just fell asleep for a moment. It's been a tiring day. How long have you been sitting next to me?'

'About an hour.'

Mary raised her eyebrows. 'You should have woken me! I can't have been asleep all that time.'

'I decided you needed your rest. And the children were happy.' He shrugged. 'Greta and I have seen Mina Maus.'

Greta grinned and jumped up and down calling out, 'Mina Maus! Mina Maus!'

Albert beamed with pride and confided to his young bride that Greta – with her brother's help – could now sing 'She'll be coming round the mountain'. The children had now seen a handful of Looney Tunes and Silly Symphonies cartoons and Greta could sing all the songs from them. 'Come along,' he said, getting up slowly himself so that his wife didn't feel rushed, and reaching over to help her tenderly out of her seat, 'it's time we were all going home.'

'No!' The children wailed in unison, and Greta whispered plaintively, 'Mina Maus?'

'Tomorrow,' her father promised. 'If you are good I will bring you back tomorrow.'

And he led them all out into the chill air in search of a taxi to take them home. Outside the cinema Mary felt as if she had emerged into a different world; the streets were bright with festive lights, she was with her family, and she felt now that there was hope. As Mary took Greta's hand the little girl bobbed about happily and sang in accented English, 'Spirits of Ammonia – brooha! – Things that creep upon ya!'

They arrived home at last and Albert took extra care of Mary. It took her by surprise because she had assumed that with having two children already and so much on his mind that he would take less interest in a third child, but he behaved for all the world as though she were made of bone china, and must be protected at all costs. He worried her through the front door, taking her coat, leading her to the sofa and taking off her shoes. He brought her a glass of water and a biscuit before he asked her questions, and Mary could tell by the noises from the kitchen that he had put the kettle on to boil while he was there.

'How far along are you? Are you and the baby quite well?'

'I think so.' She worried now about having made such a fuss. It was just like her to do well at being stoic for weeks on end and then suddenly throw it all up in one big tearful outburst. 'I saw the midwife and the doctor and they've given me things to read and told me to keep my feet up as often as I can.'

'Is this something they are very worried about in your case, or—'

'No, no, I think it's just all ladies. They tell all ladies who are . . . in the family way . . . to keep their feet up. They said I was doing quite all right, really. Healthy.'

'But the factory isn't somewhere you can keep your feet up often.'

'I know. I've already warned Diana that I'm going. I just wanted to hang on as long as I could because they need me, but I know my family need me more.'

'We should have Bess here more often,' he said, 'you will need more help with the children, and she likes to help.'

'I was going to ask . . .' Mary hesitated; it was a large request. 'Do you think, once the baby is born, we might move Bess in here to live with us? I don't like leaving her in a boarding house, and once the baby comes I'll be even more glad of her help.'

Albert seemed delighted at this excellent solution to their practical necessity. 'Why don't we move her in now? She's part of the family, why wait?'

Mary sighed in relief. She glanced over at the dining table where Max and Greta had taken the opportunity to set up Greta's Mickey Mouse puppet theatre and were relishing the opportunity to act out every single cartoon they had seen, repeating the English dialogue word for word. She and her brother chattered away in German about who would play each part, and what was happening in the background of their scene, but the lines Minnie Mouse spoke were all English. Greta was the happiest she had seemed since her arrival in England, and another weight was lifted from Mary's shoulders.

'You will miss your life at Mack's, I think,' Albert said.

'I will. But it's time now. I've got a family – and they need me.'

Chapter Forty-Eight

It was at the end of her shift that Ada found her anonymous gift. The other girls were hurrying out of the workroom and into the cloakrooms to change out of their overalls and into their many layers of winter wear. The sky beyond their windows had already darkened and although the factory was warm as toast, they knew they needed to wrap up. They could be waiting outside in the yard for some time for their various chaperones to see them home.

The usual nattering rumbled on. Phyllis Furnell was giving out Christmas cards; Sarah Handscomb wanted to know who had borrowed her copy of American *Vogue*; Jessica Pullman was hunting for her missing bobble hat; and Dale Bookman had brought in a tin of gingerbread men she'd baked at home and wanted to share with her friends and strangers alike. Everyone was busy with their own thoughts and plans and festive anticipation, and so no one noticed until it was too late that Ada was about to throw something. The jar of pickled calves' tongues had been waiting for Ada on the bench below her coat hook with a yellow ribbon, and a note which only gave her name and 'thinking of you', but no sender. At first Ada was confused – the light in the cloakrooms was on the cosy side of dim and it was difficult to see clearly – but when she realised what the jar contained she gasped in shock and threw it away from her instinctively, smashing the jar against the edge of the cast-iron bench and sending glass, brine, and limp, pink meat skidding across the floor.

'Ada! Whatever's the matter?'

'Was that from the Slasher?'

'Quick, someone call an overlooker!'

The girls surged into action and the little drama played itself out while, unnoticed, two of their number remained on the sidelines.

It was not a coincidence that Dolly Dunkley had been lurking in the corridor outside the cloakroom. She had arranged to meet her new best friend Caroline at the end of the shift, and it was pure coincidence that she should have been there to witness the third wave of sympathy from the girls of the Quality Street production line for Ada Helliwell.

'First she cuts her hand on a window, then she's attacked by a razor-wielding Slasher, then she's left a jar of tongues and has to throw them across a room.' Dolly's voice didn't carry to the other end of the room where the commotion was happening, and it was a good job too, because the rest of the girls were showing a great deal of care and sympathy for Ada and they wouldn't have taken kindly to comments of that sort.

Caroline huffed. 'And now she's so famous and it's not fair. *I* want to be famous for something. Why is she getting *all* of the attention?'

'I think we deserve the attention more than she does.'

'Exactly!' Caroline was delighted to find someone who thought as she did. 'She's not even making the most of it; she's being all odd and reluctant and simpering about it which makes everyone feel uncomfortable. If I were in her shoes I would be the most magnificent victim. I'd swoon and accept presents and sympathy left, right, and centre.'

Dolly's ears pricked up at the suggestion of presents. 'Have people been giving her things for being attacked?'

'Oh yes, heaps.'

'What sort of things?'

'Oh, you know, flowers, toffee tins, home-baked cakes; all that sort of stuff.'

Dolly was partial to home-baked cakes, and she had once braved potential criminal prosecution to get her hands on a special sack of toffees so she was beginning to wonder how she might get in on the act. 'Do you know, I don't think it sounds half bad this Slasher victim stuff. He never seems to do anyone any proper harm – I mean, no one has any terrible injuries or anything – and you get given a load of presents. Maybe we should risk walking home on our own and see what happens? If we met him it might not be so bad.'

Caroline smiled. 'Maybe we don't have to meet him . . .'

Less than an hour later the Slasher struck again. And Caroline and Dolly played their parts with glee.

Chapter Forty-Nine

Reenie was disappointed to realise that the troubles of Ada Helliwell had not endeared the girl to her any more than before; in fact, they had only made her a greater source of frustration. Reenie wanted to look charitably on the original victim of the Halifax Slasher – not to mention motherless, almost friendless, and evidently miserable victim – but the girl's determination to look on Reenie's beloved factory as anything but a healing balm was incomprehensible.

'I thought I wouldn't have to go on any more outings with you now that I'm not new anymore.' Ada's plaintive response to being accosted by Reenie in the factory dining hall might have deterred any other employee, but Reenie wasn't there for her health, she was determined to help Ada settle in and tell Harry Swallow about what a help Reenie had been.

'Well, you don't *have* to spend time with me, it's not compulsory, but your cousin Harry asked me to show you something and if I don't he'll want to know the reason why. He's my manager you see, so I want to do as he says.' Reenie disliked badgering the girl, it went against the grain for her, but she really did think it would be worth it in the end. Like chivvying her younger siblings on to help her wash up the pots straight after their Sunday dinner and not leave them till later, so they'd have the whole glorious Sunday afternoon stretching before them without the leaden anticipation of uncompleted housework.

Ada pursed her lips, cast a look in the direction of the friend who she was often seen with, but rarely seen talking to, and then reluctantly rose to follow Reenie.

'That's the ticket! You won't regret it, Ada, I've got such a surprise in store for you.' But Ada would regret it – because they were about to be trapped in a lift hoist together.

The great treat didn't take long to go wrong. Reenie had arranged with a friend in stores to get a chance for herself and Ada to go up to the roof of the Albion Mills building in the goods hoist which would give them one of the best views of the factory estate, and be something Ada could talk about with the new friends Ada was going to make with Reenie's help. The excitement of the journey in the hoist was short-lived because before they'd reached the fourth floor a creak and a judder ground them to a halt, and a shout down from the top of the shaft told them that it was stuck and they'd have to sit tight while the stores' foreman got the fire brigade.

The wait for the fire brigade was long, and Reenie was glad because if they'd had to get stuck anywhere, they had at least not got stuck on the roof where they'd have perished of cold. The time passed slowly, and after they'd settled down to sit on the floor in the dim quiet. Reenie wanted to start a conversation – but about what?

'Did you know,' Ada offered to break the silence, 'that Lord Byron took a pet bear cub to university with him because there was a rule about not having dogs, but no rule about bears?'

'I'll be honest with you, Ada, I did not know that about Lord Byron.' Hoping that this was the conversation starter that would draw Ada out, Reenie asked, 'Did you read that somewhere?' Ada twitched her nose in an almost imperceptible nod. This was going to be hard work. 'Do you like to read?' Another shiver of a nod. 'I like to read,' Reenie said enthusiastically. 'I like biographies best. I like reading about real people who have forged ahead to achieve great things against incredible odds. Do you like reading biographies, Ada?'

'If they're about people from the Regency period. Or the Romantic poets.' Ada hesitated before offering, 'I like Georgette Heyer's books.'

'My sister *loves* Georgette Heyer!' Reenie burst out, relieved at last to find something they could talk about. '*Devil's Cub* is her favourite. What's your favourite?'

'My favourite's *Devil's Cub* too!' For the first time Ada's face lit up and Reenie felt she might have reached the girl.

'You have to meet my sister Kathleen. She lives to read. She borrows other people's library cards so as she can get out more books than they let her on her own.' Reenie pressed on. 'Perhaps if you came out to our farm one Sunday for dinner you could talk to her about books? She'd like that, she doesn't often meet people who like reading as much as she does. My mother would like you too, but she shows she likes people by mothering them and making them eat twice as much as they have room for, so you best come hungry.'

There was another long silence and Reenie could see that Ada was upset. 'I'm sorry, was it because I mentioned mothers? I know that you—'

'No, no, it's all right.'

Reenie didn't believe this at all. 'Well, it's obviously something. You can talk to me, if you want to, but you don't have to.'

'It's just that . . .' Ada appeared to be struggling to find the words to express what she needed to say. 'Do you ever think you can hear what your mother would say to you, even when she's not there?'

'I can now. She'd say, "Reenie Calder, what were you doing getting in that lift?"'

'I think I can hear what my mother would say to me if she was here. I can hear it all the time now, and I don't know where to turn.'

'What does she say?'

There was a long silence, but Reenie waited patiently.

'I've done something wrong,' Ada whispered, 'and I don't know what to do about it.'

'Well, I'm sure you didn't mean to do whatever it was, and there's not much can't be solved with a sincere apology. Perhaps if you apologise to whoever you did wrong to, you'll feel better about it.'

'That won't make it right.'

'What will make it right?'

'I don't know. I just don't know. It's all got so big.'

'You could tell me about it and perhaps together we could come up with a way of—'

'No.' Ada was firm. 'I can't tell anyone. Only one other person knows, but I don't know who they are, I just know that they left a message for me today in the cloakrooms.'

'What did the message say?'

'I think they were saying something about wagging tongues; about me having said something I shouldn't.'

'That doesn't sound to me like you can just leave it be. Do you have a friend you can trust who you can talk to?'

Ada shook her head.

'Could you talk to your cousin Harry?'

Ada shook her head, turning a little paler. 'He'd be so angry with me.'

Reenie considered. 'Well, I don't think I'll be angry with you. You know I don't get angry. You've seen me lots of times in situations where people might ordinarily get angry – like when the bee got into the kitchen – and I muddled on. Maybe I'm just the person you need?'

Ada seemed to consider, and to wrestle with a rising emotion which had been waiting to catch her out if she thought too long about her predicament. 'My friend asked me to walk out with a lad she knew. We were just going to the dance together, but it all went wrong, and I was frightened and I wanted to go home, and I was so unhappy, and I didn't know how to get away. I heard another girl say that there were foreigners on the loose attacking young girls and I thought that if I said I'd been attacked by one of them people I'd be able to go home without my friend being angry with me.'

Reenie didn't quite take in all that Ada was saying at first. 'And do you think that's why the Slasher attacked you after that dance? Do you think the Slasher is someone who saw you . . .' She trailed off, trying to make sense of what Ada had told her, but she couldn't. It didn't make sense.

'No,' Ada said tearfully. 'What I mean is that there wasn't any Slasher. I took a razor blade to my own clothes because I wanted to get away from the Mack's dance.'

'But you were the first one to be attacked by the Slasher. How could you possibly have known that there were about to be attacks just the same as yours? This doesn't sound right. Are you sure you're not blaming yourself, or—'

'No. I made it up and then other people started saying they'd been attacked, and the police are looking for a man I described, but he doesn't exist and I don't know what to do. I should tell the police not to waste time looking for a man who doesn't exist, but then I would have to tell them what I did, and it's all so awful.'

Chapter Fifty

The meeting was to take place on a park bench at the far end of the boating lake. Shibden Park was not so busy this close to Christmas; the people had gone to the markets in town, the geese had gone back to Canada, and the rowing dinghies had been taken away to bide out the winter in a dry warehouse somewhere near Hipperholme. Even the distant notes of church bells were muffled by the wind.

'Sergeant Metcalf.'

'Reenie.' The policeman wore plain clothes and took the opposite end of the bench, looking out across the park and not directly at the girl who he knew to be honest after a fashion, but who had a reputation for making a monkey out of him when it suited her.

'You understand that this is a matter of some delicacy?'

Sergeant Metcalf gave her a dry look.

Reenie whispered, 'I'm very serious.'

'I'm off duty. What do you want?'

'I want to tell you what I know about that first attack of the Halifax Slasher.'

Metcalf's demeanour changed. 'I'm listening.'

Reenie held her breath. She was reluctant to launch immediately into the business at hand.

'I *am* off duty, but I don't have all day.'

Reenie pursed her lips and then asked, 'Do you have daughters, Mr Metcalf?'

'Do you have specific information, or are you trying to tell me a theory?'

Reenie tried hard not to look at the boating hut. 'There's someone here who wants to talk to you, but first I want to know if you have daughters.'

'Yes, Reenie, I have a daughter.'

Reenie nodded. 'Wait here please.' Reenie slid off the bench, eyeing the policeman as she went to make certain that he stayed where he was. She walked to the edge of the boating hut and beckoned someone to come out. After much coaxing, Ada Helliwell emerged, reluctantly returning with Reenie to the bench, her mousy hair falling over her face while she tried to make herself appear as small as possible.

'Ada,' Sergeant Metcalf nodded, 'was there something you wanted to tell me?'

Ada held her breath for a while, hugging herself with crossed arms and clenched fists. 'I'm very sorry.'

Sergeant Metcalf looked from Ada to Reenie, then back to Ada. 'What do you have to be sorry for, Ada?'

297

There was a long silence and they all waited for the older girl to work up the courage to break it. 'There wasn't any Slasher,' she said.

Sergeant Metcalf seemed to understand, and to be remembering something which only now made sense. He composed his features into a neutral expression. 'Do you want to tell me what happened?'

Ada shook her head.

The seasoned professional and father pressed her again, undaunted. 'Do you think you *ought* to tell me what happened?'

Ada nodded and wrung her hands, then looked down at them and wrestled with the part of herself which most feared the consequences. 'I was with a young man, see?' A scowl crossed her features, but she was looking at the ground. 'I didn't want to go to the dance with him, not really, but my friend said that I should, and then . . .' There was a long pause while Ada took a deep gulp of air. 'Well, he started to press his advantage, and I got away, but my friend told me off because I wasn't being attentive enough to him and she thought I should try to keep him happy, and I was so miserable that I cut my clothes with a razor I found because I couldn't see another way to get away from him. I'd have run away, but there was my friend, and he knew where I lived, and I couldn't ask her for help because she thought I was being a nuisance, and I just didn't know how else to get away.'

Sergeant Metcalf looked out over the steel grey boating lake, pausing just long enough perhaps to see the ghosts of summer parents with summer children steering them away from the water's edge. He asked, as though confirming an answer he already knew, 'Are you saying that the statement you gave about a man cutting your clothes was invented, or did the young man you went to the dance with cut your clothes?'

'No one cut my clothes. I did it myself. I just wanted to get away, I didn't know how else to get away.'

Sergeant Metcalf nodded and asked, 'Where did you obtain the razor?'

'It fell out of a bicycle pannier bag that I knocked over in the cycle sheds. There was a shaving tackle bag in there.'

'And how many people did you tell that you had created a false attack?'

Ada looked confused. 'No one. No one except Reenie. I told her this morning because I was worried about all the attacks which keep happening that all look like mine. I thought I'd given someone the idea and I didn't know what to do. I didn't mean any harm, truly I didn't, but I was frightened and—'

'You understand that you've caused a lot of fear and trouble in the town, don't you, Ada?' He said it as a father might to a child he didn't want to chastise, but had to teach. 'Lots of people have had to stay indoors while we've had curfews; lots of people have given up their time to patrol the streets and act as chaperones. Shops have lost custom; people have lost sleep.'

Ada's voice cracked with remorse, 'I'll never do anything like it again.' She took out a balled-up handkerchief and buried her face in it. 'I never even wanted to go to a job with dances. I just wanted to work in a file room somewhere and be quiet and keep my head down and read things.'

Sergeant Metcalf raised an eyebrow, introducing some levity at last. 'Don't say that round the station, they'll put you on fingerprint filing.'

Reenie sat forward on the bench, her chance to solve Ada's problem suddenly looking more hopeful. 'Would they really, though? I mean, even after what she's done?' Reenie saw a possibility. 'If Ada has to answer for what she did, could she make it up in public service? Work in the police file room, help with something for the public good? That would be the public good, wouldn't it? Helping you solve some real crimes?'

Sergeant Metcalf said carefully, 'Making a false statement *is* a real crime.'

'But she had a good reason.' Reenie hadn't wanted to say this, but she did. 'If it had been your daughter, and she'd been frighted and not known what to do to get away . . .'

Sergeant Metcalf straightened up in his seat on the bench; a flake of forest-green paint coming away from the wood as he shifted. 'You're talking about lawful excuse. That's a very technical matter.'

Ada blanched in the cold. 'Am I going to be arrested?'

'Not today.' He looked out over the lake. 'Anyone who my inspector deems to have made a false statement to the police without lawful excuse is likely going to be arrested and face charges once he hears about this.'

Reenie asked in a whisper, 'Does your inspector have daughters?'

Sergeant Metcalf watched the ghosts of summer families drifting as mist across the lake. 'He did.'

Chapter Fifty-One

'Is now a good time?' Reenie stood on the threshold of the engineering maintenance office, looking round the door for signs of her other colleagues, but Harry sat alone at his desk, working his way through dockets and memorandums with a stubby pencil and notepad.

'If you're still trying to get your old job back I don't think I'm the person you need a recommendation from anymore.' Harry leaned back in his chair, pushing his work away and folding his arms.

'Are you in a lot of trouble?'

'Not with Men's Employment, they're not fussed; managers do this sort of thing all the time so I could have fathered eight sets of twins across three departments and they'd just tell me to keep an eye on my clocking-in times and not be late for the start of my shifts. Diana Moore, however, is another matter.'

'Yes, she gave me a bit of a telling off.'

'You? She led me to understand that this was entirely my fault and that if she had her way she'd have had my guts for garters and my kidneys for breakfast.' Harry stretched his neck with a twist and it seemed to signal a change in his tone, a change in mood. 'She's right, though. I am – or I was – your manager, and that gives me an unfair position of power. I can make you feel obliged to do things you might not have done in other circumstances, and you have to go along with them because if you don't you've got no way of knowing if I'll pull your living out from under your feet. I flatter myself you liked me enough to want to spend a bit of time in my company, but—'

'I did,' Reenie burst in to reassure him, 'oh, I did.'

'But *I'm* not a kid,' he said, and the implication that she was hung uneasily in the words. 'I knew what I was doing. I knew when I took you out walking there might be something between us. I was risking your job and mine, but most importantly, I knew I wasn't risking it for a great love, I was just risking it for a bit of company and a chance to see some Christmas lights with someone who was good company.' He looked at her with clear-hearted honesty. 'I hope you're not disappointed.'

Reenie gave him a wry smile. 'No, I'm not disappointed. I'm fond of you, but you know that I'm not in love with you. My heart's bruised and so is yours. We were in the same boat and understood each other, that was all.' Reenie sighed and took a step forward. She had an envelope with her, and she gave it to him.

'What's this? Christmas cards already?'

'No. It's my resignation. I've decided to leave Mack's.'

Harry stood up abruptly. 'But you mustn't do that! Not because of me. You love this place, there must be a way we can find you a job somewhere I don't—'

Reenie shook her head. 'It's not the same. I love my work, and I have always loved this place, but it's changed. My friends are all gone or are on their way out the door, and they were what made this place special. I could stay, but I miss them, and I'd rather miss them some place new than some place that reminds me of all of them.' They looked at each other earnestly, wishing they could turn back the clock and undo so many things, or perhaps keep everything the same. Reenie tried to look plucky and said, 'Besides, there's a war coming.'

Harry nodded and took the envelope with reluctance. 'Where will you go?'

'I don't know yet. Perhaps I'll join up,' she said, with a twinkle in her eye. 'We'll see.'

'I still don't know if I can join up. I think I'm a reserved occupation. I suppose I ought to check. If there's a war I'll probably be stuck here with the old men mending machines and going slowly round the bend.'

'Aye, but you'll be able to dance with all the girls when the lads are away.'

'Well now, there is that. We've got to look on the bright side. I'll certainly have less competition at dances.'

A shadow passed over Harry's features and he suddenly became serious again. 'I think I will try and join up though. I don't think I could stick it out here while all my mates are fighting.'

'You'd miss a lot of dances.'

'You know I take a different girl to the dances every time because I don't want to break any more hearts than I've already broken, but my God it's lonely. I think I might as well be lonely fighting at war as lonely dancing at home.'

'I didn't realise you were lonely. You seem so self-assured.'

'A part of me wishes there was one special girl to write home to; someone to send me a postcard and tell me what the weather's like. But whoever she was I'd be stringing her along, giving her false expectations for when I come back, and I can't bring myself to do that.'

Reenie thought a moment. 'What about me? Can I be your girl, Harry?' She didn't say it with her usual gusto; this wasn't one of her grand schemes. She asked gently, seriously, 'I could send you postcards and badly knitted socks? You know that I love someone else, and I'll never love you in that way, and I don't want to be married or engaged, or worrying about what impression I've given, I just want to keep what we have and not say any more.'

Harry lost his habitual scowl and a half-smile pulled at his features. 'Badly knitted socks, eh? Who could resist an offer like that?'

'And postcards, don't forget the postcards.'

Harry tapped Reenie's letter of resignation against the back of his hand. 'Are you certain I can't persuade you to stay? Once I pass this on there's no going back. Can you really bear to leave your beloved Mack's?'

Reenie looked around her, took a deep breath, and sighed with what might have been relief. 'Nothing lasts forever,' she said. 'I grew up here, and I made friends here, and I found my wings here, but now it's time for me to fly the nest. Perhaps I'll be back when the war is over, or perhaps I won't.'

'Don't forget to send me those postcards,' he said.

'Of course I won't.' She spoke as she headed out the door. 'I'm your girl.'

Chapter Fifty-Two

The angel which sat atop the Hunter household's Christmas tree was an annual reminder that they were no ordinary family. While other matriarchs might have fussed over the scheme of colours, or the quality of the baubles, Lydia Hunter delighted in nothing so much as a mismatch of garish decorations made with enthusiasm by her children. Some branches bowed low under the weight of bulbous salt-dough shapes on string which had been made by Lara with help from cook and painted with oxblood boot dye. Other branches supported light but complex embroidery samplers from the older girls, and balsa wood carved camels from the boys. Finally, at the very top of the tree was the archangel Gabriel, resplendent in a sash of tatty red ribbon, which had been Gracie's favourite thing to carry around when she was six. Two Christmases had passed since her adoption, and the Hunters could have been forgiven for quietly discarding the keepsake, but they weren't that sort of family and Diana knew it.

They had always been different. From the moment she had met the Hunters in the courtroom where Gracie was given for adoption she had seen that they were people who didn't care for the appearance of things. Even to the point of living with public shame for being known as a bigamist rather than allow a risk that his children might suffer the consequences of not being legitimised, Mr Hunter would do what was right, and not what was easy. Diana hoped that she had got the measure of them, because her next move relied entirely on them being the people she thought they were.

'Diana,' the solicitor broke her reverie, 'Judge Evans is here now. Would you like to come through to the study?'

Diana rose from her seat beside the sitting-room fire, took one last glance at the archangel for luck, and then followed.

A collection of papers lay in neat piles on Mr Hunter's desk and a fountain pen was uncapped beside them. Diana charged at them without hesitation, a deep breath fortifying her to do battle with administrative forces which were painful, but necessary.

The old judge stayed her hand. 'You understand that you are signing over your daughter to the adoptive custody of Mr and Mrs Lydia Hunter in perpetuity?'

'Yes, I understand. They're her mother and father now. I wouldn't want her to know the pain of losing a mother again as she did when my stepmother was taken to prison. This is the best thing for her, the best life.'

Mr Hunter stood beside the window, looking out onto the gloomy December day. 'Even if it means she stays here in Halifax with us through a war, instead of fleeing to Canada as so many of our friends have?'

Diana nodded, asked where her place was to sign, and, signing, relinquished Gracie once and for all. She stepped aside to let the Judge witness her signature, and took her chance. 'I understand that you can't leave Halifax. I respect you more for that. You know that other lives and livelihoods rely on you staying, and so you've chosen to stay, even though you wish your children could all be safe across the sea. I want to make you an offer, and it's one I don't want you to dismiss lightly. Think on this because I've thought on it. I know you can't send all of your children to your cousins because they're elderly people and they wouldn't manage, but *I* would manage. If you send me with them as guardian you could get all of your children to safety in Canada.'

The Hunters exchanged a look which Diana couldn't read, and so she pressed on.

'You know that you can trust me, I think I've proved that today. I could have taken Gracie away myself, but I wanted what was best for her above all. I feel that way about *all* your children. You have been like a family to me and you also know that I'm capable, that I can be relied upon; you've seen that, I think, in your refugee work when I've helped you.

'We all know better than most how awful this war could be. Lydia and I know the situation in Spain better than most, and you yourself, Mr Hunter, have seen a front line. War is coming quickly and there isn't much time to act. I know your reasons for staying, and I know from personal experience how hard it is to give your children away to another. But consider it.'

'Call me George.' Mr Hunter squeezed his wife's hand and she nodded. 'I think we have gone long beyond "Mr" don't you? My wife and I had something we wanted to ask you, but we thought it best to wait until the adoptions were completed in case we appeared to be attempting to influence your decision.'

'Diana,' Lydia Hunter reached for Diana's hand, 'we have two particular requests to make of you. First, we would like you to consider changing your name to Hunter. We have taken the liberty of asking our solicitor to draw up the necessary documentation and we would pay to have it done. Legally, you are too old for us to adopt, but we feel you are family and if we arrange to change your name, everyone will know it. You will become one of us for all the world to see, an adopted aunt, if you like. You can take time to think on it because we realise that we carry a stain which will exclude us from some circles for a long while yet, and you may not want to—'

'Yes! I'll do, it, yes please!' Diana gasped as hot tears rolled rapidly down her cheeks and she lost her tight grip on her own self-reliance.

George gestured to the solicitor to bring out the other papers. 'And the second request was that you take the children – all of them – to Canada. But first you must understand what this truly means. If we stay here there is a chance we may be killed, both of us. Gas attacks, invasion, our political activity with the refugees; there are any number of dangers. If we are killed you would then be head of the household until the children are grown-up. I am arranging to have my company registered in Canada and make the English business a subsidiary. I will be sending my business manager, Stevie Ransom, to New Brunswick to operate it from there. In the event of an invasion – or a collapse of the English business – all the money will be on the other side of the Atlantic and will be invested by Stevie to provide you all with an income.'

Diana deflated in shock, crumpling into the nearest vacant chair. 'You really do trust me?' she said, all her determination and confidence suddenly gone, and the real Diana, so rarely seen, gazed around at the older and wiser people.

'We really trust you.' Mrs Hunter rubbed Diana's back as a mother might her child. 'And we owe you a great deal. If you hadn't made the hard choice to give up Gracie two years ago you would never have come into our lives, and now, in our hour of need, we would have no one to save our children. You are giving us a lifeline, and we'll be grateful for as long as we live.'

'You were right, George,' Judge Evans said as he passed Gracie's certificate of adoption over to his friend, 'she will be a fine influence on the children.'

Chapter Fifty-Three

Mary sat on the sprung horsehair sofa with her feet elevated on a pouf. She had been told that this was very important and that she must do her utmost to rest during her pregnancy. She was reading the information the midwife had given her and, despite Mary's protestations that she wasn't a clever reader, she had no trouble understanding it. She now realised that she had been too hard on herself when she hadn't been able to teach Greta English from books – of course you can't teach a five-year-old anything from a book!

Max and Greta played happily on the hearthrug before the clean electric fire. They had their Mickey Mouse puppets and were re-enacting all the scenes from the Mickey Mouse cartoons they'd been taken to see, repeating the English lines of the characters word for English word. Greta was always Minnie Mouse, and

Max took turns to be Mickey, Pluto, and Donald Duck. They had made other puppets with the help of Bess and they were recreating other cartoons characters too, like Warner Brothers' Daffy Duck and Paramount Pictures' Popeye. The house rang with noisy English phrases and exclamations, and the sound was more welcome to Mary's ears than any Christmas chimes. This meant that Greta would have a chance at an education, but more than that, she'd have a chance at friendship, and friendships had changed Mary's own life.

Perhaps learning English would even help them to safety. If a chance came to go to America they could take it, safe in the knowledge that Greta would be more willing to travel to the land of her hero than she had been to England.

Mary caught a glimpse of movement through the living-room windows. An unexpected visitor, but not an unwelcome one. Mary hurried to the door before the doorbell rang, keen to avoid disturbing the very productive game which was taking place all over the sitting-room floor.

'Hullo. What's all this?' Mary beamed a rare and dazzling smile at her friend Diana who waited on the step with parcels tied with string weighing down both arms.

'Let me in and I'll show you.'

Mary, feeling that a visit from an old friend was a treat to be savoured, ushered Diana into her kitchen to set the parcels on the table which pulled out from her dresser, and set the kettle on to boil.

'I've got to hand it to you, Mary,' Diana said as she looked around, 'you know how to make a house a home.'

'I think that's the nicest thing you've ever said to me.'

Diana laughed. 'Try not to get used to it.'

'Don't worry, I shan't tell anyone at Mack's that you've got a heart.'

'You're looking well. I heard your news officially from Albert; he's practically piped it onto the coconut eclairs he's so eager to tell everyone.' Diana pulled at the string on the first of her parcels. 'Are you happy?'

Mary nodded with a look of sincerity. 'I really am. It's not been easy, and there's still all the same things to worry about, like how long we've got here before there's an invasion, or what I'll find for the kids to wear, but—' Mary's eyes opened wide as Diana turned back the paper wrappings.

'Call it a Christmas present. Clothes for Greta and Max. They're not new, but they're good quality and they'll grow into them.'

'Wherever did you get them from?'

Diana looked squarely at her old friend and decided, for the first time in years, not to master her emotion. With tears in her eyes she spread out the contents of the first parcel of clothes and said, 'These belonged to my daughter, Gracie, and I was keeping them for sentiment's sake.'

Mary was stunned into silence. She had always known Diana had a much younger sister, but perhaps her own troubles had been enough to keep her from ever dwelling on the age gap, or perhaps she was merely shocked to hear the secret finally released from Diana's broken heart.

'Some others are things her adoptive family wanted giving away. The boys' clothes come from her adoptive brothers. I've kept a lot of Gracie's things over the years as keepsakes in case we were ever parted, but I don't need to do that now.'

'Don't you?' Mary asked in a whisper, the intimacy taking her by surprise.

'No, not anymore. Our ship has come in. All these years working like stink because I thought there was no such things as miracles, and I get one all the same.' Diana smiled sheepishly and wiped her eyes. 'The family who adopted Gracie want to send all their children to Canada as evacuees ahead of the war. They can't go with them, so they've appointed me guardian to the lot of them. I'm not just getting Gracie back, I'm getting a whole ruddy family – and a new start, too, in Canada.'

'But what if they find out that you're Gracie's mother, and—'

'They already know, and they aren't fussed. They're the liberal type. They've said I'm part of their family now. I'm too old to adopt but they want me to think about changing my name to Hunter, before I sail for British Columbia, make it halfway official, like.'

Mary smoothed out a powder-blue smock from the bundle of clothes before her and looked at her old friend anew. 'You're not really going away, are you? I mean it would only be if there was a war that you'd go to Canada.'

'I can't quite believe it's real, but my passage is booked and I sail with the children two months from now.'

Mary took in a sharp breath. 'So soon! Oh, I'm so happy for you, but I wish you weren't leaving. I don't think you realise how much I—' Mary pursed her lips.

Diana reached out to take her friend's hand. 'I shall miss you, Mrs Baum. I remember when you were plain old Mary Norcliffe and the girls on the line used to call you Bad Queen Mary because you could freeze the air with a look.'

'Oh, don't! I don't want to think of how much I used to lose my temper in those days.'

'I always rather admired that in you; you took no prisoners. Life had dealt you a hard hand and you needed to put up a hard fight to save your family. You might think you're a worrier, but the way I see it you've always had more courage than most. Just look at where you are now. What would the Mary of two years ago say if she could see you married and a mother in a new house with a good husband, and your Bess coming into her own? You've saved two families; the Norcliffe sisters and the Baums. You've pulled yourself and your sister out of the slum in Back Ripon Street, you've mastered three skilled jobs in a prestigious toffee factory, and you've fought the Home Office and won.' Diana refolded one of the cardigans from the pile. 'I know that if war comes you'll have more to worry about than most, but just remember that you've got more going for you than most. If anyone can find a way through it's you.'

Mary swallowed hard. 'Do you think you and I will ever see each other again? I can't bear the thought that we might not. We've been through a lot together, you and I.'

'Are you still dead set on trying to get to America?'

'Albert keeps trying, but I don't think we'll ever get there. Even then, it's still a long way to go to visit Canada.'

'So don't visit. Mack's have got a factory in Toronto and I can write to them and ask if they can use a confectioner. If you want to try for immigration to Canada, I'll help. Let's get you, Albert, his sister, the kids, and your Bess onto the other side of the Atlantic, away from anyone who would do you harm.'

'Do you mean it? Would you really do that for us? It's more work than you would think getting permits for immigrants.'

Diana raised an eyebrow. 'I've secured permits for eighty-seven Spaniards and three Germans so far this year, I think I can manage the forms.' Diana took a deep breath and made ready to leave. 'Merry Christmas, Mary Norcliffe. Let's see what we can find for you to worry about in Canada, shall we?' And with that she left.

Chapter Fifty-Four

'What's *she* doing here?' Dolly Dunkley wrinkled her nose in disgust as she tried to point at Ada Helliwell, but found her handcuffs chafed when she moved.

Ada, who had come out from the station file room momentarily to collect a stack of fingerprint cards, froze behind the custody sergeant's desk. The uniform Ada wore was new and the stiff white collar cut into her neck, making it difficult to turn her head. She had always thought that the offer of the job at the police station was too good to be true, and now it was surely going to be taken away from her as all the people who heard about it objected.

Caroline, following beside Dolly, straightening up a little with indignation, looked at her arresting officer and said, 'I don't understand. If we're being arrested for saying the Slasher attacked us, then why isn't Ada being arrested? She was the very first person to say that the Slasher got her, and if you think that the Slasher is all make-believe then she ought to have it worse than anyone else.' The Halifax Borough Police Station did not fall silent for Caroline Caffrey, and it seemed to make her more agitated as she looked around desperately for some person of importance on whom to exercise her golden cloud of charm. '*Well?*' she demanded, '*Shouldn't* she?'

'I don't think you need concern yourself with our file-room clerk, Miss Caffrey.' Sergeant Metcalf smiled benignly. 'Now, if you'd step up to the custody sergeant's desk for me we'll start taking your fingerprints.'

'But *she* ought to be arrested before us!' Dolly wailed, 'She was the one who made it all up first, we just copied her. If anyone's in the wrong, she is!'

Metcalf and the custody sergeant exchanged looks. 'You understand that you are under caution, don't you, Miss Dunkley?'

'What's that got to do with anything?'

'Anything you say can be given in evidence and at present you appear to be saying that you invented your attack by the Halifax Slasher.'

Caroline rolled her eyes. This was evidently not a situation in which she believed that the police had any real power over her. 'My friend didn't ever say she'd actually been attacked by the Slasher; we said we *thought* we'd been attacked by the Slasher.'

Dolly thought she saw where this was going and launched into her own version of events which now involved someone else telling her that the police wanted her to claim to be a victim in order to help them with their investigation by posing as a decoy. Sergeant Metcalf wrote it all down.

Ada held her place behind the sergeant's desk and watched. She watched as Caroline and Dolly let their lies writhe over each other like a nest of vipers, unaware that they themselves were being bitten over and over again. To Ada it was as though she were seeing the real Caroline for the first time. Dolly and Caroline were so different to look at; Dolly was over-dressed, over-coiffured, and overdone, where Caroline was a cool breeze of rose petals, but they were peas in a pod. For years Ada had wrestled with the guilt she felt that she did not always trust her best friend, that she did not always believe her best friend. Sometimes Ada would doubt her own sanity as she heard Caroline's memory of events which differed so far from her own. In her own mind Ada had always made excuses for Caroline because she loved her dearly and was convinced that there was so much good in her, but now, set against the backdrop of the police station where sensible, level-headed policemen failed to be taken in by her, Ada had to accept that her friend had always been trouble.

'Are you saying that you put your friend in a position where she had no choice but to cut her own clothes to escape from a notorious womaniser?' Sergeant Metcalf, the caring father of a young daughter, was really letting Caroline have a piece of his mind.

Caroline flushed scarlet and looked as if she was going to turn on the waterworks to wriggle out of the trouble she'd been caught in. 'I asked her to protect *me* from him! I'm the victim here! He was harassing me on the dance floor and she had said that she would talk to him. You have no idea how upsetting it was for me.'

Caroline babbled on and Ada realised that at that moment she – the new filing clerk of the Halifax Borough Police Station – was completely invisible. It was a good feeling, and though the circumstances gave her a tingle of anxiety, she felt the comfort of knowing that the file room offered sanctuary and was only a few steps away. She wondered if she dared step into it and close the door. But any moment now Caroline or Dolly might tell some new lie which the policemen would believe and if she, Ada, wasn't there to refute it she could risk losing her new position. Ada wondered if she would ever have the courage to stand up for herself in those circum- stances; she might panic and fail and Caroline might win and go off into the Mackintosh's sunset with her new friend Dolly Dunkley. Ada started to worry that the sanctuary of the file room might not be as secure as she had hoped.

'Would you give us a moment, Miss Heliwell?' Sergeant Metcalf indicated the door and Ada realised with a jolt that she was being sent away so that the policemen could speak to Dolly and Caroline alone. But now she really felt she ought to stay in case she needed to set the record straight, but then she thought that she couldn't because once Caroline started giving her side of the story Ada would doubt her own and find herself overwhelmed. 'Ada?' Sergeant Metcalf asked again, and Ada reluctantly stepped away from the desk, went through the file room door with its frosted-glass panes, and carefully turned the handle to allow the brass latch only the quietest of clicks.

Muffled voices beyond the door rose and fell, and Ada wondered if the policemen were all changing their opinion of her. Caroline was probably telling them about how Ada had let Sidney kiss her in the bike sheds, which was true, and that Ada had asked interested questions about him before agreeing to go to the dance, which was also true. Caroline was probably telling them lots of true things which would make them all change their minds about their newest recruit, and Ada accepted that it was probably all over. She slumped down into a chair beside the window and waited for the end to come. The voices rose a final time, and then she heard shuffling footsteps as Caroline and Dolly left. It was only a minute or two before Sergeant Metcalf let himself into the file room.

'Two more sets of fingerprint cards to file when you're ready, Miss Heliwell.'

Ada looked aghast. 'Have they been charged?'

'Yes, I'm afraid we've had to charge both of them with a breach of the peace and wasting police time. I think they'll be lucky if they get off with a binding over – the magistrate might want them to serve a week or two in prison.'

Ada's hand shook as she took the fingerprint cards. 'But what about me? I mean, it doesn't seem right or fair. Caroline was—'

Sergeant Metcalf sighed. 'You know what you did, and we know why you did it.' He was fatherly now. 'I don't think you'll ever do anything like it again, but then I hope you won't have to.'

'She's my best friend and I never wanted anything bad to happen to her. I feel it's all my fault, and she was just doing as I did.'

'You may not have wanted anything bad to happen to your friend, but I have just listened to her wishing all sorts of ills on you if only to see you suffer more than she does. She made her own choices and you didn't force them on her, but she forced some distressing choices on you and cared not at all for the consequences or the distress to you.' Sergeant Metcalf put a fatherly hand on his clerk's shoulder. 'Make friends with care, Ada. You're young and you're only just starting out in life. Make friends who make you bloom like a flower in the sun, that's my advice. Make time for the ones who want to care for you as much as you care for them.'

Chapter Fifty-Five

It was the week before Christmas and the Calder family farmhouse was groaning under the weight of preserved fruits of all hues. Mincemeat tarts filled old toffee tins, and the giant Quality Street tin on the table was piled high with gingerbread biscuits. They suspected it would be their last peacetime Christmas, and Mrs Calder was determined to cater lavishly for it. Katherine was sitting in her usual place by the window, enjoying a view of the valley, and John was munching on a slice of Christmas cake with a wedge of sharp farmhouse cheese, reading a dog-eared edition of *Stirring Tales for British Lads*, and grunting with derision every so often.

'Mother!' Kathleen called out, sitting up to press her face against the window. 'Are we expecting a visitor?'

Mrs Calder left off washing the dishes and walked over to the window to take a look, 'Not that I know of. Is it someone on a horse, or is it on shanks's pony?'

'It's neither,' Kathleen said. 'It's a motorcar!'

'Where?' John dropped his cake, cheese, and comic and squeezed onto the window seat beside his sister to get a better look. 'We don't know any motorists.'

'It better not be someone coming after our Reenie for making trouble at Mack's.' Then Mrs Calder called up the stairs, 'Reenie! There's a motorist coming up the hill! Are you in trouble at work again?'

Reenie came down the stairs to see what all the fuss was about. 'I can't be. I handed in my letter of resignation. I'm working a week's notice and that's my lot.'

'You did what?' Mrs Calder was too astonished to know how to respond and called her husband in from the barn instead. 'Arthur! Arthur! Did you know about this?'

'It's Peter!' Kathleen cried, 'He's driving the motorcar! It's Reenie's Peter!'

And Peter's Clare, Reenie thought to herself, but didn't say. She hadn't expected a visit from them, but she supposed that Peter had heard that she wanted to leave Mack's and had come to talk her round. She went out into the yard to meet him, wondering idly if the car came from his important new job, or his soon to be father-in-law.

The car pulled up beside the kitchen door and the various Calder family members spilled out to greet it. Peter alighted and went round to the passenger side to lift out the car's only other occupant: a large, trussed up Christmas tree.

'Is that for us?' John asked, not sure whether he was more pleased to see a Christmas tree or a car.

Peter smiled. 'Well, I didn't know if you'd have one yet, but I thought I'd get you one on the off-chance.' Peter passed the tree to John and then seemed to remember something and dived back into the car to retrieve it. 'And this is for you, Mrs Calder. I know you can be a bit of a worrier, so I thought it might set your mind at rest to see the latest extra edition from the *Halifax Courier*. It says the investigation is concluded and there was no Slasher in Halifax. The curfews are lifted and there's nothing to fear.'

'Oh, you darling boy!' Mrs Calder threw her arms around Peter and then began trying to usher him into the kitchen where she would have better opportunities to feed him gingerbread men with a glass of milk.

Mrs Calder's many and varied offers of homemade foods were declined, and her energies were redirected by her children into the decorating of the Christmas tree which was already being investigated by the cat. Reenie took the opportunity to slip away with Peter, and in the early closing darkness of a December afternoon they walked down the lane to see Ruffian.

'There's no Clare with you?' Reenie tried to sound casual.

'No.' Peter put his hands in his pockets and looked at the horizon. 'We went our separate ways in the end.'

'Oh,' Reenie said, genuinely surprised. 'I'm sorry to hear that. Are you . . . are you bearing up all right?'

'I wish I hadn't wasted Clare's time. I never should have proposed so quickly.'

'I'm sure you had the best of intentions.' Reenie was beginning to wonder why Peter had come out to see her. Was she about to have to go through it all again?

'I thought I knew what I wanted,' Peter said. 'I thought I needed to be married and make a home for my life to start, but you were right, Reenie. All that stuff – the house, the dinner plans, the life predictable – that's not how you make your life start.'

'I'm sorry she couldn't help you find what you were looking for.'

'No one else can, can they?' Peter was rueful. 'I think that's when life really starts; when you finally realise that no one else can help you find what you're looking for. Poor girl. I didn't mean to hurt her, but I couldn't marry her, I just couldn't. The life she wanted wasn't the one I wanted. I know it's selfish of me, but . . .'

'I think you'll find that I understand better than most people.'

Peter said nothing. There was a shared weight of pain in their silence. There was no easy or simple way forward. There was a bond between them which couldn't be broken, no matter how hard they tried, but it was a burden too.

'Where do we go from here?' Reenie was looking toward the path, but Peter chose to take her other meaning.

'I thought I could ask if I could be sent to work nearer Halifax, and then maybe—'

'I won't be here, Peter.'

Peter stopped still on the rocky ground. 'Are Mack's sending you to Norwich again?'

'No, I handed in my notice. I'm leaving Mack's. It was time. I'm growing up and I should try to spread my wings.'

'I still love you,' he said.

'And I still love you. But we're too young, Peter, and there's a war coming. England needs us.'

Epilogue

31 March 1939

The RMS *Empress of Britain* set sail for Canada on a bright and hopeful spring tide. The passengers aboard, who numbered over a thousand, had waited with mixed patience during winter, and then a little longer still while the great ocean liner was readied for her first Atlantic crossing of the St Lawrence season. 'The World's Wondership' had passed her early morning inspection by Captain WG Busk-Wood, and now crisply uniformed crew were exchanging optimistic pleasantries as they busied about the boat. The tiles on all the swimming pools glistened azure blue; the counters of the department store were bright with polished bronze; and the prancing wooden horses of the carousel on the port deck gleamed with a coat of new pink paint.

It wasn't only the first-class passengers who enjoyed the luxury of apartments rather than berths; the *Empress of Britain* had space enough to allow passengers comfort during their five-day crossing, and they had radio receiving sets for bedside entertainment too. The liner was a paradise of all the things which Halifax had never offered to Diana. Should she want to play squash or racquet or have a Turkish bath, she had only to say the word and she could book a court or a masseuse. The Empress Ballroom, the Cathay Lounge, the two fine orchestras, and the endless delights of the recreation level were hers to luxuriate in.

But here she was instead, on the deck, leaning on the starboard rail, her hair swirling in the wind, watching England vanish before her very eyes. How could a place where she had known such pain and unhappiness cause her so much distress to leave? She sighed as Southampton became a speck on the horizon.

'Well, we got out in the nick of time.' The woman standing beside Diana lit a cigarette with some difficulty in the teeth of the sea breeze and took a long, deep drag.

Mr Hunter had warned Diana that she might find his business manager Stevie a little eccentric, but Diana didn't think her so at all. She wore slacks habitually, and she had shorn her hair like Storm Jameson, but these things seemed more a concession to practicality than eccentricity. She had a certain stylishness which eschewed femininity and this appealed to Diana, who had herself never had much time for the fussiness so often associated with her gender. Diana liked her cabin-mate immediately. There was a certain reserve, perhaps even a superciliousness about the woman which would need to be got round, but Diana was confident that she could manage that. She herself had been a woman in business and she could only imagine what lengths Stevie had been forced to go to in order to be taken seriously by other businessmen.

'George tells me you're the children's adopted aunt.' Now that she'd got her cigarette safely lit, Stevie looked Diana up and down with undisguised curiosity.

Diana returned the look and said, 'And Mrs Hunter tells me you're university educated.' Diana's first step in breaking down her cabinmate's imperious facade was first to acknowledge her achievements.

Stevie shrugged and gazed out to sea with no particular interest. 'Have you made this crossing before?'

Diana shook her head.

'Well, it's calm now, but it will get choppy in an hour or two. Do you need to tend to the children?'

'No, the nanny will see to them.' Diana thought it best to establish her position now; she was not there to take orders from Stevie, or anyone else. 'If they wake it's better that we don't all pile into the cabin and make a fuss or they won't go back to sleep. I'm here as guardian, not nanny.'

'All the same, you seem to know a lot about children.' She took another long drag on her cigarette. It smelled of strong Egyptian tobacco and just a hint of liquorice.

Diana felt herself go a little lightheaded and she wasn't certain whether it was the smoke, the woman, or the sea. 'Are you the maternal type, perhaps?' Stevie asked with just a hint of condescension, 'Looking to settle down with a family of your own in Canada?'

Diana inhaled a little more deeply and, leaning against the iron rail of the ship, said calmly, 'It is a matter of public record that I am the natural mother of Gracie Hunter, the youngest Hunter child.' She fixed Stevie with those steel-banded irises which seemed sharp with determination. 'I was forced by circumstance to put her up for adoption when her father died. She was adopted officially by the Hunters, but they adopted me unofficially. They gave me their name, and have entrusted me with all of their children for the duration of the war, and beyond, if – if it should come to that.'

Stevie dropped her cigarette in surprise and then snatched hopelessly at the air as she tried to catch it. The other woman's cool, superior air of detachment was lost, and now Diana felt she had the upper hand.

'Goodness, I'm so sorry.' Diana looked over the side of the ship in the direction of the lost cigarette and the foaming ocean many decks below. 'I do hope that wasn't your last one.'

Stevie sighed in irritation. 'It was, as it happens.'

'Well, I can't offer you another, but I can offer you a nightcap. Mrs Hunter sent me with a bottle of brandy in case any of the children got upset. She told me to have a nip before I turn in as it's my first time on board a ship.'

Stevie allowed herself to break into a half-smile, 'Well, if your employer has given you specific instructions to take a glass then I think you really ought to, and as we're sharing a cabin I could be persuaded to join you.'

'Are you usually so easily persuadable?' Diana felt she had the upper hand now, but they were fast becoming equals, the old English class barriers tumbling down.

'You know, I don't know. How about you try and we'll see where that gets us?' The other woman had a twinkle in her eye and Diana felt a thrill of excitement. A new life awaited her and her daughter in safety and comfort on the other side of the Atlantic, and another possibility was occurring to her. For the first time in many years Diana thought she could ask herself what she *wanted* in life, not what she could make do with. She could have excitement and adventure, and perhaps Stevie would share in some of them.

'And just so we're clear,' Diana smiled warmly as they made their way back to the cabin, 'Lydia Hunter isn't my employer – I'm one of the family now.'

Historical Note

On 16th November 1938 Halifax was seized with panic over an imaginary terror. Two girls claimed they'd been attacked by an unknown man wielding a mallet. Just a few days later, on 21st November, another girl claimed to have been attacked with a razor. Over the next eight days another six attacks were reported and the newspapers were quick to name the assailant *The Slasher*. News travelled fast, and the exploits of the man who stalked the streets at night was valuable local currency. A reward was offered and groups of vigilantes patrolled the streets hoping to catch the Slasher and claim the money. Various volunteer groups acted as chaperones, walking women to and from their places of business, but many businesses had to close because Halifax had become, in effect, a ghost town.

When one of the Slasher's original victims reported that she had been attacked a second time – and two attacks appeared to occur simultaneously in different locations – the authorities became suspicious. Two Scotland Yard detectives were called in and in just four and a half hours they established the truth: there had been no Slasher, each of the victims had invented their own attack, none of it was real.

A month and a half before the first so-called Slasher attack, Britain had believed she was going to war. Adolf Hitler had broken another treaty by invading Sudetenland, and Britain was poised for armed conflict. The Prime Minister, Neville Chamberlain, flew to Munich to hold talks with Hitler, but few people at home in Britain believed these talks would bear good fruit. Even the BBC was preparing the nation for war; Virginia Woolf wrote in her diaries at the time about the broadcast of prayers, words from the Archbishop of Canterbury, messages from the Admiralty to ships off the coast, and instructions to the populace to wear warm clothes if they fled their homes. It would have been impossible to live in England in 1938 and not know that war was very, very close.

An announcement beyond the eleventh hour brought a collective sense of relief. Hitler agreed not to invade anywhere else, and Chamberlain returned to Britain with his written agreement which secured 'Peace for our time'. What did the British people think? We are able to know what they thought with an unusual degree of accuracy for the time. A large-scale scientifically conducted poll was published which showed that 90 per cent of Britons believed Hitler would not stop his march across Europe.

A month after the high anxiety of that day of almost-war, news came from the continent that synagogues, schools, businesses, hospitals, and homes belonging to Jewish citizens were being smashed and burned all over German-controlled territories. Tens of thousands of Jewish men were being rounded up and sent to prison camps, and brutal beatings were being dealt out in the street. The night was later named 'Kristallnacht' or 'The Night of Broken Glass'. It was a turning point in European history for so many reasons, but the one which has always fascinated me is that it was the first time an event of such enormity could be reported on in real time around the world through the radio.

I've often wondered how much of the Halifax Slasher affair owed its eruption to the tensions which were running high after Kristallnacht at the start of November, and the near-declaration of war by the British on 30th September 1938. How many people were feeling so overwhelmed by grief and fear at the news from Nazi-occupied territories that they wanted to do themselves harm? To cry out in pain and be heard?

In this book I haven't used the details of the real, historical Slasher Panic, but have re-imagined it with fictional actors who behave for reasons all of their own. I've imagined what might have been going on in the minds of the 'Slasher victims' to make them do the things they did, and tell the lies they told. I've tried to recreate the fearful climate they lived in, and show that they aren't so different from us in the twenty-first century, navigating changes which have sprung up suddenly, and completely up-ended our way of life.

Through all of my research into British life in 1938 I wondered why more Britons didn't simply leave the country. A new life in Canada or Australia may have meant enormous upheaval and expense, but surely anything was better than staying to see out a war? Apparently not. Deserting Britain in her hour of need was seen as not only a cowardly, but also a wicked action, and when the poets Christopher Isherwood and W. H. Auden left for America they caused a national scandal. Questions were asked in parliament, and some politicians were genuinely demanding that the pair be extradited back to the United Kingdom for immediate conscription.

The story of the Hunter family and Diana touches on this problem of staying through the war, or leaving for safety. Many parents opted to send their children abroad, while they themselves remained to fight on the home front. In Diana's case her move wasn't cowardly or wicked; she was enabling even more children to get away to safety in Canada and on her arrival she'd still be making herself useful to the war effort. The story of her daughter's readoption was inspired by a real court case which took place shortly after war had ended. A couple who had adopted a child together found themselves in a bitter battle over custody and maintenance payments when it became apparent that the adoptive father had entered into a bigamous marriage with the adoptive mother, and the adoption itself was not lawful. In reality, the legal custody of the child would revert to the court as 'guardians ad litem', but in this story I used artistic licence to return custody to Diana. This is the end of a long journey for her, and I wanted her to finally get her daughter back, but not in the way she had planned.

I took another piece of artistic licence in the extent of Mackintosh's gas mask assembly line. Although the toffee girls really did assemble gas masks in 1938, they didn't make nearly such heavy weather of them as my characters. Mackintosh's workers assembled 40,000 of them, but the real Mackintosh workers were much quicker and more efficient than mine. They didn't need as much space (they worked in a church hall) and they didn't need as much time (they completed the order in a matter of weeks). The gas masks in this book are really just a stand-in for the all-pervading fear of war which was very real. I could never have imagined when I started writing the book in September 2021 that we would be watching history repeat itself so vividly.

Acknowledgements

With thanks to:

Kate Bradley, Jemima Forrester, Kati Nicholl, Graham and Penny Hutchinson, Claire Walker, Richard Long, Annie Medcalf, Alison Murray, Edoardo Brandani, Joelle Monkman, Sam Plummer, Pippa Joyce, Kirstie Lount, Beth Morrey, Sheila Cartwright, Fiona McIntosh, Selina Wu, Magdalena Ross, Gareth Bissmire, and Lottie.

Have you discovered Penny's other
Quality Street novels?

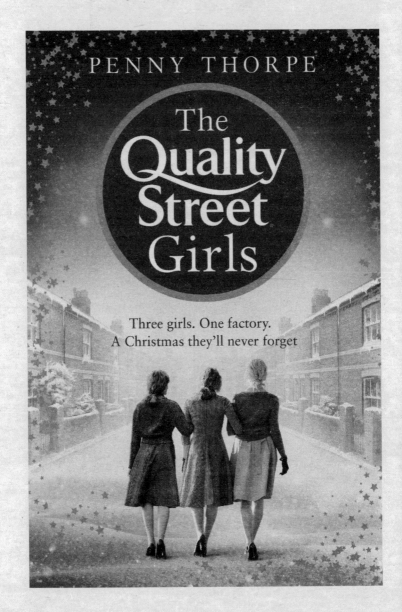

PENNY THORPE

The Mothers of Quality Street

Can the factory girls pull together for
a very special day?

PENNY THORPE

The Quality Street Wedding

Love is in the air for the factory girls